LADIES OF HORROR

Two Centuries of Supernatural Stories by the Gentle Sex

Contrary to nineteenth-century popular opinion, the woman writer did not neglect her home for her "art," but many amusing drawings implied that she did. This print, entitled "My Wife Is a Woman of Mind," is by the famous artist George Cruikshank.

Ladies of Horror

TWO CENTURIES OF SUPERNATURAL STORIES BY THE GENTLE SEX

Selected and With Introductions by
SEON MANLEY AND
GOGO LEWIS

Lothrop, Lee & Shepard Company New York

This book is for
Eftihia, Katie, and Margarita Siafaca
. . . Ladies of Charm

*Inquiries should be addressed to Lothrop, Lee and Shepard Company,
105 Madison Ave., New York, N. Y. 10016. Printed in the
United States of America. Library of Congress Catalog
Card Number: 77-148485*

ACKNOWLEDGMENTS

We are grateful to the authors, agents, publishers, and photographers who have given us permission to reprint the following selections:

The Werewolf by Clemence Housman. Reprinted by permission of The Bodley Head.

Man-Size in Marble by E. Nesbit. Reprinted by permission of John Farquharson Ltd.

Hand in Glove by Elizabeth Bowen from *A Day in the Dark*. Reprinted by permission of Jonathan Cape Ltd. and Curtis Brown Ltd.

Whitewash by Rose Macaulay. Reprinted by permission of A. D. Peters & Company.

The Birds from *Kiss Me Again Stranger* by Daphne du Maurier. Copyright 1952 by Daphne du Maurier. Reprinted by permission of Doubleday & Company, Inc.

The Tree's Wife by Mary Elizabeth Counselman. Copyright 1950 by Popular Fiction Pub. Co., and the author. Reprinted by permission of the author.

Moonlight–Starlight by Virginia Layefsky. Reprinted by permission of Curtis Publishing Co., © 1959.

The Lovely House by Shirley Jackson. Copyright 1952 by The New American Library of World Literature, Inc. Reprinted by permission of Brandt & Brandt.

The Last Seance by Agatha Christie. Reprinted by permission of Dodd, Mead & Company, Inc., from *Double Sin and Other Stories* by Agatha Christie. Copyright © 1926 by Agatha Christie. Copyright renewed 1954 by Agatha Christie. Permission to reprint also granted by Hughes Massie Ltd.

Universal Studios for the photograph of Boris Karloff as the monster in *Frankenstein* used on the jacket.

The Vanguard Press for the photograph of the effigy in a German cathedral on page 110.

The Italian Government Travel Office for the photograph of Capri on page 176.

Irene Winsby for the photograph of Daphne du Maurier on page 182.

Erich Hartmann for the photograph of Shirley Jackson on page 238.

Howard Thompson for the photograph of Agatha Christie and her husband on page 264.

Our thanks also to Mrs. Betty Shalders; Mrs. Susan Belcher; Mr. Henry Matseo; Mr. Howard Thompson; the staff of the Bellport Memorial Library, Bellport, New York; the staff of the Patchogue Library, Patchogue, New York; the staff of the Greenwich Library, Greenwich, Connecticut; the Greenwich Book Store; our husbands, Robert R. Manley and William W. Lewis; and those devotees of supernatural stories, our daughters, Sara Lewis, Carol Lewis, and Shivaun Manley.

CONTENTS

Nineteenth Century

Twentieth Century

Many horror stories originate in dreams, as did Mary Shelley's Frankenstein. *This painting called "The Nightmare" is by Henry Fuseli, a friend of Mary's mother Mary Wollstonecraft Godwin, the author of* Vindication of the Rights of Woman, *the first great feminist document.*

Nineteenth Century

The eighteenth and nineteenth centuries saw the birth of the horror story. Vampires, monsters, and ghosts became not just creatures of folklore but the substance of literature. The monster tale was created by Mary W. Shelley, a young girl when she was challenged by Lord Byron's comment one evening, "We shall each write a ghost story." His was an unfinished, forgotten sketch about a vampire; hers was Frankenstein. *Women have always had a gift for weird tales, a penchant for macabre happenings, a delightful way with a ghost. Gentle Victorian ladies of the last century tossed them off with the dexterity of needlework—the stories were not so gentle.*

1818

THE MAKING OF A MONSTER

by Mary W. Shelley

No creature of horror has so fascinated readers for nearly two centuries as the monster created by Mary W. Shelley in her novel *Frankenstein,* written when she was barely out of her teens. This was the prototype of the horror story, and it has never been excelled.

The macabre and the weird have been major elements in literature since man—and woman—first put pen to paper. Our dreams, indeed our spirits, are often filled with a mystery we cannot comprehend. Great writers have been unusually haunted by the dark, strange patterns of the human imagination. Lafcadio Hearn, himself a writer of fine ghost stories, said, "There is scarcely any great author in European literature, old or new, who has not distinguished himself in his treatment of the supernatural. In English literature, I believe, there is no exception from the time of the Anglo-Saxon poets to Shakespeare, and from Shakespeare to our own day." Indeed, Lafcadio Hearn felt that there was something "ghostly" in all the arts—architecture, sculpture, and music as well as literature. In great literature we find this "strangeness" particularly apparent. Some critics feel it is because of the writer's own desire for infinity and for immortality.

Mary Wollstonecraft Shelley was born into a highly creative family and nurtured deeply on literature. When she eloped with the poet Percy Bysshe Shelley she aligned herself with another creative genius. Shelley was fascinated with not only the beauty of words, but also the great emerging ideas of his time—the phenomenon of electricity, for example, as well as the search for the elixir of life, which man has sought from time immemorial. Today experiments to try to find the nature of life itself are being carried on in the laboratory with remarkable results: man has been able to break the genetic code, and has even been able, in a small way, to recreate life in a test tube. But this is the twentieth century, whereas Mary Shelley was a girl of the early nineteenth century, which makes her achievement all the more impressive.

Many authorities feel that all stories of the supernatural originate in our dream life. Mary Shelley has given us an accurate account of the creation of her own story. She was often asked "how I, then a young girl, came to think of and to dilate upon so very hideous an idea." One evening Lord Byron challenged the guests at his home in Geneva to write a ghost story. The other stories were abortive, but Mary's took shape in her mind, particularly after a dream.

"Night," she said, "waned upon this talk, and even the witching hour had gone by, before we retired to rest. When I placed my head on my pillow I did not sleep, nor could I be said to think. My imagination, unbidden, possessed and guided me, gifting the successive images that arose in my mind with a vividness far beyond the usual bounds of reverie. I saw—with shut eyes, but acute mental vision—I saw the pale student of unhallowed arts kneeling beside the thing he had put together. I saw the hideous phantasm of a man stretched out, and then, on the working of some powerful engine, show signs of life, and stir with an uneasy, half vital motion. Frightful must it be; for supremely frightful would be the effect of any human endeavor to mock the stupendous mechanism of the Creator of the world. His success would terrify the artist; he would rush away from his odious handiwork, horror-stricken. He would hope that, left to itself, the slight spark of life which he had communicated would fade; that this thing, which had received such imperfect animation, would subside into dead matter; and he might sleep in the belief that the silence of the grave would quench for ever the transient existence of the hideous corpse which he had looked upon as the cradle of life. He sleeps; but he is awakened; he opens his eyes; behold the horrid thing stands at his bedside, opening his curtains, and looking on him with yellow, watery, but speculative eyes.

"I opened mine in terror. The idea so possessed my mind that a thrill of fear ran through me, and I wished to exchange the ghastly image of my fancy for the realities around. I see them still; the very room, the dark *parquet*, the closed shutters, with the moonlight struggling through, and the sense I had that the glassy lake and white high Alps were beyond. I could not so easily get rid of my hideous phantom; still it haunted me. I must try to think of something else. I recurred to my ghost story—my tiresome unlucky ghost story. . . . On the morrow I announced that I had *thought of a story*."

The story, of course, was *Frankenstein*. Mary W. Shelley chose for her narrator a learned student, Doctor Frankenstein, and here he looks for the first time on the monster he has created.

I had sufficient leisure for these and many other reflections during my journey to Ingolstadt, which was long and fatiguing. At length the high white steeple of the town met my eyes. I alighted, and was conducted to my solitary apartment, to spend the evening as I pleased.

The next morning I delivered my letters of introduction and paid a visit to some of the principal professors. Chance—or rather the evil influence, the Angel of Destruction, which asserted omnipotent sway over me from the moment I turned my reluctant steps from my father's door—led me first to M. Krempe, professor of natural philosophy. He was an uncouth man, but deeply embued in the secrets of his science. He asked me several questions concerning my progress in the different branches of science appertaining to natural philosophy. I replied carelessly; and, partly in contempt, mentioned the names of my alchemists as the principal authors I had studied. The professor stared: "Have you," he said, "really spent your time in studying such nonsense?"

I replied in the affirmative. "Every minute," continued M. Krempe with warmth, "every instant that you have wasted on those books is utterly and entirely lost. You have burdened your memory with exploded systems and useless names. Good God! in what desert land have you lived, where no one was kind enough to inform you that these fancies, which you have so greedily imbibed, are a thousand years old, and as musty as they are ancient? I little expected, in this enlightened and scientific age, to find a disciple of Albertus Magnus and Paracelsus. My dear sir, you must begin your studies entirely anew."

So saying, he stepped aside, and wrote down a list of several books treating of natural philosophy, which he desired me to procure; and dismissed me, after mentioning that in the beginning of the following week he intended to commence a course of lectures upon natural philosophy in its general relations, and that M. Waldman, fellow-professor, would lecture upon chemistry the alternate days that he omitted.

I returned home, not disappointed, for I have said that I had long considered those authors useless whom the professor reprobated; but I returned, not at all the more inclined to recur to these studies in any shape. M. Krempe was a little squat man, with a gruff voice and a repulsive countenance; the teacher, therefore, did not prepossess me in favor of his pursuits. In rather a too philosophical and connected a strain, perhaps, I have given an account of the conclusions I had come to concerning them in my early years. As a child, I had not been content with the results promised by the modern professors of natural science. With a confusion of ideas only to be accounted for by my extreme youth, and my want of a guide on such matters, I had retrod the steps of knowledge along the paths of time, and exchanged the discoveries of recent inquirers for the dreams of forgotten alchemists. Besides, I had a contempt for the uses of modern natural philosophy. It was very different when the masters of the science sought immortality and power; such views, although futile, were grand: but now the scene was changed. The ambition of the inquirer seemed to limit itself to the annihilation of those visions on which my interest in science was chiefly founded. I was required to exchange chimeras of boundless grandeur for realities of little worth.

Such were my reflections during the first two or three days of my residence at Ingolstadt, which were chiefly spent in becoming acquainted with the localities, and the principal residents in my new abode. But as the ensuing week commenced, I thought of the information which M. Krempe had given me concerning the lectures. And although I could not consent to go and hear that little conceited fellow deliver sentences out of a pulpit, I recollected what he had said of M. Waldman, whom I had never seen, as he had hitherto been out of town.

Partly from curiosity, and partly from idleness, I went into the lecturing room, which M. Waldman entered shortly after. This professor was very unlike his colleague. He appeared about fifty years of age, but with an aspect expressive of the greatest benevolence; a few gray hairs covered his temples, but those at the back of his head were nearly black. His person was short, but remarkably erect; and his voice the sweetest I had ever heard. He began his lecture by a recapitulation of the history of chemistry, and the various improvements made by different men of learning, pronouncing with fervor the names of the most distinguished discoverers. He then took a cursory view of the present state of the science, and explained many of its elementary terms. After having made a few preparatory experiments, he concluded with a panegyric upon modern chemistry, the terms of which I shall never forget:—

"The ancient teachers of this science," said he, "promised impossibilities, and performed nothing. The modern masters promise very little; they know that metals cannot be transmuted, and that the elixir of life is a chimera. But these philosophers, whose hands seem only made to dabble in dirt, and their eyes to pore over the microscope or crucible, have indeed performed miracles. They penetrate into the recesses of nature, and show how she works in her hiding places. They ascend into the heavens: they have discovered how the blood circulates, and the nature of the air we breathe. They have acquired new and almost unlimited powers; they can command the thunders of heaven, mimic the earthquake, and even mock the invisible world with its own shadows."

Such were the professor's words—rather let me say such the words of fate, enounced to destroy me. As he went on, I felt as if my soul were grappling with a palpable enemy; one by one the various keys were touched which formed the mechanism of my being: chord after chord was sounded, and soon my mind was filled with one thought, one conception, one purpose. So much has been done, exclaimed the soul of Frankenstein—more, far more, will I achieve: treading in the steps already marked, I will pioneer a new way, explore unknown powers, and unfold to the world the deepest mysteries of creation.

I closed not my eyes that night. My internal being was in a state of insurrection and turmoil; I felt that order would thence arise, but I had no power to produce it. By degrees, after the morning's dawn, sleep came. I awoke, and my yesternight's thoughts were as a dream. There only remained a resolution to return to my ancient studies, and to devote myself to a science for which I believed myself to possess a natural talent. On the same day, I paid M. Waldman a visit. His manners in private were even more mild and attractive than in public; for there was a certain dignity in his mien during his lecture, which in his own house was replaced by the greatest affability and kindness. I gave him pretty nearly the same account of my former pursuits as I had given to his fellow-professor. He heard with attention the little narration concerning my studies, and smiled at the names of Cornelius Agrippa and Paracelsus, but without the contempt that M. Krempe had exhibited. He said, that "these were men to whose indefatigable zeal modern philosophers were indebted for most of the foundations of their knowledge. They had left to us, as an easier task, to give new names, and arrange in connected classifications, the facts which they in a great degree had been the instruments of bringing to light. The labors of men of genius, however erroneously directed, scarcely ever fail in ultimately turning to the solid advantage of mankind." I listened to his statement, which was delivered without any presumption or affectation; and then added, that his lecture had removed my prejudices against modern chemists; I expressed myself in measured terms, with the modesty and deference due from a youth to his instructor, without letting escape (inexperience in life would have made me ashamed) any of the enthusiasm which stimulated my intended labors. I requested his advice concerning the books which I ought to procure.

"I am happy," said M. Waldman, "to have gained a disciple; and if your application equals your ability, I have no doubt of your success. Chemistry is that branch of natural philosophy in which the greatest improvements have been and may be made: it is on that account that I have made it my peculiar study; but at the same time I have not neglected the other branches of science. A man would make but a very sorry chemist if he attended to that department of human knowledge alone. If your wish is to become really a man of science, and not merely a petty experimentalist, I should advise you to apply to every branch of natural philosophy, including mathematics."

He then took me into his laboratory, and explained to me the uses of his various machines; instructing me as to what I ought to procure, and promising me the use of his own when

I should have advanced far enough in the science not to derange their mechanism. He also gave me the list of books which I had requested; and I took my leave.

Thus ended a day memorable to me: it decided my future destiny.

FROM this day natural philosophy, and particularly chemistry, in the most comprehensive sense of the term, became nearly my sole occupation. I read with ardor those works, so full of genius and discrimination, which modern inquirers have written on these subjects. I attended the lectures, and cultivated the acquaintance, of the men of science of the university; and I found even in M. Krempe a great deal of sound sense and real information, combined, it is true, with a repulsive physiognomy and manners, but not on that account the less valuable. In M. Waldman I found a true friend. His gentleness was never tinged by dogmatism; and his instructions were given with an air of frankness and good nature that banished every idea of pedantry. In a thousand ways he smoothed for me the path of knowledge, and made the most abstruse inquiries clear and facile to my apprehension. My application was at first fluctuating and uncertain; it gained strength as I proceeded, and soon became so ardent and eager that the stars often disappeared in the light of morning whilst I was yet engaged in my laboratory.

As I applied so closely, it may be easily conceived that my progress was rapid. My ardor was indeed the astonishment of the students, and my proficiency that of the masters. Professor Krempe often asked me, with a sly smile, how Cornelius Agrippa went on? whilst M. Waldman expressed the most heartfelt exultation in my progress. Two years passed in this manner, during which I paid no visit to Geneva, but was engaged, heart and soul, in the pursuit of some discoveries, which I hoped to make. None but those who have experienced them can conceive of the enticements of science. In other studies you go as far as others have gone before you, and there is nothing more to know; but in a scientific pursuit there is continual food for discovery and wonder. A mind of moderate capacity, which closely pursues one study, must infallibly arrive at great proficiency in that study; and I, who continually sought the attainment of one object of pursuit, and was solely wrapt up in this, improved so rapidly that, at the end of two years, I made some discoveries in the improvement of some chemical instruments which procured me great esteem and admiration at the university. When I had arrived at this point, and had become as well acquainted with the theory and practice of natural philosophy as depended on the lessons of any of the professors at Ingolstadt, my residence there being no longer conducive to my improvement, I thought of returning to my friends and my native town, when an incident happened that protracted my stay.

One of the phenomena which had peculiarly attracted my attention was the structure of the human frame, and, indeed, any animal endued with life. Whence, I often asked myself, did the principle of life proceed? It was a bold question, and one which has ever been considered as a mystery; yet with how many things are we upon the brink of becoming acquainted, if cowardice or carelessness did not restrain our inquiries. I revolved these circumstances in my mind, and determined thenceforth to apply myself more particularly to those branches of natural philosophy which relate to physiology. Unless I had been animated by an almost supernatural enthusiasm, my application to this study would have been irksome, and almost intolerable. To examine the causes of life, we must first have recourse to death. I became acquainted with the science of anatomy: but this was not sufficient; I must also observe the natural decay and corruption of the human body. In my education my father had taken the greatest precautions that my mind should be impressed with no supernatural horrors. I do not ever remember to have trembled at a tale of superstition, or to have feared the apparition of a spirit. Darkness had no effect upon my fancy; and a churchyard was to me merely the receptacle of bodies deprived of life, which, from being the seat of beauty and strength, had become food for the worm. Now I was led to examine the cause and progress of this decay, and forced to spend days and nights in vaults and charnel-houses. My attention was fixed upon every object the most insupportable to the delicacy of the human feelings. I saw how the fine form of man was degraded and wasted; I beheld the corruption of death succeed to the blooming cheek of life; I saw how the worm inherited the wonders of the eye and brain. I paused, examining and analyzing all the minutiæ of causation, as exemplified in the change from life to death, and death to life, until from the midst of this darkness a sudden light broke in upon me—a light so brilliant and wondrous, yet so simple, that while I became dizzy with the immensity of the prospect which it illustrated, I was surprised, that among so many men of genius who had directed their inquiries towards the same science, that I alone should be reserved to discover so astonishing a secret.

Remember, I am not recording the vision of a madman. The sun does not more certainly shine in the heavens, than that which I now affirm is true. Some miracle might have produced it, yet the stages of the discovery were distinct and probable. After days and nights of incredible labor and fatigue, I succeeded in discovering the cause of generation and life; nay, more, I became myself capable of bestowing animation upon lifeless matter.

The astonishment which I had at first experienced on this discovery soon gave place to delight and rapture. After so much time spent in painful labor, to arrive at once at the summit of my desires was the most gratifying consummation of my toils. But this discovery was so great and overwhelming that all the steps by which I had been progressively led to it were obliterated, and I beheld only the result. What had been the study and desire of the wisest men since the creation of the world was now within my grasp. Not that, like a magic scene, it all opened upon me at once: the information I had obtained was of a nature rather to direct my endeavors so soon as I should point them towards the object of my search, than to exhibit that object already accomplished. I was like the Arabian who had been buried with the dead, and found a passage to life, aided only by one glimmering, and seemingly ineffectual, light.

I see by your eagerness, and the wonder and hope which your eyes express, my friend, that you expect to be informed of the secret with which I am acquainted; that cannot be: listen patiently until the end of my story, and you will easily perceive why I am reserved upon that subject. I will not lead you on, unguarded and ardent as I then was, to your destruction and infallible misery. Learn from me, if not by my precepts, at least by my example, how dangerous is the acquirement of knowledge, and how much happier that man is who believes his native town to be the world, than he who aspires to become greater than his nature will allow.

When I found so astonishing a power placed within my hands, I hesitated a long time concerning the manner in which I should employ it. Although I possessed the capacity of bestowing animation, yet to prepare a frame for the reception of it, with all its intricacies of fibers, muscles, and veins, still remained a work of inconceivable difficulty and labor. I doubted at first whether I should attempt the creation of a being like myself, or one of simpler organization; but my imagination was too much exalted by my first success to permit me to doubt of my ability to give life to an animal as complex and wonderful as man. The materials at present within my command hardly appeared adequate to so arduous an undertaking; but I doubted not that I should ultimately succeed. I prepared myself for a multitude of reverses; my operations might be incessantly baffled, and at last my work be imperfect: yet, when I considered the improvement which every day takes place in science and mechanics, I was encouraged to hope my present attempts would at least lay the foundations of future success. Nor could I consider the magnitude and complexity of my plan as any argument of its impracticability. It was with these feelings that

I began the creation of a human being. As the minuteness of the parts formed a great hindrance to my speed, I resolved, contrary to my first intention, to make the being of a gigantic stature; that is to say, about eight feet in height, and proportionately large. After having formed this determination, and having spent some months in successfully collecting and arranging my materials, I began.

No one can conceive the variety of feelings which bore me onwards, like a hurricane, in the first enthusiasm of success. Life and death appeared to me ideal bounds, which I should first break through, and pour a torrent of light into our dark world. A new species would bless me as its creator and source; many happy and excellent natures would owe their being to me. No father could claim the gratitude of his child so completely as I should deserve theirs. Pursuing these reflections, I thought, that if I could bestow animation upon lifeless matter, I might in process of time (although I now found it impossible) renew life where death had apparently devoted the body to corruption.

These thoughts supported my spirits, while I pursued my undertaking with unremitting ardor. My cheek had grown pale with study, and my person had become emaciated with confinement. Sometimes, on the very brink of certainty, I failed; yet still I clung to the hope which the next day or the next hour might realize. One secret which I alone possessed was the hope to which I had dedicated myself; and the moon gazed on my midnight labors, while, with unrelaxed and breathless eagerness, I pursued nature to her hiding-places. Who shall conceive the horrors of my secret toil, as I dabbled among the unhallowed damps of the grave, or tortured the living animal to animate the lifeless clay? My limbs now tremble and my eyes swim with the remembrance; but then a resistless, and almost frantic, impulse urged me forward; I seemed to have lost all soul or sensation but for this one pursuit. It was indeed but a passing trance that only made me feel with renewed acuteness so soon as, the unnatural stimulus ceasing to operate, I had returned to my old habits. I collected bones from charnel-houses; and disturbed, with profane fingers, the tremendous secrets of the human frame. In a solitary chamber, or rather cell, at the top of the house, and separated from all the other apartments by a gallery and staircase, I kept my workshop of filthy creation: my eyeballs were starting from the sockets in attending to the details of my employment. The dissecting room and the slaughterhouse furnished many of my materials; and often did my human nature turn with loathing from my occupation, whilst, still urged on by an eagerness which perpetually increased, I brought my work near to a conclusion.

The summer months passed while I was thus engaged, heart and soul, in one pursuit. It was a most beautiful season; never did the fields bestow a more plentiful harvest, or the vines yield a more luxuriant vintage: but my eyes were insensible to the charms of nature. And the same feelings which made me neglect the scenes around me caused me also to forget those friends who were so many miles absent, and whom I had not seen for so long a time. I knew my silence disquieted them; and I well remembered the words of my father: "I know that while you are pleased with yourself, you will think of us with affection, and we shall hear regularly from you. You must pardon me if I regard any interruption in your correspondence as a proof that your other duties are equally neglected."

I knew well, therefore, what would be my father's feelings; but I could not tear my thoughts from my employment, loathsome in itself, but which had taken an irresistible hold of my imagination. I wished, as it were, to procrastinate all that related to my feelings of affection until the great object, which swallowed up every habit of my nature, should be completed.

I then thought that my father would be unjust if he ascribed my neglect to vice, or faultiness on my part; but I am now convinced that he was justified in conceiving that I should not be altogether free from blame. A human being in perfection ought always to preserve a calm and peaceful mind, and never to allow passion or a transitory desire to disturb his tranquillity. I do not think that the pursuit of knowledge is an exception to this rule. If the study to which you apply yourself has a tendency to weaken your affections, and to destroy your taste for those simple pleasures in which no alloy can possibly mix, then that study is certainly unlawful, that is to say, not befitting the human mind. If this rule were always observed; if no man allowed any pursuit whatsoever to interfere with the tranquillity of his domestic affections, Greece had not been enslaved: Caesar would have spared his country; America would have been discovered more gradually; and the empires of Mexico and Peru had not been destroyed.

But I forget that I am moralizing in the most interesting part of my tale; and your looks remind me to proceed.

My father made no reproach in his letters, and only took notice of my silence by inquiring into my occupations more particularly than before. Winter, spring, and summer passed away during my labors; but I did not watch the blossom or the expanding leaves—sights which before always yielded me supreme delight—so deeply was I engrossed in my occupation. The leaves of that year had withered before my work drew near to a close; and now every day showed me more plainly how well I had succeeded. But my enthusiasm was checked by my anxiety, and I appeared rather like one doomed by slavery to toil in the mines, or any other unwholesome trade, than an artist occupied by his favorite employment. Every night I was oppressed by a slow fever, and I became nervous to a most pitiful degree; the fall of a leaf startled me, and I shunned my fellow-creatures as if I had been guilty of a crime. Sometimes I grew alarmed at the wreck I perceived that I had become; the energy of my purpose alone sustained me: my labors would soon end, and I believed that exercise and amusement would then drive away incipient disease; and I promised myself both of these when my creation should be complete.

It was on a dreary night of November that I beheld the accomplishment of my toils. With an anxiety that almost amounted to agony, I collected the instruments of life around me, that I might infuse a spark of being into the lifeless thing that lay at my feet. It was already one in the morning; the rain pattered dismally against the panes, and my candle was nearly burnt out, when, by the glimmer of the half-extinguished light, I saw the dull yellow eye of the creature open; it breathed hard, and a convulsive motion agitated its limbs.

How can I describe my emotions at this catastrophe, or how delineate the wretch whom with such infinite pains and care I had endeavored to form? His limbs were in proportion, and I had selected his features as beautiful. Beautiful!—Great God! His yellow skin scarcely covered the work of muscles and arteries beneath; his hair was of a lustrous black, and flowing; his teeth of a pearly whiteness; but these luxuriances only formed a more horrid contrast with his watery eyes, that seemed almost of the same color as the dun white sockets in which they were set, his shriveled complexion and straight black lips.

The different accidents of life are not so changeable as the feelings of human nature. I had worked hard for nearly two years, for the sole purpose of infusing life into an inanimate body. For this I had deprived myself of rest and health. I had desired it with an ardor that far exceeded moderation; but now that I had finished, the beauty of the dream vanished, and breathless horror and disgust filled my heart. Unable to endure the aspect of the being I had created, I rushed out of the room, and continued a long time traversing my bedchamber, unable to compose my mind to sleep. At length lassitude succeeded to the tumult I had before endured; and I threw myself on the bed in my clothes, endeavoring to seek a few moments of forgetfulness. But it was in vain: I slept, indeed, but I was disturbed by the wildest dreams. I thought I saw Elizabeth, in the bloom of health, walking in the streets of Ingolstadt. Delighted and surprised, I embraced her; but as I imprinted the first kiss on her lips, they became livid with the hue of death; her features appeared to change, and I thought that I held the corpse of my dead mother in my arms; a shroud enveloped her form, and I saw the grave-worms crawling in the folds of the flannel. I started from my sleep with horror; a cold dew covered my forehead, my teeth chattered, and every limb became convulsed: when, by the dim and yellow light of the moon, as it forced its way through the window shutters, I beheld the wretch—the miserable monster whom I had created. He held up the curtain of the bed; and his eyes, if eyes they may be called, were fixed on me. His jaws opened, and he muttered some inarticulate sounds, while a grin wrinkled his cheeks. He might have spoken, but I did not hear; one hand was stretched out, seemingly to detain me, but I escaped, and rushed down stairs. I took refuge in the courtyard belonging to the house which I inhabited; where I remained during the rest of the night, walking up and down in the greatest agitation, listening attentively, catching and fearing each sound as if it were to announce the approach of the demoniacal corpse to which I had so miserably given life.

Oh! no mortal could support the horror of that countenance. A mummy again endued with animation could not be so hideous as that wretch. I had gazed on him while unfinished; he was ugly then; but when those muscles and joints were rendered capable of motion, it became a thing such as even Dante could not have conceived.

I passed the night wretchedly. Sometimes my pulse beat so quickly and hardly that I felt the palpitation of every artery; at others, I nearly sank to the ground through languor and extreme weakness. Mingled with this horror, I felt the bitterness of disappointment; dreams that had been my food and pleasant rest for so long a space were now become a hell to me; and the change was so rapid, the overthrow so complete!

Morning, dismal and wet, at length dawned, and discovered to my sleepless and aching eyes the church of Ingolstadt, its white steeple and clock, which indicated the sixth hour. The porter opened the gates of the court, which had that night been my asylum, and I issued into the streets, pacing them with quick steps, as if I sought to avoid the wretch whom I feared every turning of the streets would present to my view. I did not dare return to the apartment which I inhabited, but felt impelled to hurry on, although drenched by the rain which poured from a black and comfortless sky.

I continued walking in this manner for some time, endeavoring, by bodily exercise, to ease the load that weighed upon my mind. I traversed the streets, without any clear conception of where I was, or what I was doing. My heart palpitated in the sickness of fear; and I hurried on with irregular steps, not daring to look about me:—

> "Like one who, on a lonely road,
> Doth walk in fear and dread,
> And, having once turned round, walks on,
> And turns no more his head;
> Because he knows a frightful fiend
> Doth close behind him tread."*

* Coleridge's *Ancient Mariner*

Werewolves are very ancient creatures of legend. It was said that some men could charm wolves. This is John LaFarge's painting called "The Wolf Charmer."

·⊱| 1896 |⊰·

THE WEREWOLF

by Clemence Housman

One of the oldest supernatural motifs in literature is that of the werewolf, a man or woman transformed into a wolf, who, with a vengeance he cannot control, goes out to slay a fellow human being—often one he loves. The ancient Roman writers Herodotus and Ovid wrote of werewolves, and such stories have appeared in literature ever since. The werewolf was a favorite topic of legend, particularly in eastern Europe and in France where it was known as the *loup-garou,* deeply to be feared. In the popular imagination werewolves did exist. Many antiquarian writers have claimed to have seen such animals, and have given dates of their appearance. In India, for example, the werewolf legend has still not died out.

All primitive peoples felt that man and animal were closely attuned to each other. Many primitive tribes have some animal as a totem, a further extension of a human personality, a good or bad presence that is closely identified with the tribe. Our own Indians of the American Northwest, for example, have particularly strong feelings for animals. Their totems are the animals depicted on totem poles. But werewolf stories are rare in the United States. English and European writers, with their legacies of medieval tales, have been far more obsessed with portraying werewolves. As time went by, in most civilized areas the werewolf was no longer considered real, but rather a projection of some of the horror and fear that man contains within his own unconscious.

Few writers have used the werewolf plot with as much poignancy and drama as Clemence Housman, the sister of the far better known A. E. Housman, who published her story in 1896.

The great farm hall was ablaze with the fire-light, and noisy with laughter and talk and many-sounding work. None could be idle but the very young and the very old—little Rol, who was hugging a puppy, and old Trella, whose palsied hand fumbled over her knitting. The early evening had closed in, and the farm servants had come in from the outdoor work and assembled in the ample hall, which had space for scores of workers. Several of the men were engaged in carving, and to these were yielded the best place and light; others made or repaired fishing tackle and harness, and a great seine net occupied three pairs of hands. Of the women, most were sorting and mixing eider feather and chopping straw of the same. Looms were there, though not in present use, but three wheels whirred emulously, and the finest and swiftest thread of the three ran between the fingers of the house mistress. Near her were some children, busy, too, plaiting wicks for candles and lamps. Each group of workers had a lamp in its centre, and those farthest from the fire had extra warmth from two braziers filled with glowing wood embers, replenished now and again from the generous hearth. But the flicker of the great fire was manifest to remotest corners, and prevailed beyond the limits of the lesser lights.

Little Rol grew tired of his puppy, dropped it incontinently, and made an onslaught on Tyr, the old wolfhound, who basked, dozing, whimpering and twitching in his hunting dreams. Prone went Rol beside Tyr, his young arms round the shaggy neck, his curls against the black jowl. Tyr gave a perfunctory lick, and stretched with a sleepy sigh. Rol growled and rolled and shoved invitingly, but could gain nothing from the old dog but placid toleration and a half-observant blink. "Take that, then!" said Rol, indignant at this ignoring of his advances, and sent the puppy sprawling against the dignity that disdained him as playmate. The dog took no notice, and the child wandered off to find amusement elsewhere.

The baskets of white eider feathers caught his eye far off in a distant corner. He slipped under the table and crept along on all-fours, the ordinary commonplace custom of walking down a room upright not being to his fancy. When close to the women he lay still for a moment watching, with his elbows on the floor and his chin in his palms. One of the women seeing him nodded and smiled, and presently he crept out behind her skirts and passed, hardly noticed, from one to another, till he found opportunity to possess himself of a large handful of feathers. With these he traversed the length of the room, under the table again, and emerged near the spinners. At the feet of the youngest he curled himself round, sheltered by her knees from the observation of the others, and disarmed her of interference by secretly displaying his handful with a confiding smile. A dubious nod satisfied him, and presently he proceeded with the play he had planned. He took a tuft of the white down, and gently shook it free of his fingers close to the whirl of the wheel. The wind of the swift motion took it, spun it round and round in widening circles, till it floated above like a slow white moth. Little Rol's eyes danced, and the row of his small teeth shone in a silent laugh of delight. Another and another of the white tufts was sent whirling round like a winged thing in a spider's web, and floating clear at last. Presently the handful failed.

Rol sprawled forward to survey the room and contemplate another journey under the table. His shoulder thrusting forward checked the wheel for an instant; he shifted hastily. The wheel flew on with a jerk and the thread snapped. "Naughty Rol!" said the girl. The swiftest wheel stopped also, and the house mistress, Rol's aunt, leaned forward and sighting the low curly head, gave a warning against mischief, and sent him off to old Trella's corner.

Rol obeyed, and, after a discreet period of obedience, sidled out again down the length of the room farthest from his aunt's eye. As he slipped in among the men, they looked up to see that their tools might be, as far as possible, out of reach of Rol's hands, and close to their own. Nevertheless, before long he managed to secure a fine chisel and take off its point on the leg of the table. The carver's strong objections to this disconcerted Rol, who for five minutes thereafter effaced himself under the table.

During this seclusion he contemplated the many pairs of legs that surrounded him and almost shut out the light of the fire. How very odd some of the legs were; some were curved where they should be straight; some were straight where they should be curved; and as Rol said to himself, "They all seemed screwed on differently." Some were tucked away modestly, under the benches, others were thrust far out under the table, encroaching on Rol's own particular domain. He stretched out his own short legs and regarded them critically, and, after comparison, favorably. Why were not all legs made like his, or like his?

These legs approved by Rol were a little apart from the rest. He crawled opposite and again made comparison. His face grew quite solemn as he thought of the innumerable days to come before his legs could be as long and strong. He hoped they would be just like those, his models, as straight as to bone, as curved as to muscle.

A few moments later Sweyn of the long legs felt a small hand caressing his foot, and looking down met the upturned eyes of his little cousin Rol. Lying on his back, still softly patting and stroking the young man's foot, the child was quiet and happy for a good while. He watched the movements of the strong, deft hands and the shifting of the bright tools. Now and then minute chips of wood puffed off by Sweyn fell down upon his face. At last he raised himself very gently, lest a jog should wake impatience in the carver, and crossing his own legs round

Sweyn's ankle, clasping with his arms too, laid his head against the knee. Such an act is evidence of a child's most wonderful hero worship. Quite content was Rol, and more than content when Sweyn paused a minute to joke, and pat his head and pull his curls. Quiet he remained, as long as quiescence is possible to limbs young as his. Sweyn forgot he was near, hardly noticed when his leg was gently released, and never saw the stealthy abstraction of one of his tools.

Ten minutes thereafter was a lamentable wail from low on the floor, rising to the full pitch of Rol's healthy lungs, for his hand was gashed across and the copious bleeding terrified him. Then there was soothing and comforting, washing and binding, and a modicum of scolding, till the loud outcry sank into occasional sobs, and the child, tear-stained and subdued, was returned to the chimney-corner, where Trella nodded.

In the reaction after pain and fright, Rol found that the quiet of that fire-lit corner was to his mind. Tyr, too, disdained him no longer, but roused by his sobs, showed all the concern and sympathy that a dog can by licking and wistful watching. A little shame weighed also upon his spirits. He wished he had not cried quite so much. He remembered how once Sweyn had come home with his arm torn down from the shoulder, and a dead bear; and how he had never winced nor said a word, though his lips turned white with pain. Poor little Rol gave an extra sighing sob over his own faint-hearted shortcomings.

The light and motion of the great fire began to tell strange stories to the child, and the wind in the chimney roared a corroborative note now and then. The great black mouth of the chimney, impending high over the hearth, received the murky coils of smoke and brightness of aspiring sparks as into a mysterious gulf, and beyond, in the high darkness, were muttering and wailing and strange doings, so that sometimes the smoke rushed back in panic, and curled out and up to the roof, and condensed itself to invisibility among the rafters. And then the wind would rage after its lost prey, rattling and shrieking at window and door.

In a lull, after one such loud gust, Rol lifted his head in surprise and listened. A lull had also come on the babble of talk, and thus could be heard with strange distinctness a sound without the door—the sound of a child's voice, a child's hands. "Open, open; let me in!" piped the little voice from low down, lower than the handle, and the latch rattled as though a tip-toe child reached up to it, and soft small knocks were struck. One near the door sprang up and opened it. "No one is here," he said. Tyr lifted his head and gave utterance to a howl, loud, prolonged, most dismal.

Sweyn, not able to believe that his ears had deceived him, got up and went to the door. It was a dark night; the clouds were heavy with snow, that had fallen fitfully when the wind lulled. Untrodden snow lay up to the porch; there was no sight nor sound of any human being. Sweyn strained his eyes far and near, only to see dark sky, pure snow, and a line of black fir trees on a hill brow, bowing down before the wind. "It must have been the wind," he said, and closed the door.

Many faces looked scared. The sounds of a child's voice had been so distinct—and the words, "Open, open; let me in!" The wind might creak the wood or rattle the latch, but could not speak with a child's voice; nor knock with the soft plain blows that a plump fist gives. And the strange unusual howl of the wolf-hound was an omen to be feared, be the rest what it might. Strange things were said by one and other, till the rebuke of the house mistress quelled them into far-off whispers. For a time after there was uneasiness, constraint, and silence; then the chill fear thawed by degrees, and the babble of talk flowed on again.

Yet half an hour later a very slight noise outside the door sufficed to arrest every hand, every tongue. Every head was raised, every eye fixed in one direction. "It is Christian; he is late," said Sweyn.

No, no; this is a feeble shuffle, not a young man's tread. With the sound of uncertain feet came the hard tap tap of a stick against the door, and the high-pitched voice of eld, "Open,

open; let me in!" Again Tyr flung up his head in a long doleful howl.

Before the echo of the tapping stick and the high voice had fairly died way, Sweyn had sprung across to the door and flung it wide. "No one again," he said in a steady voice, though his eyes looked startled as he stared out. He saw the lonely expanse of snow, the clouds swagging low, and between the two the line of dark fir trees bowing in the wind. He closed the door without word of comment, and recrossed the room.

A score of blanched faces were turned to him as though he were the solver of the enigma. He could not be unconscious of this mute eye-questioning, and it disturbed his resolute air of composure. He hesitated, glanced toward his mother, the house mistress, then back at the frightened folk, and gravely, before them all, made the sign of the cross. There was a flutter of hands as the sign was repeated by all, and the dead silence was stirred as by a huge sigh, for the held breath of many was freed as if the sign gave magic relief.

Even the house mistress was perturbed. She left her wheel and crossed the room to her son, and spoke with him for a moment in a low tone that none could overhear. But a moment later her voice was high-pitched and loud, so that all might benefit by her rebuke of the "heathen chatter" of one of the girls. Perhaps she essayed to silence thus her own misgivings and forebodings.

No other voice dared speak now with its natural fulness. Low tones made intermittent murmurs, and now and then silence drifted over the whole room. The handling of tools was as noiseless as might be, and suspended on the instant if the door rattled in a gust of wind. After a time Sweyn left his work, joined the group nearest the door, and loitered there on the pretence of giving advice and help to the unskillful.

A man's tread was heard outside in the porch, "Christian!" said Sweyn and his mother simultaneously, he confidently, she authoritatively, to set the checked wheels going again. But Tyr flung up his head with an appalling howl.

"Open, open; let me in!"

It was a man's voice, and the door shook and rattled as a man's strength beat against it. Sweyn could feel the planks quivering, as on the instant his hand was upon the door, flinging it open, to face the blank porch, and beyond only snow and sky, and firs aslant in the wind.

He stood for a long minute with the open door in his hand. The bitter wind swept in with its icy chill, but a deadlier chill of fear came swifter, and seemed to freeze the beating of hearts. Sweyn snatched up a great bearskin cloak.

"Sweyn, where are you going?"

"No farther than the porch, mother," and he stepped out and closed the door.

He wrapped himself in the heavy fur, and leaning against the most sheltered wall of the porch, steeled his nerves to face the devil and all his works. No sound of voices came from within; but he could hear the crackle and roar of the fire.

It was bitterly cold. His feet grew numb, but he forebore stamping them into warmth lest the sound should strike panic within; nor would he leave the porch, nor print a foot-mark on the untrodden snow that testified conclusively to no human voices and hands having approached the door since snow fell two hours or more ago. "When the wind drops there will be more snow," thought Sweyn.

For the best part of an hour he kept his watch, and saw no living thing—heard no unwonted sound. "I will freeze here no longer," he muttered, and reentered.

One woman gave a half-suppressed scream as his hand was laid on the latch, and then a gasp of relief as he came in. No one questioned him, only his mother said, in a tone of forced unconcern, "Could you not see Christian coming?" as though she were made anxious only by the absence of her younger son. Hardly had Sweyn stamped near to the fire than clear knocking was heard at the door. Tyr leaped from the hearth—his eyes red as the fire—his fangs showing white in the black jowl—

his neck ridged and bristling; and overleaping Rol, ramped at the door, barking furiously.

Outside the door a clear, mellow voice was calling. Tyr's bark made the words undistinguishable.

No one offered to stir toward the door before Sweyn.

He stalked down the room resolutely, lifted the latch, and swung back the door.

A white-robed woman glided in.

No wraith! Living—beautiful—young.

Tyr leapt upon her.

Lithely she balked the sharp fangs with folds of her long fur robe, and snatching from her girdle a small two-edged axe, whirled it up for a blow of defence.

Sweyn caught the dog by the collar and dragged him off, yelling and struggling. The stranger stood in the doorway motionless, one foot set forward, one arm flung up, till the house mistress hurried down the room, and Sweyn, relinquishing to others the furious Tyr, turned again to close the door and offer excuses for so fierce a greeting. Then she lowered her arm, slung the axe in its place at her waist, loosened the furs about her face, and shook over her shoulder the long white robe—all, as it were, with the sway of one movement.

She was a maiden, tall and very fair. The fashion of her dress was strange—half masculine, yet not unwomanly. A fine fur tunic, reaching but little below the knee, was all the skirt she wore; below were the cross-bound shoes and leggings that a hunter wears. A white fur cap was set low upon the brows, and from its edge strips of fur fell lappet-wise about her shoulders, two of which at her entrance had been drawn forward and crossed about her throat, but now, loosened and thrust back, left unhidden long plaits of fair hair that lay forward on shoulder and breast, down to the ivory-studded girdle where the axe gleamed.

Sweyn and his mother led the stranger to the hearth without question or sign of curiosity, till she voluntarily told her tale of a long journey to distant kindred, a promised guide unmet, and signals and landmarks mistaken.

"Alone!" exclaimed Sweyn, in astonishment. "Have you journeyed thus far—a hundred leagues—alone?"

She answered "Yes," with a little smile.

"Over the hills and the wastes! Why, the folk there are savage and wild as beasts."

She dropped her hand upon her axe with a laugh of scorn.

"I fear neither man nor beast; some few fear me," and then she told strange tales of fierce attack and defence, and of the bold, free huntress life she had led.

Her words came a little slowly and deliberately, as though she spoke in a scarce familiar tongue; now and then she hesitated, and stopped in a phrase, as if for lack of some word.

She became the centre of a group of listeners. The interest she excited dissipated, in some degree, the dread inspired by the mysterious voices. There was nothing ominous about this bright, fair reality, though her aspect was strange.

Little Rol crept near, staring at the stranger with all his might. Unnoticed, he softly stroked and patted a corner of her soft white robe that reached to the floor in ample folds. He laid his cheek against it caressingly, and then edged close up to her knees.

"What is your name?" he asked.

The stranger's smile and ready answer, as she looked down, saved Rol from the rebuke merited by his question.

"My real name," she said, "would be uncouth to your ears and tongue. The folk of this country have given me another name, and from this"—she laid her hand on the fur robe—"they call me 'White Fell.'"

Little Rol repeated it to himself, stroking and patting as before. "White Fell, White Fell."

The fair face, and soft, beautiful dress pleased Rol. He knelt up, with his eyes on her face and an air of uncertain determination, like a robin's on a doorstep, and plumped his elbows into her lap with a little gasp at his own audacity.

"Rol!" exclaimed his aunt; but, "Oh, let him!" said White Fell, smiling and stroking his head; and Rol stayed.

He advanced farther, and, panting at his own adventurousness, in the face of his aunt's authority, climbed up on to her knees. Her welcoming arms hindered any protest. He nestled happily, fingering the axe head, the ivory studs in her girdle, the ivory clasp at her throat, the plaits of fair hair; rubbing his head against the softness of her fur-clad shoulder, with a child's confidence in the kindness of beauty.

White Fell had not uncovered her head, only knotted the pendant fur loosely behind her neck. Rol reached up his hand toward it, whispering her name to himself, "White Fell, White Fell," then slid his arms round her neck, and kissed her—once—twice. She laughed delightedly and kissed him again.

"The child plagues you?" said Sweyn.

"No, indeed," she answered, with an earnestness so intense as to seem disproportionate to the occasion.

Rol settled himself again on her lap and began to unwind the bandage bound round his hand. He paused a little when he saw where the blood had soaked through, then went on till his hand was bare and the cut displayed, gaping and long, though only skin-deep. He held it up toward White Fell, desirous of her pity and sympathy.

At sight of it and the blood-stained linen she drew in her breath suddenly, clasped Rol to her—hard, hard—till he began to struggle. Her face was hidden behind the boy, so that none could see its expression. It had lighted up with a most awful glee.

Afar, beyond the fir grove, beyond the low hill behind, the absent Christian was hastening his return. From daybreak he had been afoot, carrying summons to a bear hunt to all the best hunters of the farms and hamlets that lay within a radius of twelve miles. Nevertheless, having been detained till a late hour, he now broke into a run, going with a long smooth stride that fast made the miles diminish.

He entered the midnight blackness of the fir grove with scarcely slackened pace, though the path was invisible, and, passing through into the open again, sighted the farm lying a furlong off down the slope. Then he sprang out freely, and almost on the instant gave one great sideways leap and stood still. There in the snow was the track of a great wolf.

His hand went to his knife, his only weapon. He stooped, knelt down, to bring his eyes to the level of a beast, and peered about, his teeth set, his heart beating—a little harder than the pace of his running had set it. A solitary wolf, nearly always savage and of large size, is a formidable beast that will not hesitate to attack a single man. This wolf track was the largest Christian had ever seen, and, as far as he could judge, recently made. It led from under the fir-trees down the slope. Well for him, he thought, was the delay that had so vexed him before; well for him that he had not passed through the dark fir grove when that danger of jaws lurked there. Going warily, he followed the track.

It led down the slope, across a broad ice-bound stream, along the level beyond, leading toward the farm. A less sure knowledge than Christian's might have doubted of it being a wolf track, and guessed it to be made by Tyr or some large dog; but he was sure, and knew better than to mistake between a wolf's and a dog's footmark.

Straight on—straight on toward the farm.

Christian grew surprised and anxious at a prowling wolf daring so near. He drew his knife and pressed on, more hastily, more keenly eyed. Oh, that Tyr were with him!

Straight on, straight on, even to the very door, where the snow failed. His heart seemed to give a great leap and then stop. There the track ended.

Nothing lurked in the porch, and there was no sign of return. The firs stood straight against the sky, the clouds lay low; for the wind had fallen and a few snowflakes came drifting down. In a horror of surprise Christian stood dazed a moment; then he lifted the latch and went in. His glance took in all the old familiar forms and faces, and with them that of the stranger, fur-clad and beautiful. The awful truth flashed upon him. He knew what she was.

Only a few were startled by the rattle of the latch as he entered. The room was filled with bustle and movement, for it was the supper hour, and all tools were being put aside and trestles and tables shifted. Christian had no knowledge of what he said and did; he moved and spoke mechanically, half thinking that soon he must wake from this horrible dream. Sweyn and his mother supposed him to be cold and dead-tired, and spared all unnecessary questions. And he found himself seated beside the hearth, opposite that dreadful Thing that looked like a beautiful girl, watching her every movement, curdling with horror to see her fondle Rol.

Sweyn stood near them both, intent upon White Fell also, but how differently! She seemed unconscious of the gaze of both—neither aware of the chill dread in the eyes of Christian, nor of Sweyn's warm admiration.

These two brothers, who were twins, contrasted greatly, despite their striking likeness. They were alike in regular profile, fair brown hair, and deep blue eyes; but Sweyn's features were perfect as a young god's, while Christian's showed faulty details. Thus, the line of his mouth was set too straight, the eyes shelved too deeply back, and the contour of the face flowed in less generous curves than Sweyn's. Their height was the same, but Christian was too slender for perfect proportion, while Sweyn's well-knit frame, broad shoulders and muscular arms made him pre-eminent for manly beauty as well as for strength. As a hunter Sweyn was without rival; as a fisher without rival. All the countryside acknowledged him to be the best wrestler, rider, dancer, singer. Only in speed could he be surpassed, and in that only by his younger brother. All others Sweyn could distance fairly; but Christian could out-run him easily. Ay, he could keep pace with Sweyn's most breathless burst, and laugh and talk the while. Christian took little pride in his fleetness of foot, counting a man's legs to be the least worthy of his limbs. He had no envy of his brother's athletic superiority, though to several feats he had made a moderate second. He loved as only a twin can love—proud of all that Sweyn did, content with all that Sweyn was, humbly content also that his own great love should not be so exceedingly returned, since he knew himself to be so far less loveworthy.

Christian dared not, in the midst of women and children, launch the horror that he knew into words. He waited to consult his brother; but Sweyn did not, or would not, notice the signal he made, and kept his face always turned toward White Fell. Christian drew away from the hearth, unable to remain passive with that dread upon him.

"Where is Tyr?" he said, suddenly. Then catching sight of the dog in a distant corner, "Why is he chained there?"

"He flew at the stranger," one answered.

Christian's eyes glowed. "Yes?" he said interrogatively, and, rising, went without a word to the corner where Tyr was chained. The dog rose up to meet him, as piteous and indignant as a dumb beast can be. He stroked the black head. "Good Tyr! Brave dog!"

They knew—they only—and the man and the dumb dog had comfort of each other.

Christian's eyes turned again toward White Fell. Tyr's also, and he strained against the length of the chain. Christian's hand lay on the dog's neck, and he felt it ridge and bristle with the quivering of impotent fury. Then he began to quiver in like manner, with a fury born of reason, not instinct; as impotent morally as was Tyr physically. Oh, the woman's form that he dare not touch! Anything but that, and he with Tyr, would be free to kill or be killed.

Then he returned to ask fresh questions.

"How long has the stranger been here?"

"She came about half an hour before you."

"Who opened the door to her?"

"Sweyn. No one else dared."

The tone of the answer was mysterious.

"Why?" queried Christian. "Has anything strange happened? Tell me."

For answer he was told in a low undertone of the summons at the door, thrice repeated, without human agency; and of Tyr's ominous howls, and of Sweyn's fruitless watch outside.

Christian turned toward his brother in a torment of impatience for a word apart. The board was spread and Sweyn was leading White Fell to the guest's place. This was more awful! She would break bread with them under the roof tree.

He started forward and, touching Sweyn's arm, whispered an urgent entreaty. Sweyn stared, and shook his head in angry impatience.

Thereupon Christian would take no morsel of food.

His opportunity came at last. White Fell questioned of the landmarks of the country, and of one Cairn Hill, which was an appointed meeting place at which she was due that night. The house mistress and Sweyn both exclaimed.

"It is three long miles away," said Sweyn, "with no place for shelter but a wretched hut. Stay with us this night and I will show you the way to-morrow."

White Fell seemed to hesitate. "Three miles," she said, "then I should be able to see or hear a signal."

"I will look out," said Sweyn; "then, if there be no signal, you must not leave us."

He went to the door. Christian silently followed him out.

"Sweyn, do you know what she is?"

Sweyn, surprised at the vehement grasp and low hoarse voice, made answer:

"She? Who? White Fell?"

"Yes."

"She is the most beautiful girl I have ever seen."

"She is a were-wolf."

Sweyn burst out laughing. "Are you mad?" he asked.

"No; here, see for yourself."

Christian drew him out of the porch, pointing to the snow where the footmarks had been—had been, for now they were not. Snow was falling, and every dint was blotted out.

"Well?" asked Sweyn.

"Had you come when I signed to you, you would have seen for yourself."

"Seen what?"

"The footprints of a wolf leading up to the door; none leading away."

It was impossible not to be startled by the tone alone, though it was hardly above a whisper. Sweyn eyed his brother anxiously, but in the darkness could make nothing of his face. Then he laid his hands kindly and reassuringly on Christian's shoulders and felt how he was quivering with excitement and horror.

"One sees strange things," he said, "when the cold has got into the brain behind the eyes; you came in cold and worn out."

"No," interrupted Christian. "I saw the track first on the brow of the slope, and followed it down right here to the door. This is no delusion."

Sweyn in his heart felt positive that it was. Christian was given to day dreams and strange fancies, though never had he been possessed with so mad a notion before.

"Don't you believe me?" said Christian desperately. "You must. I swear it is sane truth. Are you blind? Why, even Tyr knows."

"You will be clearer-headed to-morrow, after a night's rest. Then come, too, if you will, with White Fell, to the Hill Cairn, and, if you have doubts still, watch and follow, and see what footprints she leaves."

Galled by Sweyn's evident contempt, Christian turned abruptly to the door. Sweyn caught him back.

"What now, Christian? What are you going to do?"

"You do not believe me; my mother shall."

Sweyn's grasp tightened. "You shall not tell her," he said, authoritatively.

Customarily Christian was so docile to his brother's mastery that it was now a surprising thing when he wrenched himself free vigorously and said as determinedly as Sweyn: "She shall know." But Sweyn was nearer the door, and would not let him pass.

"There has been scare enough for one night already. If this notion of yours will keep, broach it to-morrow." Christian would not yield.

"Women are so easily scared," pursued Sweyn, "and are ready to believe any folly without proof. Be a man, Christian, and fight this notion of a were-wolf by yourself."

"If you would believe me," began Christian.

"I believe you to be a fool," said Sweyn, losing patience. "Another, who was not your brother, might think you a knave, and guess that you had transformed White Fell into a were-wolf because she smiled more readily on me than on you."

The jest was not without foundation, for the grace of White Fell's bright looks had been bestowed on him—on Christian never a whit. Sweyn's coxcombry was always frank and most forgivable, and not without justifiableness.

"If you want an ally," continued Sweyn, "confide in old Trella. Out of her stores of wisdom—if her memory holds good—she can instruct you in the orthodox manner of tackling a were-wolf. If I remember aright, you should watch the suspected person till midnight, when the beast's form must be resumed, and retained ever after if a human eye sees the change; or, better still, sprinkle hands and feet with holy water, which is certain death! Oh, never fear, but old Trella will be equal to the occasion."

Sweyn's contempt was no longer good-humored, for he began to feel excessively annoyed at this monstrous doubt of White Fell. But Christian was too deeply distressed to take offence.

"You speak of them as old wives' tales, but if you had seen the proof I have seen, you would be ready at least to wish them true, if not also to put them to the test."

"Well," said Sweyn, with a laugh that had a little sneer in

it, "put them to the test—I will not mind that, if you will only keep your notions to yourself. Now, Christian, give me your word for silence, and we will freeze here no longer."

Christian remained silent.

Sweyn put his hands on his shoulders again and vainly tried to see his face in the darkness.

"We have never quarreled yet, Christian?"

"I have never quarreled," returned the other, aware for the first time that his dictatorial brother had sometimes offered occasion for quarrel, had he been ready to take it.

"Well," said Sweyn, emphatically, "if you speak against White Fell to any other, as to-night you have spoken to me—we shall."

He delivered the words like an ultimatum, turned sharp round and re-entered the house. Christian, more fearful and wretched than before, followed.

"Snow is falling fast—not a single light is to be seen."

White Fell's eyes passed over Christian without apparent notice, and turned bright and shining upon Sweyn.

"Nor any signal to be heard?" she queried. "Did you not hear the sound of a sea-horn?"

"I saw nothing and heard nothing; and signal or no signal, the heavy snow would keep you here perforce."

She smiled her thanks beautifully. And Christian's heart sank like lead with a deadly foreboding, as he noted what a light was kindled in Sweyn's eyes by her smile.

That night, when all others slept, Christian, the weariest of all, watched outside the guest chamber till midnight was past. No sound, not the faintest, could be heard. Could the old tale be true of the midnight change? What was on the other side of the door—a woman or a beast—he would have given his right hand to know. Instinctively he laid his hand on the latch, and drew it softly, though believing that bolts fastened the inner side. The door yielded to his hand; he stood on the threshold; a keen gust of air cut at him. The window stood open; the room was empty.

So Christian could sleep with a somewhat lightened heart.

In the morning there was surprise and conjecture when White Fell's absence was discovered. Christian held his peace; not even to his brother did he say how he knew that she had fled before midnight; and Sweyn, though evidently greatly chagrined, seemed to disdain reference to the subject of Christian's fears.

The elder brother alone joined the bear hunt; Christian found pretext to stay behind. Sweyn, being out of humor, manifested his contempt by uttering not one expostulation.

All that day, and for many a day after, Christian would never go out of sight of his home. Sweyn alone noticed how he manoeuvred for this, and was clearly annoyed by it. White Fell's name was never mentioned between them, though not seldom was it heard in general talk. Hardly a day passed without little Rol asking when White Fell would come again; pretty White Fell, who kissed like a snowflake. And if Sweyn answered, Christian would be quite sure that the light in his eyes, kindled by White Fell's smile, had not yet died out.

Little Rol! Naughty, merry, fair-haired little Rol! A day came when his feet raced over the threshold never to return; when his chatter and laugh were heard no more; when tears of anguish were wept by eyes that never would see his bright head again—never again—living or dead.

He was seen at dusk for the last time, escaping from the house with his puppy, in freakish rebellion against old Trella. Later, when his absence had begun to cause anxiety, his puppy crept back to the farm, cowed, whimpering, and yelping—a pitiful, dumb lump of terror—without intelligence or courage to guide the frightened search.

Rol was never found, nor any trace of him. How he had perished was known only by an awful guess—a wild beast had devoured him.

Christian heard the conjecture, "a wolf," and a horrible certainty flashed upon him that he knew what wolf it was. He tried to declare what he knew, but Sweyn saw him start at the words with white face and struggling lips, and, guessing his purpose, pulled him back and kept him silent, hardly, by his imperious grip and wrathful eyes, and one low whisper. Again Christian yielded to his brother's stronger words and will, and against his own judgment consented to silence.

Repentance came before the new moon—the first of the year—was old. White Fell came again, smiling as she entered as though assured of a glad and kindly welcome; and, in truth, there was only one who saw again her fair face and strange white garb without pleasure. Sweyn's face glowed with delight, while Christian's grew pale and rigid as death. He had given his word to keep silence, but he had not thought that she would dare to come again. Silence was impossible—face to face with that Thing—impossible. Irrepressibly he cried out:

"Where is Rol?"

Not a quiver disturbed White Fell's face; she heard, yet remained bright and tranquil—Sweyn's eyes flashed round at his brother dangerously. Among the women some tears fell at the poor child's name, but none caught alarm from its sudden utterance, for the thought of Rol rose naturally. Where was Rol, who had nestled in the stranger's arms, kissing her, and watched for her since, and prattled of her daily?

Christian went out silently. Only one thing there was that he could do, and he must not delay. His horror overmastered any curiosity to hear White Fell's glib excuses and smiling apologies for her strange and uncourteous departure; or her easy tale of the circumstances of her return; or to watch her bearing as she heard the sad tale of little Rol.

The swiftest runner of the countryside had started on his hardest race—little less than three leagues and back, which he reckoned to accomplish in two hours, though the night was moonless and the way rugged. He rushed against the still cold air till it felt like a wind upon his face. The dim homestead sank below the ridges at his back, and fresh ridges of snowlands rose out of the obscure horizon level to drive past him as the stirless air drove, and sink away behind into obscure level again. He took no conscious heed of landmarks, not even when all sign of a path was gone under depths of snow. His will was set to reach his goal with unexampled speed, and thither by instinct his physical forces bore him, without one definite thought to guide.

And the idle brain lay passive, inert, receiving into its vacancy, restless siftings of past sights and sounds; Rol weeping, laughing, playing, coiled in the arms of that dreadful Thing; Tyr—O Tyr!—white fangs in the black jowl; the women who wept on the foolish puppy, precious for the child's last touch; footprints from pinewood to door; the smiling face among furs, of such womanly beauty—smiling—smiling; and Sweyn's face.

"Sweyn, Sweyn, O Sweyn, my brother!"

Sweyn's angry laugh possessed his ear within the sound of the wind of his speed; Sweyn's scorn assailed more quick and keen than the biting cold at his throat. And yet he was unimpressed by any thought of how Sweyn's scorn and anger would rise if this errand were known.

To the younger brother all life was a spiritual mystery, veiled from his clear knowledge by the density of flesh. Since he knew his own body to be linked to the complex and antagonistic forces that constitute one soul, it seemed to him not impossibly strange that one spiritual force should possess divers forms for widely various manifestation. Nor, to him, was it great effort to believe that as pure water washes away all natural foulness, so water holy by consecration must needs cleanse God's world from that supernatural evil Thing. Therefore, faster than ever man's foot had covered those leagues, he sped under the dark, still night, over the waste trackless snow ridges to the far-away church where salvation lay in the holy-water stoop at the door. His faith was as firm as any that wrought miracles in days past, simple as a child's wish, strong as a man's will.

He was hardly missed during these hours, every second of which was by him fulfilled to its utmost extent by extremest effort that sinews and nerves could attain. Within the homestead the while the easy moments went bright with words and looks of unwonted animation, for the kindly hospitable instincts of the inmates were roused into cordial expression of welcome and interest by the grace and beauty of the returned stranger.

But Sweyn was eager and earnest, with more than a host's courteous warmth. The impression that at her first coming had charmed him, that had lived since through memory, deepened now in her actual presence. Sweyn, the matchless among men, acknowledged in this fair White Fell a spirit high and bold as his own, and a frame so firm and capable that only bulk was lacking for equal strength. Yet the white skin was moulded most smoothly, without such muscular swelling as made his might evident. Such love as his frank self-love could concede was called forth by an ardent admiration for this supreme stranger. More admiration than love was in his passion, and therefore he was free from a lover's hesitancy, and delicate reserve and doubts. Frankly and boldly he courted her favor by looks and tones, and an address that was his by natural ease.

Nor was she a woman to be wooed otherwise. Tender whispers and sighs would never gain her ear; but her eyes would brighten and shine if she heard of a brave feat, and her prompt hand in sympathy fall swiftly on the axe haft and clasp it hard. That movement ever fired Sweyn's admiration anew; he watched for it, strove to elicit it and glowed when it came. Wonderful and beautiful was that wrist, slender and steel-strong; the smooth shapely hand that curved so fast and firm, ready to deal instant death.

Desiring to feel the pressure of these hands, this bold lover schemed with palpable directness, proposing that she should hear how their hunting songs were sung, with a chorus that signalled hands to be clasped. So his splendid voice gave the verses, and, as the chorus was taken up, he claimed her hands, and, even through the easy grip, felt, as he desired, the strength that was latent, and the vigor that quickened the very finger tips, as the song fired her, and her voice was caught out of her by the rhythmic swell and rang clear on the top of the closing surge.

Afterward she sang alone. For contrast, or in the pride of swaying moods by her voice, she chose a mournful song that drifted along in a minor chant, sad as a wind that dirges:

"Oh, let me go!
Around spin wreaths of snow;
The dark earth sleeps below.

"Far up the plain
Moans on a voice of pain;
'Where shall my babe be lain,'

"In my white breast
Lay the sweet life to rest!
Lay, where it can be best!

" 'Hush! hush!' it cries;
'Tense night is on the skies;
'Two stars are in thine eyes.'

"Come, babe away!
But lie thou till dawn be gray,
Who must be dead by day.

"This cannot last;
But, o'er the sickening blast,
All sorrows shall be past;

"All kings shall be
Low bending at thy knee,
Worshipping life from thee.

"For men long sore
To hope of what's before—
To leave the things of yore.

"Mine, and not thine,
How deep their jewels shine!
Peace laps thy head, not mine!"

Old Trella came tottering from her corner, shaken to additional palsy by an aroused memory. She strained her dim eyes toward the singer, and then bent her head that the one ear yet sensible to sound might avail of every note. At the close, groping forward, she murmured with the high pitched quaver of old age:

"So she sang, my Thora; my last and brightest. What is she like—she, whose voice is like my dead Thora's? Are her eyes blue?"

"Blue as the sky."

"So were my Thora's! Is her hair fair and in plaits to the waist?"

"Even so," answered White Fell herself, and met the advancing hands with her own, and guided them to corroborate her words by touch.

"Like my dead Thora's," repeated the old woman; and then her trembling hands rested on the fur-clad shoulders and she bent forward and kissed the smooth fair face that White Fell upturned, nothing loath to receive and return the caress.

So Christian saw them as he entered.

He stood a moment. After the starless darkness and the icy night air, and the fierce silent two hours' race, his senses reeled on sudden entrance into warmth and light and the cheery hum of voices. A sudden unforeseen anguish assailed him, as now first he entertained the possibility of being overmatched by her wiles and her daring, if at the approach of pure death she should start up at bay transformed to a terrible beast, and achieve a savage glut at the last. He looked with horror and pity on the harmless helpless folk, so unwitting of outrage to their comfort and security. The dreadful Thing in their midst, that was veiled from their knowledge by womanly beauty, was a centre of pleasant interest. There, before him, signally impressive, was poor old Trella, weakest and feeblest of all, in fond nearness. And a moment might bring about the revelation of a monstrous horror—a ghastly, deadly danger, set loose and at bay, in a circle of girls and women, and careless, defenceless men.

And he alone of the throng prepared!

For one breathing space he faltered, no longer than that, while over him swept the agony of compunction that yet could not make him surrender his purpose.

He alone? Nay, but Tyr also, and he crossed to the dumb sole sharer of his knowledge.

So timeless is thought that a few seconds only lay between his lifting of the latch and his loosening of Tyr's collar; but in those few seconds succeeding his first glance, as lightning-swift had been the impulses of others, their motion as quick and sure. Sweyn's vigilant eye had darted upon him, and instantly his every fiber was alert with hostile instinct; and half divining, half incredulous, of Christian's object in stooping to Tyr, he came hastily, wary, wrathful, resolute to oppose the malice of his wild-eyed brother.

But beyond Sweyn rose White Fell, blanching white as her furs, and with eyes grown fierce and wild. She leapt down the room to the door, whirling her long robe closely to her. "Hark!" she panted. "The signal horn! Hark, I must go!" as she snatched at the latch to be out and away.

For one precious moment Christian had hesitated on the half loosened collar; for, except the womanly form were exchanged for the bestial, Tyr's jaws would gnash to rags his honor of manhood. He heard her voice, and turned—too late.

As she tugged at the door, he sprang across grasping his flask, but Sweyn dashed between and caught him back irresistibly, so that a most frantic effort only availed to wrench one arm free. With that, on the impulse of sheer despair, he cast at her with all his force. The door swung behind her, and the flask flew into fragments against it. Then, as Sweyn's grasp slackened, and he met the questioning astonishment of surrounding faces, with a hoarse inarticulate cry: "God help us all!" he said; "she is a were-wolf!"

Sweyn turned upon him, "Liar, coward!" and his hands gripped his brother's throat with deadly force as though the spoken word could be killed so, and, as Christian struggled, lifted him clear off his feet and flung him crashing backward. So furious was he that, as his brother lay motionless, he stirred him roughly with his foot, till their mother came between, crying, "Shame!" and yet then he stood by, his teeth set, his brows knit, his hands clenched, ready to enforce silence again violently, as Christian rose, staggering and bewildered.

But utter silence and submission was more than he expected, and turned his anger into contempt for one so easily cowed and held in subjection by mere force. "He is mad!" he said, turning on his heel as he spoke, so that he lost his mother's look of pained reproach at this sudden free utterance of what was a lurking dread within her.

Christian was too spent for the effort of speech. His hard drawn breath labored in great sobs; his limbs were powerless and unstrung in utter relax after hard service. His failure in this endeavor induced a stupor of misery and despair. In addition was the wretched humiliation of open violence and strife with his brother, and the distress of hearing misjudging contempt expressed without reserve, for he was aware that Sweyn had turned to allay the scared excitement half by imperious mastery, half by explanation and argument that showed painful disregard of brotherly consideration.

Sweyn the while was observant of his brother, despite the continual check of finding, turn and glance where he would, Christian's eyes always upon him, with a strange look of helpless distress, discomposing enough to the angry aggressor. "Like a beaten dog!" he said to himself, rallying contempt to withstand compunction. Observation set him wondering on Christian's exhausted condition. The heavy laboring breath and the slack, inert fall of the limbs told surely of unusual and prolonged exertion. And then why had close upon two hours' absence been followed by manifestly hostile behavior toward White Fell? Suddenly, the fragments of the flask giving a clue, he guessed all, and faced about to stare at his brother in amaze. He forgot that the motive scheme was against White Fell, demanding derision and resentment from him; that was swept out of remembrance by astonishment and admiration for the feat of speed and endurance.

That night Sweyn and his mother talked long and late together, shaping into certainty the suspicion that Christian's mind had lost its balance, and discussing the evident cause. For Sweyn, declaring his own love for White Fell, suggested that his unfortunate brother with a like passion—they being twins in love as in birth—had through jealousy and despair turned from love to hate, until reason failed at the strain, and a craze developed, which the malice and treachery of madness made a serious and dangerous force.

So Sweyn theorized; convincing himself as he spoke; convincing afterward others who advanced doubts against White Fell; fettering his judgment by his advocacy, and by his staunch defence of her hurried flight, silencing his own inner consciousness of the unaccountability of her action.

But a little time and Sweyn lost his vantage in the shock of a fresh horror at the homestead. Trella was no more, and her end a mystery. The poor old woman crawled out in a bright gleam to visit a bed-ridden gossip living beyond the fir grove. Under the trees she was last seen halting for her companion, sent back for a forgotten present. Quick alarm sprang, calling every man to the search. Her stick was found among the brushwood near the path, but no track or stain, for a gusty wind was sifting the snow from the branches and hid all sign of how she came by her death.

So panic-stricken were the farm folk that none dared go singly on the search. Known danger could be braced, but not this stealthy Death that walked by day invisible, that cut off alike the child in his play and the aged woman so near to her quiet grave.

"Rol she kissed; Trella she kissed!" So rang Christian's frantic cry again and again, till Sweyn dragged him away and strove to keep him apart from the rest of the household.

But thenceforward all Sweyn's reasoning and mastery could not uphold White Fell above suspicion. He was not called upon to defend her from accusation, when Christian had been brought to silence again; but he well knew the significance of this fact, that her name, formerly uttered freely and often, he never heard now—it was huddled away into whispers that he could not catch.

For a time the twins' variance was marked on Sweyn's part by an air of rigid indifference, on Christian's by heavy downcast silence, and a nervous, apprehensive observation of his brother. Superadded to his remorse and foreboding, Sweyn's displeasure weighed upon him intolerably, and the remembrance of their violent rupture was ceaseless misery. The elder brother, self-sufficient and insensitive, could little know how deeply his unkindness stabbed. A depth and force of affection such as Christian's was unknown to him, and his brother's ceaseless surveillance annoyed him greatly. Therefore, that suspicion might be lulled, he judged it wise to make overtures for peace. Most easily done. A little kindliness, a few evidences of consideration, a slight return of the old brotherly imperiousness, and Christian replied by a gratefulness and relief that might have touched him had he understood all, but instead increased his secret contempt.

So successful was his finesse that when, late on a day, a message summoning Christian to a distance was transmitted by Sweyn no doubt of its genuineness occurred. When, his errand proving useless, he set out to return, mistake or misapprehension was all that he surmised. Not till he sighted the homestead, lying low between the night-gray snow ridges, did vivid recollection of the time when he had tracked that horror to the door rouse an intense dread, and with it a hardly defined suspicion.

His grasp tightened on the bear-spear that he carried as a

staff; every sense was alert, every muscle strung; excitement urged him on, caution checked him, and the two governed his long stride, swiftly, noiselessly to the climax he felt was at hand.

As he drew near to the outer gates, a light shadow stirred and went, as though the gray of the snow had taken detached motion. A darker shadow stayed and faced Christian.

Sweyn stood before him, and surely the shadow that went was White Fell.

They had been together—close. Had she not been in his arms, near enough for lips to meet?

There was no moon, but the stars gave light enough to show that Sweyn's face was flushed and elate. The flush remained, though the expression changed quickly at sight of his brother. How, if Christian had seen all, should one of his frenzied outbursts be met and managed—by resolution? by indifference? He halted between the two, and as a result, he swaggered.

"White Fell?" questioned Christian, breathlessly.

"Yes?" Sweyn's answer was a query, with an intonation that implied he was clearing the ground for action.

From Christian came, "Have you kissed her?" like a bolt direct, staggering Sweyn by its sheer, prompt temerity.

He flushed yet darker, and yet half smiled over this earnest of success he had won. Had there been really between himself and Christian the rivalry that he imagined, his face had enough of the insolence of triumph to exasperate jealous rage.

"You dare ask this!"

"Sweyn, O Sweyn, I must know! You have!"

The ring of despair and anguish in his tone angered Sweyn, misconstruing it. Jealousy so presumptuous was intolerable.

"Mad fool!" he said, constraining himself no longer. "Win for yourself a woman to kiss. Leave mine without question. Such a one as I should desire to kiss is such a one as shall never allow a kiss to you."

Then Christian fully understood his supposition.

"I—I—I!" he cried. "White Fell—that deadly Thing! Sweyn, are you blind, mad? I would save you from her—a were-wolf!"

Sweyn maddened again at the accusation—a dastardly way of revenge, as he conceived; and instantly, for the second time, the brothers were at strife violently. But Christian was now too desperate to be scrupulous; for a dim glimpse had shot a possibility into his mind, and to be free to follow it the striking of his brother was a necessity. Thank God! he was armed, and so Sweyn's equal.

Facing his assailant with the bear-spear, he struck up his arms, and with the butt end hit so hard that he fell. Then the matchless runner leapt away, to follow a forlorn hope.

Sweyn, on regaining his feet, was as amazed as angry at this unaccountable flight. He knew in his heart that his brother was no coward, and that it was unlike him to shrink from an encounter because defeat was certain, and cruel humiliation from a vindictive victor probable. Of the uselessness of pursuit he was well aware; he must abide his chagrin until his time for advantage should come. Since White Fell had parted to the right, Christian to the left, the event of a sequent encounter did not occur to him.

And now Christian, acting on the dim glimpse he had had, just as Sweyn turned upon him, of something that moved against the sky along the ridge behind the homestead, was staking his only hope on a chance, and his own superlative speed. If what he saw was really White Fell, he guessed she was bending her steps toward the open wastes; and there was just a possibility that, by a straight dash, and a desperate, perilous leap over a sheer bluff, he might yet meet her or head her. And then—he had no further thought.

It was past, the quick, fierce race, and the chance of death at the leap, and he halted in a hollow to fetch his breath and to look—did she come? Had she gone?

She came.

She came with a smooth, gliding, noiseless speed, that was neither walking nor running; her arms were folded in her furs that were drawn tight about her body; the white lappets from her head were wrapped and knotted closely beneath her face;

her eyes were set on a far distance. Then the even sway of her going was startled to a pause by Christian.

"Fell!"

She drew a quick, sharp breath at the sound of her name thus mutilated, and faced Sweyn's brother. Her eyes glittered; her upper lip was lifted and showed the teeth. The half of her name, impressed with an ominous sense as uttered by him, warned her of the aspect of a deadly foe. Yet she cast loose her robes till they trailed ample, and spoke as a mild woman.

"What would you?"

Christian answered with his solemn, dreadful accusation:

"You kissed Rol—and Rol is dead! You kissed Trella—she is dead! You have kissed Sweyn, my brother, but he shall not die!"

He added: "You may live till midnight."

The edge of the teeth and the glitter of the eyes stayed a moment, and her right hand also slid down to the axe haft. Then, without a word, she swerved from him, and sprang out and away swiftly over the snow.

And Christian sprang out and away, and followed her swiftly over the snow, keeping behind, but half a stride's length from her side.

So they went running together, silent, toward the vast wastes of snow where no living thing but they two moved under the stars of night.

Never before had Christian so rejoiced in his powers. The gift of speed and the training of use and endurance were priceless to him now. Though midnight was hours away he was confident that go where that Fell Thing would hasten as she would, she could not outstrip him, nor escape from him. Then, when came the time for transformation, when the woman's form made no longer a shield against a man's hand, he could slay or be slain to save Sweyn. He had struck his dear brother in dire extremity, but he could not, though reason urged, strike a woman.

For one mile, for two miles they ran; White Fell ever foremost, Christian ever at an equal distance from her side, so near that, now and again, her outflying furs touched him. She spoke no word; nor he. She never turned her head to look at him, nor swerved to evade him; but, with set face looking forward, sped straight on, over rough, over smooth, aware of his nearness by the regular beat of his feet, and the sound of his breath behind.

In a while she quickened her pace. From the first Christian had judged of her speed as admirable, yet with exulting security in his own excelling and enduring whatever her efforts. But, when the pace increased, he found himself put to the test as never had been done before in any race. Her feet indeed flew faster than his; it was only by his length of stride that he kept his place at her side. But his heart was high and resolute, and he did not fear failure yet.

So the desperate race flew on. Their feet struck up the powdery snow, their breath smoked into the sharp, clear air, and they were gone before the air was cleared of snow and vapor. Now and then Christian glanced up to judge, by the rising of the stars, of the coming of midnight. So long—so long!

White Fell held on without slack. She, it was evident, with confidence in her speed proving matchless, as resolute to outrun her pursuer, as he to endure till midnight and fulfil his purpose. And Christian held on, still self-assured. He could not fail; he would not fail. To avenge Rol and Trella was motive enough for him to do what man could do; but for Sweyn more. She had kissed Sweyn, but he should not die, too—with Sweyn to save he could not fail.

Never before was such a race as this; no, not when in old Greece man and maid raced together with two fates at stake; for the hard running was sustained unabated, while star after star rose and went wheeling up toward midnight—for one hour, for two hours.

Then Christian saw and heard what shot him through with fear. Where a fringe of trees hung round a slope he saw something dark moving, and heard a yelp, followed by a full, horrid cry, and the dark spread out upon the snow—a pack of wolves in pursuit.

Of the beasts alone he had little cause for fear; at the pace he held he could distance them, four footed though they were. But of White Fell's wiles he had infinite apprehension, for how might she not avail herself of the savage jaws of these wolves, akin as they were to half her nature. She vouchsafed to them nor look nor sign; but Christian, on an impulse, to assure himself that she should not escape him, caught and held the back-flung edge of her furs, running still.

She turned like a flash with a beastly snarl, teeth and eyes gleaming again. Her axe shone on the upstroke, on the downstroke, as she hacked at his hand. She had lopped it off at the wrist, but that he parried with the bear-spear. Even then she shore through the shaft and shattered the bones of the hand, so that he loosed perforce.

Then again they raced on as before, Christian not losing a pace, though his left hand swung bleeding and broken.

The snarl, indubitably, though modified from a woman's organs; the vicious fury revealed in teeth and eyes; the sharp, arrogant pain of her maiming blow, caught away Christian's heed of the beasts behind, by striking into him close, vivid realization of the infinitely greater danger that ran before him in that deadly Thing.

When he bethought him to look behind, lo! the pack had but reached their tracks, and instantly slunk aside, cowed; the yell of pursuit changed to yelps and whines. So abhorrent was that fell creature to beast as to man.

She had drawn her furs more closely to her, disposing them so that, instead of flying loose to her heels, no drapery hung lower than her knees, and this without a check to her wonderful speed, nor embarrassment by the cumbering of the folds. She held her head as before; her lips were firmly set, only the tense nostrils gave her breath; not a sign of distress witnessed to the long sustaining of that terrible speed.

But on Christian by now the strain was telling palpably. His head weighed heavy, and his breath came laboring in great sobs; the bear-spear would have been a burden now. His heart was beating like a hammer, but such a dullness oppressed his brain that it was only by degrees he could realize his helpless state; wounded and weaponless, chasing that Thing, that was a fierce, desperate, axe-armed woman, except she should assume the beast with fangs yet more deadly.

And still the far, slow stars went lingering nearly an hour from midnight.

So far was his brain astray that an impression took him that she was fleeing from the midnight stars, whose gain was by such slow degrees that a time equalling days and days had gone in the race round the northern circle of the world, and days and days as long might last before the end—except she slackened, or except he failed.

But he would not fail yet.

How long had he been praying so? He had started with a self-confidence and reliance that had felt no need for that aid; and now it seemed the only means by which to restrain his heart from swelling beyond the compass of his body; by which to cherish his brain from dwindling and shriveling quite away. Some sharp-toothed creature kept tearing and dragging on his maimed left hand; he never could see it, he could not shake it off, but he prayed it off at times.

The clear stars before him took to shuddering and he knew why; they shuddered at sight of what was behind him. He had never divined before that strange Things hid themselves from men, under pretence of being snow-clad mounds of swaying trees; but now they came slipping out from their harmless covers to follow him, and mock at his impotence to make a kindred Thing resolve to truer form. He knew the air behind him was thronged; he heard the hum of innumerable murmurings together; but his eyes could never catch them—they were too swift and nimble; but he knew they were there, because, on a backward glance, he saw the snow mounds surge as they grovelled flatlings out of sight; he saw the trees reel as they screwed themselves rigid past recognition among the boughs.

And after such glance the stars for a while returned to steadfastness, and an infinite stretch of silence froze upon the chill, gray world, only deranged by the swift, even beat of the flying feet, and his own—slower from the longer stride, and the sound of his breath. And for some clear moments he knew that his only concern was to sustain his speed regardless of pain and distress, to deny with every nerve he had her power to outstrip him or to widen the space between them, till the stars crept up to midnight.

A hideous check came to the race. White Fell swirled about and leapt to the right, and Christian, unprepared for so prompt a lurch, found close at his feet a deep pit yawning, and his own impetus past control. But he snatched at her as he bore past, clasping her right arm with his one whole hand, and the two swung together upon the brink.

And her straining away in self-preservation was vigorous enough to counterbalance his headlong impulse, and brought them reeling together to safety.

Then, before he was verily sure that they were not to perish so, crashing down, he saw her gnashing in wild, pale fury, as she wrenched to be free; and since her right arm was in his grasp, used her axe left-handed, striking back at him.

The blow was effectual enough even so; his right arm dropped powerless, gashed and with the lesser bone broken that jarred with horrid pain when he let it swing, as he leaped out again, and ran to recover the few feet she had gained from his pause at the shock.

The near escape and this new, quick pain made again every faculty alive and intense. He knew that what he followed was most surely Death animate; wounded and helpless, he was utterly at her mercy if so she should realize and take action. Hopeless to avenge, hopeless to save, his very despair for Sweyn swept him on to follow and follow and precede the kiss-doomed to death. Could he yet fail to hunt that Thing past midnight, out of the womanly form, alluring and treacherous, into lasting restraint of the bestial, which was the last shred of hope left from the confident purpose of the outset.

The last hour from midnight had lost half its quarters, and the stars went lifting up the great minutes, and again his greatening heart and his shrinking brain and the sickening agony that swung at either side conspired to appal the will that had only seeming empire over his feet.

Now White Fell's body was so closely enveloped that not a lap nor an edge flew free. She stretched forward strangely aslant, leaning from the upright poise of a runner. She cleared the ground at times by long bounds, gaining an increase of speed that Christian agonized to equal.

He grew bewildered, uncertain of his own identity, doubting of his own true form. He could not be really a man, no more than that running Thing was really a woman; his real form was only hidden under embodiment of a man, but what it was he did not know. And Sweyn's real form he did not know. Sweyn lay fallen at his feet, where he had struck him down—his own brother—he; he stumbled over him and had to overleap him and race harder because she who had kissed Sweyn leapt so fast. "Sweyn—Sweyn—O Sweyn!"

Why did the stars stop to shudder? Midnight else had surely come!

The leaning, leaping Thing looked back at him a wild, fierce look, and laughed in savage scorn and triumph. He saw in a flash why, for within a time measureable by seconds she would have escaped him utterly. As the land lay a slope of ice sunk on the one hand; on the other hand a steep rose, shouldering forward; between the two was space for a foot to be planted, but none for a body to stand; yet a juniper bough, thrusting out, gave a handhold secure enough for one with a resolute grasp to swing past the perilous place, and pass on safe.

Though the first seconds of the last moment were going,

she dared to flash back a wicked look, and laugh at the pursuer who was impotent to grasp.

The crisis struck convulsive life into his last supreme effort; his will surged up indomitable, his speed proved matchless yet. He leapt with a rush, passed her before her laugh had time to go out, and turned short, barring the way, and braced to withstand her.

She came hurling desperate, with a feint to the right hand, and then launched herself upon him with a spring like a wild beast when it leaps to kill. And he, with one strong arm and a hand that could not hold, with one strong hand and an arm that could not guide and sustain, he caught and held her even so. And they fell together. And because he felt his whole arm slipping and his whole hand loosing, to slack the dreadful agony of the wrenched bone above, he caught and held with his teeth the tunic at her knee, as she struggled up and wrung off his hands to overleap him victorious.

Like lightning she snatched her axe, and struck him on the neck—deep—once—twice—his life-blood gushed out, staining her feet.

The stars touched midnight.

The death scream he heard was not his, for his set teeth had hardly yet relaxed when it rang out. And the dreadful cry began with a woman's shriek, and changed and ended as the yell of a beast. And before the final blank overtook his dying eyes, he saw the She gave place to It; he saw more, that Life gave place to Death—incomprehensibly.

For he did not dream that no holy water could be more holy, more potent to destroy an evil thing than the life-blood of a pure heart poured out for another in willing devotion.

His own true hidden reality that he had desired to know grew palpable, recognizable. It seemed to him just this: a great, glad, abounding hope that he had saved his brother; too expansive to be contained by the limited form of a sole man, it yearned for a new embodiment infinite as the stars.

What did it matter to that true reality that the man's brain shrank, shrank, till it was nothing; that the man's body could not retain the huge pain of his heart, and heaved it out through the red exit riven at the neck: that hurtling blackness blotted out forever the man's sight, hearing, sense?

In the early gray of day Sweyn chanced upon the footprints of a man—of a runner, as he saw by the shifted snow; and the direction they had taken aroused curiosity, since a little farther their line must be crossed by the edge of a sheer height. He turned to trace them. And so doing, the length of the stride struck his attention—a stride long as his own if he ran. He knew he was following Christian.

In his anger he had hardened himself to be indifferent to the night-long absence of his brother; but now, seeing where the footsteps went, he was seized with compunction and dread. He had failed to give thought and care to his poor, frantic twin, who might—was it possible?—have rushed to a frantic death.

His heart stood still when he came to the place where the leap had been taken. A piled edge of snow had fallen, too, and nothing lay below when he peered. Along the upper edge he ran for a furlong, till he came to a dip where he could slip and climb down, and then back again on the lower level to the pile of fallen snow. There he saw that the vigorous running had started afresh.

He stood pondering; vexed that any man should have taken that leap where he had not ventured to follow; vexed that he had been beguiled to such painful emotions; guessing vainly at Christian's object in this mad freak. He began sauntering along half-unconsciously following his brother's track, and so in a while he came to the place where the footprints were doubled.

Small prints were these others, small as a woman's, though the pace from one to another was longer than that which the skirts of women allow.

Did not White Fell tread so?

A dreadful guess appalled him—so dreadful that he recoiled from belief. Yet his face grew ashy white, and he gasped to fetch back motion to his checked heart. Unbelievable? Closer attention showed how the smaller footfall had altered for greater speed, striking into the snow with a deeper onset and a lighter pressure on the heels. Unbelievable? Could any woman but White Fell run so? Could any man but Christian run so? The guess became a certainty. He was following where alone in the dark night White Fell had fled from Christian pursuing.

Such villainy set heart and brain on fire with rage and indignation—such villainy in his own brother, till lately loveworthy, praiseworthy, though a fool for meekness. He would kill Christian; had he lives as many as the footprints he had trodden, vengeance should demand them all. In a tempest of murderous hate he followed on in haste, for the track was plain enough; starting with such a burst of speed as could not be maintained, but brought him back soon to a plod for the spent, sobbing breath to be regulated.

Mile after mile he traveled with a bursting heart; more piteous, more tragic, seemed the case at this evidence of White Fell's splendid supremacy, holding her own so long against Christian's famous speed. So long, so long, that his love and admiration grew more and more boundless, and his grief and indignation therewith also. Whenever the track lay clear he ran, with such reckless prodigality of strength that it was soon spent, and he dragged on heavily, till, sometimes on the ice of a mere, sometimes on a wind-swept place, all signs were lost; but, so undeviating had been their line, that a course straight on, and then short questing to either hand recovered them again.

Hour after hour had gone by through more than half that winter day, before ever he came to the place where the trampled snow showed that a scurry of feet had come and gone! Wolves' feet—and gone most amazingly! Only a little beyond he came to the lopped point of Christian's bear-spear—farther on he would see where the remnant of the useless shaft had been dropped. The snow here was dashed with blood, and the footsteps of the two had fallen closer together. Some hoarse sound of exultation came from him that might have been a laugh had breath sufficed. "O White Fell, my poor brave love! Well struck!" he groaned, torn by his pity and great admiration, as he guessed surely how she had turned and dealt a blow.

The sight of the blood inflamed him as it might a beast that ravens. He grew mad with a desire to once again have Christian by the throat, not to loose this time till he had crushed out his life—or beat out his life—or stabbed out his life—or all of these, and torn him piecemeal likewise—and ah! then, not till then, bleed his heart with weeping, like a child, like a girl, over the piteous fate of his poor lost love.

On—on—on—through the aching time, toiling and straining in the track of those two superb runners, aware of the marvel of their endurance, but unaware of the marvel of their speed that in the three hours before midnight had overpassed all that vast distance that he could only traverse from twilight to twilight. For clear daylight was passing when he came to the edge of an old marlpit, and saw how the two who had gone before had stamped and trampled together in desperate peril on the verge. And here fresh blood stains spoke to him of a valiant defence against his infamous brother; and he followed where the blood had dripped till the cold had staunched its flow, taking a savage gratification from the evidence that Christian had been gashed deeply, maddening afresh with desire to do likewise more excellently and so slake his murderous hate. And he began to know that through all his despair he had entertained a germ of hope, that grew apace, rained upon by his brother's blood.

He strove on as best he might, wrung now by an access of hope—now of despair, in agony to reach the end, however terrible, sick with the aching of the toiled miles that deferred it.

And the light went lingering out of the sky, giving place to uncertain stars.

He came to the finish.

Two bodies lay in a narrow place. Christian's was one, but the other beyond not White Fell's. There where the footsteps ended lay a great white wolf. At the sight Sweyn's strength was blasted; body and soul he was struck down groveling.

The stars had grown sure and intense before he stirred from where he had dropped prone. Very feebly he crawled to his dead brother, and laid his hands upon him, and crouched so, afraid to look or stir further.

Cold—stiff—hours dead. Yet the dead body was his only shelter and stay in that most dreadful hour. His soul, stripped bare of all comfort, cowered, shivering, naked, abject, and the living clung to the dead out of piteous need for grace from the soul that had passed away.

He rose to his knees, lifting the body. Christian had fallen face forward in the snow, with his arms flung up and wide, and so had the frost made him rigid; strange, ghastly, unyielding to Sweyn lifting, so that he laid him down again and crouched above, with his arms fast round him and a low, heart-wrung groan.

When at last he found force to raise his brother's body and gather it in his arms, tight clasped to his breast, he tried to face the Thing that lay beyond. The sight set his limbs in a palsy with horror and dread. His senses had failed and fainted in utter cowardice, but for the strength that came from holding dead Christian in his arms, enabling him to compel his eyes to endure the sight, and take into the brain the complete aspect of the Thing. No wound—only blood stains on the feet. The great, grim jaws had a savage grin, though dead-stiff. And his kiss—he could bear it no longer, and turned away, nor ever looked again.

And the dead man in his arms, knowing the full horror, had followed and faced it for his sake; had suffered agony and death for his sake; in the neck was the deep death-gash, one arm and both hands were dark with frozen blood, for his sake! Dead he knew him—as in life he had not known him—to give the right meed of love and worship. He longed for annihilation, that so he might lose the agony of knowing himself so unworthy such perfect love. The frozen calm of death on the face appalled him. He dared not touch it with lips that had cursed so lately, with lips fouled by a kiss of the Horror that had been Death.

He struggled to his feet, still clasping Christian. The dead man stood upright within his arms, frozen rigid. The eyes were not quite closed; the head had stiffened, bowed slightly to one side; the arms stayed straight and wide. It was the figure of one crucified, the blood-stained hands also conforming.

So living and dead went back along the track, that one had passed in the deepest passion of love, and one in the deepest passion of hate. All that night Sweyn toiled through the snow, bearing the weight of dead Christian, treading back along the steps he before had trodden when he was wronging with vilest thoughts and cursing with murderous hate the brother who all the while lay dead for his sake.

1899

THE WIND IN THE ROSE-BUSH

by Mary Wilkins Freeman

The American ghost story has a matter-of-factness about it that makes it peculiarly different from the British story. It is one thing to have strange goings-on in castles and mysterious parts of the world, but who expects to find a ghost in the cold, crisp, clear air of New England? Mary Wilkins Freeman, one of our finest regional writers, did not hesitate to seek out the ghosts in our own country, particularly in New England, where the early Salem witch trials gave rise to a brooding conscience that developed such great writers of the supernatural as Nathaniel Hawthorne.

Ghosts, too, have appeared in literature since the time of the Romans. Of all supernatural tales the ghost story has changed least. There were ghosts in classical mythology, ghosts in medieval legend, and ghosts in those great four-decker novels of the Victorian period. In our own time it is unusual to have a ghost novel such as existed in the past. But curiously enough, today such novels are re-emerging. The ghost's true expression, however, is in the short story.

In America ideal places for haunting, such as ancestral castles, old abbeys, royal courts, are hard to find. Our American ghosts rarely appear in costly raiment, in spectral clothes, in strange garb. Our ghosts are very human—to use a strange word for a ghost, very down-to-earth. There are many different types of ghosts, both seen and unseen. The unseen is, of course, a

An early portrait of Mary Wilkins Freeman

ghostly presence and in this charming, evocative story our ghost is not seen at all, but still she is there, in a rose bush.

As the ghost story emerged from classical times, the ghosts themselves became more haunting. In former days they were more frightening. The Gothic ghosts of the eighteenth century, for example, were often skeletons or terrible wraiths. They uttered ghastly cries or low painful moans. As the ghost approached modern times, it was not his appearance that became so frightening, but rather a kind of haunting of the senses that took over. For the New England puritanism of the nineteenth century, so well portrayed by Mary Wilkins Freeman, one needs no terrible cries in the night, no walking skeletons—the only skeleton is the proverbial one in the closet of a New England household.

Ford Village has no railroad station, being on the other side of the river from Porter's Falls, and accessible only by the ford which gives it its name, and a ferry line.

The ferry-boat was waiting when Rebecca Flint got off the train with her bag and lunch basket. When she and her small trunk were safely embarked she sat stiff and straight and calm in the ferry-boat as it shot swiftly and smoothly across stream. There was a horse attached to a light country wagon on board, and he pawed the deck uneasily. His owner stood near, with a wary eye upon him, although he was chewing, with as dully reflective an expression as a cow. Beside Rebecca sat a woman of about her own age, who kept looking at her with furtive curiosity; her husband, short and stout and saturnine, stood near her. Rebecca paid no attention to either of them. She was tall and spare and pale, the type of a spinster, yet with rudimentary lines and expressions of matronhood. She all unconsciously held her shawl, rolled up in a canvas bag, on her left hip, as if it had been a child. She wore a settled frown of dissent at life, but it was the frown of a mother who regarded life as a froward child, rather than as an overwhelming fate.

The other woman continued staring at her; she was mildly stupid, except for an overdeveloped curiosity which made her at times sharp beyond belief. Her eyes glittered, red spots came on her flaccid cheeks; she kept opening her mouth to speak, making little abortive motions. Finally she could endure it no longer; she nudged Rebecca boldly.

"A pleasant day," said she.

Rebecca looked at her and nodded coldly.

"Yes, very," she assented.

"Have you come far?"

"I have come from Michigan."

"Oh!" said the woman, with awe. "It's a long way," she remarked presently.

"Yes, it is," replied Rebecca, conclusively.

Still the other woman was not daunted; there was something which she determined to know, possibly roused thereto by a vague sense of incongruity in the other's appearance. "It's a long ways to come and leave a family," she remarked with painful slyness.

"I ain't got any family to leave," returned Rebecca shortly.

"Then you ain't——"

"No, I ain't."

"Oh!" said the woman.

Rebecca looked straight ahead at the race of the river.

It was a long ferry. Finally Rebecca herself waxed unexpectedly loquacious. She turned to the other woman and inquired if she knew John Dent's widow who lived in Ford Village. "Her husband died about three years ago," said she, by way of detail.

The woman started violently. She turned pale, then she flushed; she cast a strange glance at her husband, who was regarding both women with a sort of stolid keenness.

"Yes, I guess I do," faltered the woman finally.

"Well, his first wife was my sister," said Rebecca with the air of one imparting important intelligence.

"Was she?" responded the other woman feebly. She glanced at her husband with an expression of doubt and terror, and he shook his head forbiddingly.

"I'm going to see her, and take my niece Agnes home with me," said Rebecca.

Then the woman gave such a violent start that she noticed it.

"What is the matter?" she asked.

"Nothin', I guess," replied the woman, with eyes on her husband, who was slowly shaking his head, like a Chinese toy.

"Is my niece sick?" asked Rebecca with quick suspicion.

"No, she ain't sick," replied the woman with alacrity, then she caught her breath with a gasp.

"When did you see her?"

"Let me see; I ain't seen her for some little time," replied the woman. Then she caught her breath again.

"She ought to have grown up real pretty, if she takes after my sister. She was a real pretty woman," Rebecca said wistfully.

"Yes, I guess she did grow up pretty," replied the woman in a trembling voice.

"What kind of a woman is the second wife?"

The woman glanced at her husband's warning face. She continued to gaze at him while she replied in a choking voice to Rebecca:

"I—guess she's a nice woman," she replied. "I—don't know, I—guess so. I—don't see much of her."

"I felt kind of hurt that John married again so quick," said Rebecca; "but I suppose he wanted his house kept, and Agnes wanted care. I wasn't so situated that I could take her when her mother died. I had my own mother to care for, and I was school-teaching. Now Mother has gone, and my uncle died six months ago and left me quite a little property, and I've given up my school, and I've come for Agnes. I guess she'll be glad to go with me, though I suppose her stepmother is a good woman, and has always done for her."

The man's warning shake at his wife was fairly portentous.

"I guess so," said she.

"John always wrote that she was a beautiful woman," said Rebecca.

Then the ferry-boat grated on the shore.

John Dent's widow had sent a horse and wagon to meet her sister-in-law. When the woman and her husband went down the road, on which Rebecca in the wagon with her trunk soon passed them, she said reproachfully:

"Seems as if I'd ought to have told her, Thomas."

"Let her find it out herself," replied the man. "Don't you go to burnin' your fingers in other folks' puddin', Maria."

"Do you s'pose she'll see anything?" asked the woman with a spasmodic shudder and a terrified roll of her eyes.

"See!" returned her husband with stolid scorn. "Better be sure there's anything to see."

"Oh, Thomas, they say——"

"Lord, ain't you found out that what they say is mostly lies?"

"But if it should be true, and she's a nervous woman, she might be scared enough to lose her wits," said his wife, staring uneasily after Rebecca's erect figure in the wagon disappearing over the crest of the hilly road.

"Wits that so easy upset ain't worth much," declared the man. "You keep out of it, Maria."

Rebecca in the meantime rode on in the wagon, beside a flaxen-headed boy, who looked, to her understanding, not very bright. She asked him a question, and he paid no attention. She repeated it, and he responded with a bewildered and incoherent grunt. Then she let him alone, after making sure that he knew how to drive straight.

They had traveled about half a mile, passed the village square, and gone a short distance beyond, when the boy drew up with a sudden Whoa! before a very prosperous-looking house. It had been one of the aboriginal cottages of the vicinity, small and white, with a roof extending on one side over a piazza, and a tiny "L" jutting out in the rear, on the right hand. Now the cottage was transformed by dormer windows, a bay window on the piazzaless side, a carved railing down the front steps, and a modern hard-wood door.

"Is this John Dent's house?" asked Rebecca.

The boy was as sparing of speech as a philosopher. His only response was in flinging the reins over the horse's back, stretching out one foot to the shaft, and leaping out of the wagon, then going around to the rear for the trunk. Rebecca got out and went toward the house. Its white paint had a new gloss; its blinds were an immaculate apple green; the lawn was trimmed as smooth as velvet, and it was dotted with scrupulous groups of hydrangeas and cannas.

"I always understood that John Dent was well-to-do," Rebecca reflected comfortably. "I guess Agnes will have considerable. I've got enough, but it will come in handy for her schooling. She can have advantages."

The boy dragged the trunk up the fine gravel-walk, but before he reached the steps leading up to the piazza, for the house stood on a terrace, the front door opened and a fair, frizzled head of a very large and handsome woman appeared. She held up her black silk skirt, disclosing voluminous ruffles of starched embroidery, and waited for Rebecca. She smiled placidly, her pink, double-chinned face widened and dimpled, but her blue eyes were wary and calculating. She extended her hand as Rebecca climbed the steps.

"This is Miss Flint, I suppose," said she.

"Yes, ma'am," replied Rebecca, noticing with bewilderment a curious expression compounded of fear and defiance on the other's face.

"Your letter only arrived this morning," said Mrs. Dent, in a steady voice. Her great face was a uniform pink, and her china-blue eyes were at once aggressive and veiled with secrecy.

"Yes, I hardly thought you'd get my letter," replied Rebecca. "I felt as if I could not wait to hear from you before I came. I supposed you would be so situated that you could have me a little while without putting you out too much, from what John used to write me about his circumstances, and when I had that money so unexpected I felt as if I must come for Agnes. I suppose you will be willing to give her up. You know she's my own blood, and of course she's no relation to you, though you must have got attached to her. I know from her picture what a sweet girl she must be, and John always said she looked like her own mother, and Grace was a beautiful woman, if she was my sister."

Rebecca stopped and stared at the other woman in amazement and alarm. The great handsome blonde creature stood speechless, livid, gasping, with her hand to her heart, her lips parted in a horrible caricature of a smile.

"Are you sick!" cried Rebecca, drawing near. "Don't you want me to get you some water!"

Then Mrs. Dent recovered herself with a great effort. "It is nothing," she said. "I am subject to—spells. I am over it now.

Won't you come in, Miss Flint?"

As she spoke, the beautiful deep-rose colour suffused her face, her blue eyes met her visitor's with the opaqueness of turquoise—with a revelation of blue, but a concealment of all behind.

Rebecca followed her hostess in, and the boy, who had waited quiescently, climbed the steps with the trunk. But before they entered the door a strange thing happened. On the upper terrace, close to the piazza-post, grew a great rose-bush, and on it, late in the season though it was, one small red, perfect rose.

Rebecca looked at it, and the other woman extended her hand with a quick gesture. "Don't you pick that rose!" she brusquely cried.

Rebecca drew herself up with stiff dignity.

"I ain't in the habit of picking other folks' roses without leave," said she.

As Rebecca spoke she started violently, and lost sight of her resentment, for something singular happened. Suddenly the rosebush was agitated violently as if by a gust of wind, yet it was a remarkably still day. Not a leaf of the hydrangea standing on the terrace close to the rose trembled.

"What on earth——" began Rebecca, then she stopped with a gasp at the sight of the other woman's face. Although a face, it gave somehow the impression of a desperately clutched hand of secrecy.

"Come in!" said she in a harsh voice, which seemed to come forth from her chest with no intervention of the organs of speech. "Come into the house. I'm getting cold out here."

"What makes that rose-bush blow so when there isn't any wind?" asked Rebecca, trembling with vague horror, yet resolute.

"I don't see as it is blowing," returned the woman calmly. And as she spoke, indeed the bush was quiet.

"It was blowing," declared Rebecca.

"It isn't now," said Mrs. Dent. "I can't try to account for

everything that blows out-of-doors. I have too much to do."

She spoke scornfully and confidently, with defiant, unflinching eyes, first on the bush, then on Rebecca, and led the way into the house.

"It looked queer," persisted Rebecca, but she followed, and also the boy with the trunk.

Rebecca entered an interior, prosperous, even elegant, according to her simple ideas. There were Brussels carpets, lace curtains, and plenty of brilliant upholstery and polished wood.

"You're real nicely situated," remarked Rebecca, after she had become a little accustomed to her new surroundings and the two women were seated at the tea-table.

Mrs. Dent stared with a hard complacency from behind her silver-plated service. "Yes, I be," said she.

"You got all the things new?" said Rebecca hesitatingly, with a jealous memory of her dead sister's bridal furnishings.

"Yes," said Mrs. Dent; "I was never one to want dead folks' things, and I had money enough of my own, so I wasn't beholden to John. I had the old duds put up at auction. They didn't bring much."

"I suppose you saved some for Agnes. She'll want some of her poor mother's things when she is grown up," said Rebecca with some indignation.

The defiant stare of Mrs. Dent's blue eyes waxed more intense. "There's a few things up garret," said she.

"She'll be likely to value them," remarked Rebecca. As she spoke she glanced at the window. "Isn't it most time for her to be coming home?" she asked.

"Most time," answered Mrs. Dent carelessly; "but when she gets over to Addie Slocum's she never knows when to come home."

"Is Addie Slocum her intimate friend?"

"Intimate as any."

"Maybe we can have her come out to see Agnes when she's living with me," said Rebecca wistfully. "I suppose she'll be likely to be homesick at first."

"Most likely," answered Mrs. Dent.

"Does she call you mother?" Rebecca asked.

"No, she calls me Aunt Emeline," replied the other woman shortly. "When did you say you were going home?"

"In about a week, I thought, if she can be ready to go so soon," answered Rebecca with a surprised look.

She reflected that she would not remain a day longer than she could help after such an inhospitable look and question.

"Oh, as far as that goes," said Mrs. Dent, "it wouldn't make any difference about her being ready. You could go home whenever you felt that you must, and she could come afterward."

"Alone?"

"Why not? She's a big girl now, and you don't have to change cars."

"My niece will go home when I do, and not travel alone; and if I can't wait here for her, in the house that used to be her mother's and my sister's home, I'll go and board somewhere," returned Rebecca with warmth.

"Oh, you can stay here as long as you want to. You're welcome," said Mrs. Dent.

Then Rebecca started. "There she is!" she declared in a trembling, exultant voice. Nobody knew how she longed to see the girl.

"She isn't as late as I thought she'd be," said Mrs. Dent, and again that curious, subtle change passed over her face, and again it settled into that stony impassiveness.

Rebecca stared at the door, waiting for it to open. "Where is she?" she asked presently.

"I guess she's stopped to take off her hat in the entry," suggested Mrs. Dent.

Rebecca waited. "Why don't she come? It can't take her all this time to take off her hat."

For answer Mrs. Dent rose with a stiff jerk and threw open the door.

"Agnes!" she called. "Agnes." Then she turned and eyed Rebecca. "She ain't there."

"I saw her pass the window," said Rebecca in bewilderment.

"You must have been mistaken."

"I know I did," persisted Rebecca.

"You couldn't have."

"I did. I saw first a shadow go over the ceiling, then I saw her in the glass there"—she pointed to a mirror over the sideboard opposite—"and then the shadow passed the window."

"How did she look in the glass?"

"Little and light-haired, with the light hair kind of tossing over her forehead."

"You couldn't have seen her."

"Was that like Agnes?"

"Like enough; but of course you didn't see her. You've been thinking so much about her that you thought you did."

"You thought *you* did."

"I thought I saw a shadow pass the window, but I must have been mistaken. She didn't come in, or we would have seen her before now. I knew it was too early for her to get home from Addie Slocum's, anyhow."

When Rebecca went to bed Agnes had not returned. Rebecca had resolved that she would not retire until the girl came, but she was very tired, and she reasoned with herself that she was foolish. Besides, Mrs. Dent suggested that Agnes might go to the church social with Addie Slocum. When Rebecca suggested that she be sent for and told that her aunt had come, Mrs. Dent laughed meaningly.

"I guess you'll find out that a young girl ain't so ready to leave a sociable, where there's boys, to see her aunt," said she.

"She's too young," said Rebecca incredulously and indignantly.

"She's sixteen," replied Mrs. Dent; "and she's always been great for the boys."

"She's going to school four years after I get her before she thinks of boys," declared Rebecca.

"We'll see," laughed the other woman.

After Rebecca went to bed, she lay awake a long time listening for the sound of girlish laughter and a boy's voice under her window; then she fell asleep.

The next morning she was down early. Mrs. Dent, who kept no servants, was busily preparing breakfast.

"Don't Agnes help you about breakfast?" asked Rebecca.

"No, I let her lay," replied Mrs. Dent shortly.

"What time did she get home last night?"

"She didn't get home."

"What?"

"She didn't get home. She stayed with Addie. She often does."

"Without sending you word?"

"Oh, she knew I wouldn't worry."

"When will she be home?"

"Oh, I guess she'll be along pretty soon."

Rebecca was uneasy, but she tried to conceal it, for she knew of no good reason for uneasiness. What was there to occasion alarm in the fact of one young girl staying overnight with another? She could not eat much breakfast. Afterward she went out on the little piazza, although her hostess strove furtively to stop her.

"Why don't you go out back of the house? It's real pretty—a view over the river," she said.

"I guess I'll go out here," replied Rebecca. She had a purpose: to watch for the absent girl.

Presently Rebecca came hustling into the house through the sitting-room, into the kitchen where Mrs. Dent was cooking.

"That rose-bush!" she gasped.

Mrs. Dent turned and faced her.

"What of it?"

"It's a-blowing."

"What of it?"

"There isn't a mite of wind this morning."

Mrs. Dent turned with an inimitable toss of her fair head. "If you think I can spend my time puzzling over such nonsense as——" she began, but Rebecca interrupted her with a cry and a rush to the door.

"There she is now!" she cried.

She flung the door wide open, and curiously enough a breeze came in and her own gray hair tossed, and a paper blew off the table to the floor with a loud rustle, but there was nobody in sight.

"There's nobody here," Rebecca said.

She looked blankly at the other woman, who brought her rolling-pin down on a slab of pie-crust with a thud.

"I didn't hear anybody," she said calmly.

"*I saw somebody pass that window!*"

"You were mistaken again."

"I *know* I saw somebody."

"You couldn't have. Please shut that door."

Rebecca shut the door. She sat down beside the window and looked out on the autumnal yard, with its little curve of foot-path to the kitchen door.

"What smells so strong of roses in this room?" she said presently. She sniffed hard.

"I don't smell anything but these nutmegs."

"It is not nutmeg."

"I don't smell anything else."

"Where do you suppose Agnes is?"

"Oh, perhaps she has gone over the ferry to Porter's Falls with Addie. She often does. Addie's got an aunt over there, and Addie's got a cousin, a real pretty boy."

"You suppose she's gone over there?"

"Mebbe. I shouldn't wonder."

"When should she be home?"

"Oh, not before afternoon."

Rebecca waited with all the patience she could muster. She kept reassuring herself, telling herself that it was all natural, that the other woman could not help it, but she made up her mind that if Agnes did not return that afternoon she should be sent for.

When it was four o'clock she started up with resolution. She had been furtively watching the onyx clock on the sitting-room mantel; she had timed herself. She had said that if Agnes was not home by that time she should demand that she be sent for. She rose and stood before Mrs. Dent, who looked up coolly from her embroidery.

"I've waited just as long as I'm going to," she said. "I've come 'way from Michigan to see my own sister's daughter and take her home with me. I've been here ever since yesterday—twenty-four hours—and I haven't seen her. Now I'm going to. I want her sent for."

Mrs. Dent folded her embroidery and rose.

"Well, I don't blame you," she said. "It is high time she came home. I'll go right over and get her myself."

Rebecca heaved a sigh of relief. She hardly knew what she had suspected or feared, but she knew that her position had been one of antagonism if not accusation, and she was sensible of relief.

"I wish you would," she said gratefully, and went back to her chair, while Mrs. Dent got her shawl and her little white head-tie. "I wouldn't trouble you, but I do feel as if I couldn't wait any longer to see her," she remarked apologetically.

"Oh, it ain't any trouble at all," said Mrs. Dent as she went out. "I don't blame you; you have waited long enough."

Rebecca sat at the window watching breathlessly until Mrs. Dent came stepping through the yard alone. She ran to the door and saw, hardly noticing it this time, that the rose-bush was again violently agitated, yet with no wind evident elsewhere.

"Where is she?" she cried.

Mrs. Dent laughed with stiff lips as she came up the steps over the terrace. "Girls will be girls," said she. "She's gone with Addie to Lincoln. Addie's got an uncle who's conductor on the train, and lives there, and he got 'em passes, and they're goin' to stay to Addie's Aunt Margaret's a few days. Mrs. Slocum said Agnes didn't have time to come over and ask me before the train went, but she took it on herself to say it would be all right, and——"

"Why hadn't she been over to tell you?" Rebecca was angry, though not suspicious. She even saw no reason for her anger.

"Oh, she was putting up grapes. She was coming over just as soon as she got the black off her hands. She heard I had company, and her hands were a sight. She was holding them over sulphur matches."

"You say she's going to stay a few days?" repeated Rebecca dazedly.

"Yes; till Thursday, Mrs. Slocum said."

"How far is Lincoln from here?"

"About fifty miles. It'll be a real treat to her. Mrs. Slocum's sister is a real nice woman."

"It is goin' to make it pretty late about my goin' home."

"If you don't feel as if you could wait, I'll get her ready and send her on just as soon as I can," Mrs. Dent said sweetly.

"I'm going to wait," said Rebecca grimly.

The two women sat down again, and Mrs. Dent took up her embroidery.

"Is there any sewing I can do for her?" Rebecca asked finally in a desperate way. "If I can get her sewing along some——"

Mrs. Dent arose with alacrity and fetched a mass of white from the closet. "Here," she said, "if you want to sew the lace on this nightgown. I was going to put her to it, but she'll be glad enough to get rid of it. She ought to have this and one more before she goes. I don't like to send her away without some good underclothing."

Rebecca snatched at the little white garment and sewed feverishly.

That night she wakened from a deep sleep a little after midnight and lay a minute trying to collect her faculties and explain to herself what she was listening to. At last she discovered that it was the then popular strains of "The Maiden's Prayer" floating up through the floor from the piano in the sitting-room below. She jumped up, threw a shawl over her nightgown, and hurried downstairs trembling. There was nobody in the sitting-room; the piano was silent. She ran to Mrs. Dent's bedroom and called hysterically:

"Emeline! Emeline!"

"What is it?" asked Mrs. Dent's voice from the bed. The voice was stern, but had a note of consciousness in it.

"Who—who was that playing 'The Maiden's Prayer' in the sitting-room, on the piano?"

"I didn't hear anybody."

"There was some one."

"I didn't hear anything."

"I tell you there was some one. But—*there ain't anybody there.*"

"I didn't hear anything."

"I did—somebody playing 'The Maiden's Prayer' on the piano. Has Agnes got home? I *want to know.*"

"Of course Agnes hasn't got home," answered Mrs. Dent with rising inflection. "Be you gone crazy over that girl? The last boat from Porter's Falls was in before we went to bed. Of course she ain't come."

"I heard——"

"You were dreaming."

"I wasn't; I was broad awake."

Rebecca went back to her chamber and kept her lamp burning all night.

The next morning her eyes upon Mrs. Dent were wary and blazing with suppressed excitement. She kept opening her mouth as if to speak, then frowning, and setting her lips hard. After breakfast she went upstairs, and came down presently with her coat and bonnet.

"Now, Emeline," she said, "I want to know where the Slocums live."

Mrs. Dent gave a strange, long, half-lidded glance at her. She was finishing her coffee.

"Why?" she asked.

"I'm going over there and find out if they have heard anything from her daughter and Agnes since they went away. I don't like what I heard last night."

"You must have been dreaming."

"It don't make any odds whether I was or not. Does she play 'The Maiden's Prayer' on the piano? I want to know."

"What if she does? She plays it a little, I believe. I don't know. She don't half play it, anyhow; she ain't got an ear."

"That wasn't half played last night. I don't like such things happening. I ain't superstitious, but I don't like it. I'm going. Where do the Slocums live?"

"You go down the road over the bridge past the old grist mill, then you turn to the left; it's the only house for half a mile. You can't miss it. It has a barn with a ship in full sail on the cupola."

"Well, I'm going. I don't feel easy."

About two hours later Rebecca returned. There were red spots on her cheeks. She looked wild. "I've been there," she said, "and there isn't a soul at home. Something *has* happened."

"What has happened?"

"I don't know. Something. I had a warning last night. There wasn't a soul there. They've been sent for to Lincoln."

"Did you see anybody to ask?" asked Mrs. Dent with thinly concealed anxiety.

"I asked the woman that lives on the turn of the road. She's stone deaf. I suppose you know. She listened while I screamed at her to know where the Slocums were, and then she said, 'Mrs. Smith don't live here.' I didn't see anybody on the road, and that's the only house. What do you suppose it means?"

"I don't suppose it means much of anything," replied Mrs. Dent coolly. "Mr. Slocum is conductor on the railroad, and he'd be away anyway, and Mrs. Slocum often goes early when he does, to spend the day with her sister in Porter's Falls. She'd be more likely to go away than Addie."

"And you don't think anything has happened?" Rebecca asked with diminishing distrust before the reasonableness of it.

"Land, no!"

Rebecca went upstairs to lay aside her coat and bonnet. But she came hurrying back with them still on.

"Who's been in my room?" she gasped. Her face was pale as ashes.

Mrs. Dent also paled as she regarded her.

"What do you mean?" she asked slowly.

"I found when I went upstairs that—little nightgown of—Agnes's on—the bed, laid out. It was—*laid out*. The sleeves were folded across the bosom, and there was that little red rose between them. Emeline, what is it? Emeline, what's the matter? Oh!"

Mrs. Dent was struggling for breath in great, choking gasps. She clung to the back of a chair. Rebecca, trembling herself so she could scarcely keep on her feet, got her some water.

As soon as she recovered herself Mrs. Dent regarded her with eyes full of the strangest mixture of fear and horror and hostility.

"What do you mean talking so?" she said in a hard voice.

"It *is there*."

"Nonsense. You threw it down and it fell that way."

"It was folded in my bureau drawer."

"It couldn't have been."

"Who picked that red rose?"

"Look on the bush," Mrs. Dent replied shortly.

Rebecca looked at her; her mouth gaped. She hurried out of the room. When she came back her eyes seemed to protrude. (She had in the meantime hastened upstairs, and come down with tottering steps, clinging to the banisters.)

"Now I want to know what all this means?" she demanded.

"What what means?"

"The rose is on the bush, and it's gone from the bed in my room! Is this house haunted, or what?"

"I don't know anything about a house being haunted. I don't believe in such things. Be you crazy?" Mrs. Dent spoke with gathering force. The colour flashed back to her cheeks.

"No," said Rebecca shortly. "I ain't crazy yet, but I shall be if this keeps on much longer. I'm going to find out where that girl is before night."

Mrs. Dent eyed her.

"What be you going to do?"

"I'm going to Lincoln."

A faint triumphant smile overspread Mrs. Dent's large face.

"You can't," said she; "there ain't any train."

"No train?"

"No; there ain't any afternoon train from the Falls to Lincoln."

"Then I'm going over to the Slocums' again to-night."

However, Rebecca did not go; such a rain came up as deterred even her resolution and she had only her best dresses with her. Then in the evening came the letter from the Michigan village which she had left nearly a week ago. It was from her cousin, a single woman, who had come to keep her house while she was away. It was a pleasant unexciting letter enough, all the first of it, and related mostly how she missed Rebecca; how she hoped she was having pleasant weather and kept her health; and how her friend, Mrs. Greenaway, had come to stay with her since she had felt lonesome the first night in the house; how she hoped Rebecca would have no objections to this, although nothing had been said about it, since she had not realized that she might be nervous alone. The cousin was painfully conscientious, hence the letter. Rebecca smiled in spite of her disturbed mind as she read it, then her eye caught the postscript. That was in a different hand, purporting to be written by the friend, Mrs. Hannah Greenaway, informing her that the cousin had fallen down the cellar stairs and broken her hip, and was in a dangerous condition, and begging Rebecca to return at once, as she herself was rheumatic and unable to nurse her properly, and no one else could be obtained.

Rebecca looked at Mrs. Dent, who had come to her room with the letter quite late; it was half-past nine, and she had gone upstairs for the night.

"Where did this come from?" she asked.

"Mr. Amblecrom brought it," she replied.

"Who's he?"

"The postmaster. He often brings the letters that come on the late mail. He knows I ain't anybody to send. He brought yours about your coming. He said he and his wife came over on the ferry-boat with you."

"I remember him," Rebecca replied shortly. "There's bad news in this letter."

Mrs. Dent's face took on an expression of serious inquiry.

"Yes, my Cousin Harriet has fallen down the cellar stairs—they were always dangerous—and she's broken her hip, and I've got to take the first train home to-morrow."

"You don't say so. I'm dreadfully sorry."

"No, you ain't sorry!" said Rebecca, with a look as if she leaped. "You're glad. I don't know why, but you're glad. You've wanted to get rid of me for some reason ever since I came. I don't know why. You're a strange woman. Now you've got your way, and I hope you're satisfied."

"How you talk."

Mrs. Dent spoke in a faintly injured voice, but there was a light in her eyes.

"I talk the way it is. Well, I'm going to-morrow morning, and I want you, just as soon as Agnes Dent comes home, to send her out to me. Don't you wait for anything. You pack what clothes she's got, and don't wait even to mend them, and you buy her ticket. I'll leave the money, and you send her along. She don't have to change cars. You start her off, when she gets home, on the next train!"

"Very well," replied the other woman. She had an expression of covert amusement.

"Mind you do it."

"Very well, Rebecca."

Rebecca started on her journey the next morning. When she arrived, two days later, she found her cousin in perfect health. She found, moreover, that the friend had not written the postscript in the cousin's letter. Rebecca would have returned to

Ford Village the next morning, but the fatigue and nervous strain had been too much for her. She was not able to move from her bed. She had a species of low fever induced by anxiety and fatigue. But she could write, and she did, to the Slocums, and she received no answer. She also wrote to Mrs. Dent; she even sent numerous telegrams, with no response. Finally she wrote to the postmaster, and an answer arrived by the first possible mail. The letter was short, curt, and to the purpose. Mr. Amblecrom, the postmaster, was a man of few words, and especially wary as to his expressions in a letter.

"Dear madam," he wrote, "your favour rec'ed. No Slocums in Ford's Village. All dead. Addie ten years ago, her mother two years later, her father five. House vacant. Mrs. John Dent said to have neglected stepdaughter. Girl was sick. Medicine not given. Talk of taking action. Not enough evidence. House said to be haunted. Strange sights and sounds. Your niece, Agnes Dent, died a year ago, about this time.

"Yours truly,

"THOMAS AMBLECROM."

Medusa was one of the original Gorgons. The Greeks, however, found it so difficult to portray ugliness in any art form that they made even Medusa, despite the snakes in her hair, fairly attractive.

1899

THE GORGON'S HEAD

by Gertrude Bacon

British women writers of the nineteenth century were often indefatigable travelers. Sooner or later they visited Greece, a country not only rich in mythology, but at that time very much in the public eye because of extensive archaeological excavations that were often under British auspices. They heard, or so they wrote, many contemporary versions of old Greek legends.

Gertrude Bacon's story is about perhaps the most physically repellent monster in Greek legend, the Gorgon—a female creature whose head and face were so ghastly, so terrifying, that anyone who saw her turned to stone. The same theme appears in many cultures and, in one guise or another, in many stories. It is probably born of the fact that we all have had, at some time or another, a disquieting dream in which we have been terrified by a face we cannot quite identify. In popular superstition, particularly in Greece, it became associated with the idea of the "evil eye," which could throw a curse upon the object of its gaze. This type of story could be classified as a demon tale, but Miss Bacon makes it fiercely alive, evoking the primitive horror of the early legend.

The reassuring aspect of tales of horror is that they are outside us. Instead of making us afraid of our own fears, we can empathize with the fears of others in fiction. When writers skillfully and successfully evoke such fears from us, we feel a

The concept of evil changed dramatically during the eighteenth, nineteenth, and twentieth centuries. In the earlier centuries evil was often personified. This famous illustration by William Blake for Dante's Inferno *shows man in the grip of the spirit of evil.*

release. The ancient Greeks used to call this process catharsis; you'll experience such a release after this crackling good tale.

"They that go down to the sea in ships" see strange things, but what they tell is ofttimes stranger still. A faculty for romancing is imparted by a seafaring life as readily and surely as a rolling gait and weatherbeaten countenance. A fine imagination is one of the gifts of the ocean—witness the surprising and unlimited power of expression and epithet possessed by the sailor. And a fine imagination will frequently manifest itself in other ways besides swear words.

Captain Brander is one of the most gifted men in this way in the whole merchant service. His officers say of him with pride that he possesses the largest vocabulary in the great steamship company of which he is one of the oldest and most respected skippers, and his yarns are only equalled in their utter impossibility by the genius he displays in furnishing them with minute detail and all the outward circumstance of truth.

I first learned this fact from the second engineer the evening of the sixth day of our voyage, as we leant across the bulwarks and watched the sunset. The second engineer was a bit of a liar—or I should say romancer—himself. The day he took me down into the engine room he told me, as personal experiences, tales of mutinous Lascar firemen, unpopular officers who disappeared suddenly into the fiery maw of blazing furnaces, and so forth, which, whatever foundation of fact they may have possessed, certainly did not lose in the telling. As a humble aspirant in the same branch of art he naturally was quick to recognize the genius of that past master, the Captain, and his admiration for his chief was as boundless as it was sincere.

"I say, Miss Baker," he said, apropos of nothing, "have you had the skipper 'on' yet?"

"Not that I am aware of," I said. "What do you mean?"

"Why, has he been spinning you any yarns yet? There isn't a man in the service can touch him for stories. I don't deny that he has seen some service, and been in some tight places, but for a real out-and-out lie, commend me to old Monkey Brand!" (It was by this sobriquet, I regret to say, suggested partly by his name, and mostly by his undoubted resemblance to a well-known advertisement, that the worthy captain was known in the unregenerate engine room.)

"Oh, I should just love to hear him," I cried. "There is nothing I should like better. Do tell me how I can manage to draw him."

"Well, he doesn't want much drawing as a rule," said the engineer. "He likes to give vent to his imagination. Let me see," he continued, "tomorrow afternoon we shall be about passing the Grecian Islands. Ask him about them, and try and get him on the subject of Gorgons."

"Gorgons!" I said. "What a strange topic! Why, since I've left school I have almost forgotten what they were. Weren't they mythological creatures who turned people into stone when they looked at them?"

"That's about it, I believe," said the engineer, "and a fellow called Perseus cut off their heads, or something of that kind. It's a lie anyhow, but you ask the skipper."

It was the custom of Captain Brander every afternoon to make a kind of royal progress among his passengers. Going the entire circuit of the ship; passing slowly from group to group, with a joke here and a chat there, and bestowing his favors in lordly and impartial fashion—especially among the ladies. I have watched him often coming the whole length of the promenade deck, making some outrageous compliment to one girl, patting another on the shoulder, even chucking a third under the chin; a sense of supreme self-satisfaction animating his red cheeks, curling his gray hair, and suffusing his whole short, portly person. Eccentric he was; indifferent to his personal appearance—his battered old cap had seen almost as much service as he had—but a more popular man or an abler officer never walked the bridge. On this particular occasion I was at the end of the deck, and had so arranged that an inviting deck chair stood vacant beside me. Wearied by his progress by the time he reached me, he fell at once into my little trap, and sat down on the empty chair, leant back, and spread his legs. He and I were fast friends, and had been since the day when I tried to photograph him, and he had frustrated my design by unscrewing the front lens of my camera and keeping it in his pocket for the rest of the morning.

"Captain," I said, pointing to a cloudy gray outline faintly visible against the eastern horizon, "what land is that?"

"My dear young lady," said he, "I am quite sick of answering that question! If I have been asked it once I have been asked it twenty times in the last half hour. That old Mrs. Matherson in the red shawl buttonholed me on the subject to such an extent that I thought I should never get away again. Wonderful thirst for information that old party has! And she appears to think that because I'm captain I must have a complete knowledge of geography, geology, history, etymology, mythology, *and* navigation. Well, for the twenty-first time, then, we are passing the isles off the coast of Greece, and that one straight ahead is Zante."

"So that is Greece, is it?" I mused aloud. "Well, from here at least it looks old enough and romantic enough to be the home of all those ancient heroes we read about—Alexander and Hercules and—and—Gorgons and those sort of things." I felt I had introduced the subject somewhat lamely, after all, and the captain looked me full in the face as if suspecting a plot. But if I am not very adroit in conversation, I can at least look innocent upon occasions, and he merely said, "And what do you know about Gorgons, pray?"

"Oh, as much as most people, I expect!" I answered. "They are only a sort of fairy tale, you know."

"I am not so sure of that," said Captain Brander. "Those fairy tales, as you call them, have often truth at the bottom of them. And as to Gorgons, why, I could tell you a little incident that happened to me once—but it's rather a long story."

Then I urged my best persuasions—not that he needed much pressing—and pushing his old cap off his bald forehead, and speaking slowly and with that almost American accent peculiar to him, he unfolded his tale of wonder as follows:

"It's nearly thirty years ago, Miss Baker—that's long before *you* were ever born or thought of—that I was fourth officer of the *Haslar*, 2,000-ton vessel of this same company I serve to this day. How times have altered, to be sure! The *Haslar* was reckoned a fine ship in those days, and if you had told me that I should presently command an 8,000-tonner, such as I do this day, with 11,000 horsepower engines, and more men for the crew alone than the *Haslar* could hold when she was packed her tightest, I very probably wouldn't have believed you. However, that is neither here nor there. But thirty years ago in the springtime—now I come to think of it, it was in the month of April—we were cruising in this very neighborhood, and one thick foggy night our skipper lost his bearings a bit, got too near the coast, and ran us ashore off the south point of Zante.

"Of course there was a great fuss, and everybody came up on deck with lifebelts, and all the girls screamed, and all the young fellows swore to save them or die in the attempt; and the skipper turned as white as paper—not that he was afraid, for he was no coward—none of our officers are that—but because he knew his prospects were ruined, and he would be turned out of the company and perhaps lose his certificate, and he'd got a wife and a big family, poor chap! Of course that consideration didn't affect *me*, for I was in my bunk and asleep at the time, but it was certainly unfortunate for him.

"Well, it was very soon discovered that the ship wasn't going down in a hurry, and nobody got into the boats, though they were lowered ready. And when daylight came we saw we were fast on the rocks, with half the stern under water, and the saloon and a lot of the cabins flooded. But more than that the *Haslar* couldn't sink, and at low water you might almost walk dryshod on to the shore. There was no getting her off, however, and so all the passengers were landed and sent home as best they could across country, and a rough time they had of it, for Zante is not an overhospitable sort of a place; while we officers had to stick to the ship till we could get help, and then till she was repaired sufficiently to work her into dock somewhere.

"It was a tedious job, for help was slow in coming; and then all her boilers had to be taken out before she would float, and we fellows got jolly sick of it, I can tell you, for we were hard-worked, and Zante is a wretched hole to spend more than half an hour in. Our one amusement, when we were off duty, was to go ashore on foot or row round the island in a boat, shooting wild fowl and exploring the country. There was precious little to see and not much to shoot, and it was slow fun altogether till one day, the second officer came back from a tramp ashore and told us he had found his way to some very remote village on the eastern coast, where there was a cave among the hills which the villagers warned him not to enter. He could not gather for what reason, because he didn't understand enough of their outlandish tongue, but as it was then growing late he was obliged to return to the ship without further investigation.

"I was always one for adventure when I was a lad, and directly the second officer told his tale I made up my mind to go and explore that cave before any of the rest had a chance. It so happened that next day was my turn for going ashore, and I went and looked up one of the assistant engineers and persuaded him to come with me. I wanted him because he was a chum of mine, and also he was the only one of us who could talk the language a bit. He had been in those parts before, and generally acted as interpreter in our dealings with the natives. His name was Travers, a queer little dark chap, with black eyes and a hot temper, but a pleasant enough fellow, if you did not rub him the wrong way, and game for anything under the sun. He readily agreed to come with me, and we started as soon as we could get away, telling no one of our destination, for we had no wish to be forestalled.

"It was a long tramp, right across the island, to the village which Jenkins, the second officer, had indicated. But at last, after climbing a weary hill, we looked down on some clustering huts standing amid vineyards in the valley beneath, while another and much sheerer cliff rose on the opposite side, whose rugged scarp was all rent and riven as by an earthquake, and intersected by a deep ravine. Here and there among the rocks were dark shadows and black patches, which might be the entrances to caverns in the crag. 'This must be the place,' I said, 'and one of those is the forbidden cave. How are we to find out which?'

"As if in answer to my question, at this moment there came along the hilltop toward us a burly countryman with a sunburned face and tattered garments. He regarded us with astonishment, as well he might, for they get few strangers in those parts, and he made some remark to us in his queer language, which, of course, I didn't understand, but Travers did and replied to it. Finding he was understood, the countryman stopped and talked.

" 'Ah!' he said, or so Travers interpreted. 'So you have reached the valley of the Haunted Cavern! It is far to seek and hard to find, but it lies spread beneath you.'

" 'But which is the Haunted Cavern, and why is it so called?" asked Travers.

" 'It lies in yonder cleft of the hills,' answered the man, pointing to the opposite ravine, 'and it is called the Haunted Cavern because none who venture there return alive. Nay, they return not either alive or dead. They are seen no more!'

" 'Tell that to the Marines!' said Travers, only he translated it into Greek, of course, or what the Zante people think is Greek. 'You don't expect me to believe such a yarn as that! Why what is there up in that place?'

" 'That is what none can tell,' replied the peasant, 'for none come back to say. And, indeed, it is the truth I speak. Many men have attempted to find the secret. In bygone days, I have heard, a whole party of soldiers were sent there to search for brigands supposed to be in hiding, but not one was seen again. The cavern has an evil name, and now is shunned by one and all, but every now and again there arises a youth venturesome beyond the rest; and he heeds not the warnings of the old, but hopes to break the spell and find the treasure that some say is hidden there, and he starts in high hope and courage, but never again do we behold his face!'

" 'But what is the reason?' persisted Travers, the incredulous.

" 'Nay, that we cannot say,' reiterated the man. 'A short distance can one go up the ravine that leads to the cavern. I have been there myself, and truly there is nothing that can be seen except a barren valley, scattered all over with big black stones. Nothing more, and farther than the entrance none must venture.'

" 'Oh, I say!' exclaimed Travers, in delight, 'did you ever

hear such an old liar? This beats anything I could have believed possible in the nineteenth century. Come on, Brander! We are in luck this time!' and the impetuous fellow dashed off down the hill, I at his heels, leaving the countryman dumb with amazement behind us.

"At the foot of the hill we entered the little village. An old, white-haired man of rather superior appearance was crossing the road before us. Travers accosted him and asked him the way to the Haunted Cavern. The old man turned quite pale with astonishment and apprehension.

" 'The Haunted Cavern, my son!' he said, in quavering tones, 'surely you are not going thither?'

" 'Yes, we are, though,' said Travers, his eyes dancing with excitement. It is wonderful what enterprise that boy—he was little more—had in him. 'And if you won't tell us, we'll find the way out for ourselves!' and he pushed past the old man, who held out his skinny hands as if to detain him.

"Before we had got clear of the hamlet the news had somehow got circulated that we were about to explore the ravine, and the whole of the inhabitants turned out in the wildest excitement. Some were for staying us forcibly, till Travers began to get quite nasty, drew his revolver, and talked of firing. Many reiterated and emphasized alarming warnings and assurances that we should never return. All watched us with the most intense interest, and followed close on our footsteps until we began to near the fatal spot, when they fell off singly or in parties, till finally at the very entrance of the ravine we had left even the boldest spirits behind us.

"In truth, it was a strange spot to which we had penetrated. The narrow path had led us suddenly round the spur of the mountain, and now, look which way we might, the giant rocks towered up sheer above us, hundreds of feet high, in inaccessible gray walls. The sinking sun was now too low to shine within this well-like space, which his rays could only reach at midday, and the very air struck damp and chill. We were in an open valley, thus shut in by the cliffs, of considerable extent, but not to be reached by any path except that we had traversed. The ground was firm and smooth, but littered all over with the strangest black stones of all sorts of shapes, and in all positions, though of a fairly uniform size, and alike in material. There was something uncanny and weird about these queer black boulders, which strewed the valley the thicker the farther we advanced, till at the far end of the space, where a huge black hole yawned ominous in the cliff, they almost entirely blocked the way.

"The dark cavern looked terribly grim and forbidding in the fading light. A little stream issued from its mouth and trickled among the stones. It did not gurgle and glisten as most mountain streams, but flowed noiselessly, sluggish, and dull, and gathered in stagnant pools on its rocky bed. No birds sang in that dismal nook; no sound from without penetrated to its recesses. All was silent, dim, and chill as the tomb itself.

"Despite my utmost efforts, I felt the spell of the weird, wild spot stealing over me, and a cold shudder crept down my backbone. There was but room for one at a time in the ever-narrowing track, and I was at first leading. My steps became slower and slower, and finally I paused altogether and turned to look back on Travers to see if he too was feeling the oppressive sense of evil that seemed to hang heavy in the very air. But in his face was only visible an ecstasy almost of eagerness and delight. His dark eyes sparkled again, his cheeks were flushed, his breath came quick, and his whole body was quivering with excitement.

" 'Go on, Brander!' he cried. 'What are you stopping for, man? This is grand! This is luck, indeed! Did you ever see such a place? Come on, I want to get to that cave!'

"I felt utterly ashamed to confess my weakness, but it was that cave that I had begun to dread more and more. Whatever else I may be, Miss Baker, it is not boasting to say I am no coward. I have seen danger, aye, and courted it all my life, and until that moment I doubt if I had known what fear was.

But I knew then: the blind, unreasoning fear that saps the strength of mind and limb and melts the heart and paralyzes all thought save that one overpowering instinct to fly—somewhere. Yet, in face of Travers' eagerness, I could not bear to show the white feather. I turned my back therefore on the dark cavern, now just ahead of us, and endeavored to temporize.

" 'Travers,' I said, 'did you ever see such queer stones? How do you suppose they have got here? They are quite a different nature from these cliffs, so they could not have fallen from the sides.'

" 'Oh, bother the stones!' said Travers. 'I can't look at them now, I want to get into the cave. Quick, before it gets dark!' and as I still hesitated, he pushed past me into a more open space beyond, almost at the cavern's mouth. I did not dare to leave him, and was scrambling after him as best I might, when I suddenly heard him cry out in a voice such as I had never heard before, and hope never to again. A shrill, high-pitched cry in which there were surprise, wonder, disgust, alarm, and awful horror all combined in one: a cry of astonishment, a shriek of agony, a shout of dismay. 'Look, Brander! Look! Look!'

"I could have sworn that when he spoke my companion was in full view, close beside me, touching me almost, though at the exact moment my eyes were looking from him; but when I turned my head in answer to his cry he was gone.

"For one second only had my gaze been averted, but in that time he had utterly vanished from sight, disappeared in a flash, gone—whither? A large black stone stood close beside me, similar to the rest in that ghostly valley; yet it struck me somehow that I had not noticed it there before. I placed my hand upon it as I peered round behind to see if Travers were there, and a shudder I could not explain ran up my arm, for the stone felt warm to the touch. I had not time then to analyze my unreasonable horror at this trivial circumstance; I was too eager to find my friend. I rushed madly among the stones, I yelled his name again and again, but the weird echoes of my cry, returned in countless reflections from cliff and cavern, alone answered me.

"In a frenzy of despair I continued my search, for certain was I that by no natural means could Travers have disappeared so utterly in so brief a space. Blind panic seized me, and I knew not what I did, till my eye suddenly fell on a shallow pool of water collected in a rocky hollow at my very feet. It was not more than a couple of inches deep, and scarce a yard across, but on its placid face were reflected the overhanging rock and opening of the cavern just behind it, and also something else that glued my eyes to it in horror and rooted my flying feet to the ground.

"Just above the cavern's mouth was a narrow ledge of rock, running horizontally, and a few inches in width. On this natural shelf, reflected in the water, I saw, hanging downward, a decayed fragment of goatskin, rotten with age, but which might have been bound round something, long years before. Upon this, as if escaped from its folds, rested a Head.

"It was a human head, severed at the neck, but fresh and unfaded as if but newly dead. It bore the features of a woman —of a woman of more perfect loveliness than was ever told of in tale, or sculptured in marble, or painted on canvas. Every feature, every line, was of the truest beauty, cast in the noblest mold—the face of a goddess. But upon that perfect countenance was the mark of eternal pain, of deathless agony and suffering past words. The forehead was lined and knit, the death-white lips were tightly pressed in speechless torment; in the wide eyes seemed yet to lurk the flame of an unquenchable fire; while around the fair brows, in place of hair, curled and coiled the stark bodies of venomous serpents, stiff in death, but their loathsome forms still erect, their evil heads yet thrust forward as if to strike.

"My heart ceased beating, and the chill of death crept over my limbs, as with eyes starting from their sockets I stared at that awful head, reflected in the pool. For hours it seemed to me I gazed fascinated, as the bird by the eye of the snake that has charmed it. I was as incapable of thought as movement, till suddenly forgotten schoolroom learning began to cross my brain, and I knew that I looked at the reflection of Medusa, the Gorgon, fairest and foulest of living things, the unclean creature, half woman, half eagle, slain by the hero Perseus, and one glimpse of whose tortured face turned the luckless beholder into stone with the horror of it.

"If I once raised my eyes from the reflection to the actual head above I knew that I too should freeze in a moment into another black block, even as poor Travers, and every other who had entered the accursed valley had done before. And as this thought occurred to me, the longing to lift my eyes and look upon the real object became so overpowering that, in sheer self-preservation, I inclined my face closer and closer to the water till I seemed almost to touch it, when my senses fled and I knew no more.

"When I woke at last it was far on in the night, and a bright moon, riding high, shone full down upon the valley, revealing the ragged rocks and scattered stones with a cold brilliance that almost equalled the day. I was lying chilled and stiff beside the pool, and I started up in amazement, unable to recall to my mind, for a moment, where I was or what I was doing there. I had my back to the cavern, fortunately, and as I gazed over the ghostly and deserted scene the events of the day suddenly returned to my mind in a single flash of terror.

"To escape from this ghastly place was now my only thought, and in order to do this I resolved to look no more at the pool at my feet in case the terrible fascination should again take possession of me. What it cost me to adhere to this resolution I cannot tell you, but with the courage of despair I pressed blindly forward to the mouth of the ravine, only pausing a second to lay my hand upon the now ice-cold stone that once was Travers.

"Poor Travers! gay, light-hearted fellow! Ever in the forefront of mischief, of danger, of adventure. How eager he had been to solve the secret of the haunted valley, which now must be his tomb forever. How full of health and spirits he had scrambled a few hours before among those very boulders, one of which now, standing stiffly erect among its forest of brethren, was at once the monument and sole relic of a fearless lad, a cheery friend, and a gallant seaman. Dear old Travers! Brave, foolish boy! My heart was heavy, indeed, for his awful fate, as I reverently touched the stone and murmured to the night breeze, stealing around the rocks, 'Good-bye, old fellow; sleep sound!'

"It seemed to me, in my loneliness and terror, that my fearsome journey would never be ended: that, lost in a labyrinth, I should tread that valley forever. But at last, after endless ages, I reached the mouth of the ravine, and once on open ground I stretched my cramped limbs and ran, without ceasing, till I once more reached the ship."

Here the captain paused, more from want of breath than anything else, I think.

"Go on, Captain Brander," I cried. "You haven't half finished yet. What did they say when you returned, and how did you explain about poor Travers?"

"Young lady," said Captain Brander, "don't ask any more questions. I think I have told you enough for one afternoon," and here, an officer coming up and summoning him, he left me.

⊱ 1893 ⊰

MAN-SIZE IN MARBLE

by E. Nesbit

Our nineteenth-century ladies of the macabre had a passion for old graveyards. Places of shadows, old yew trees, moonlit nights always inspired them to flights of fancy and, happily for us, stories of stark terror. E. Nesbit, at most times a very gentle writer of family stories, showed another side when she tackled a graveyard.

One of the most frequently recurring themes in horror literature is making the inanimate animate, or, as you have read in "The Gorgon's Head," the animate inanimate. Another frequent theme is a hand of terror. The first truly Gothic novel was written by Horace Walpole in June 1764. He dreamed one night that he looked up and saw a gigantic hand in armor. His novel inspired by that hand was called *The Castle of Otranto*. It is a tremendously dull tale today, but in the eighteenth century "distinguished persons were afraid to go to bed after reading it."

This Gothic story by E. Nesbit, however, can still keep the reader awake.

Although every word of this story is as true as despair, I do not expect people to believe it. Nowadays a "rational explanation" is required before belief is possible. Let me, then,

An early photograph of E. Nesbit

at once offer the "rational explanation" which finds most favour among those who have heard the tale of my life's tragedy. It is held that we were "under a delusion," Laura and I, on that 31st of October; and that this supposition places the whole matter on a satisfactory and believable basis. The reader can judge, when he, too, has heard my story, how far this is an "explanation," and in what sense it is "rational." There were three who took part in this: Laura and I and another man. The other man still lives, and can speak to the truth of the least credible part of my story.

I never in my life knew what it was to have as much money as I required to supply the most ordinary needs—good colours, books, and cab-fares—and when we were married we knew quite well that we should only be able to live at all by "strict punctuality and attention to business." I used to paint in those days, and Laura used to write, and we felt sure we could keep the pot at least simmering. Living in town was out of the question, so we went to look for a cottage in the country, which should be at once sanitary and picturesque. So rarely do these two qualities meet in one cottage that our search was for some time quite fruitless. But when we got away from friends and house-agents, on our honeymoon, our wits grew clear again, and we knew a pretty cottage when at last we saw one.

It was at Brenzett—a little village set on a hill over against the southern marshes. We had gone there, from the seaside village where we were staying, to see the church, and two fields from the church we found this cottage. It stood quite by itself, about two miles from the village. It was a long, low building, with rooms sticking out in unexpected places. There was a bit of stone-work—ivy-covered and moss-grown, just two old rooms, all that was left of a big house that had once stood there—and round this stone-work the house had grown up. Stripped of its roses and jasmine it would have been hideous. As it stood it was charming, and after a brief examination we took it. It was absurdly cheap. There was a jolly old-fashioned garden, with grass paths, and no end of hollyhocks and sunflowers, and big lilies. From the window you could see the marsh-pastures, and beyond them the blue, thin line of the sea.

Marble and bronze effigies were fairly common in the Middle Ages. This one is in a German cathedral.

We got a tall old peasant woman to do for us. Her face and figure were good, though her cooking was of the homeliest; but she understood all about gardening, and told us all the old names of the coppices and cornfields, and the stories of the smugglers and highwaymen, and, better still, of the "things that walked," and of the "sights" which met one in lonely glens of a starlight night. We soon came to leave all the domestic business to Mrs. Dorman, and to use her legends in little magazine stories which brought in the jingling guinea.

We had three months of married happiness, and did not have a single quarrel. One October evening I had been down to smoke a pipe with the doctor—our only neighbour—a pleasant young Irishman. Laura had stayed at home to finish a comic sketch. I left her laughing over her own jokes, and came in to find her a crumpled heap of pale muslin, weeping on the window seat.

"Good heavens, my darling, what's the matter?" I cried, taking her in my arms.

"What is the matter? Do speak."

"It's Mrs. Dorman," she sobbed.

"What has she done?" I inquired, immensely relieved.

"She says she must go before the end of the month, and she says her niece is ill; she's gone down to see her now, but I don't believe that's the reason, because her niece is always ill. I believe someone has been setting her against us. Her manner was so queer——"

"Never mind, Pussy," I said; "whatever you do, don't cry, or I shall have to cry too to keep you in countenance, and then you'll never respect your man again."

"But you see," she went on, "it is really serious, because these village people are so sheepy, and if one won't do a thing you may be quite sure none of the others will. And I shall have to cook the dinners and wash up the hateful greasy plates; and you'll have to carry cans of water about and clean the boots and knives—and we shall never have any time for work or earn any money or anything."

I represented to her that even if we had to perform these duties the day would still present some margin for other toils and recreations. But she refused to see the matter in any but the greyest lights.

"I'll speak to Mrs. Dorman when she comes back, and see if I can't come to terms with her," I said. "Perhaps she wants a rise in her screw. It will be all right. Let's walk up to the church."

The church was a large and lonely one, and we loved to go there, especially upon bright nights. The path skirted a wood, cut through it once, and ran along the crest of the hill through two meadows, and round the churchyard wall, over which the old yews loomed in black masses of shadow.

This path, which was partly paved, was called "the bier-walk," for it had long been the way by which the corpses had been carried to burial. The churchyard was richly treed, and was shaded by great elms which stood just outside and stretched their majestic arms in benediction over the happy dead. A large, low porch let one into the building by a Norman doorway and a heavy oak door studded with iron. Inside, the arches rose into darkness, and between them the reticulated windows, which stood out white in the moonlight. In the chancel, the windows were of rich glass, which showed in faint light their noble colouring, and made the black oak of the choir pews hardly more solid than the shadows. But on each side of the altar lay a grey marble figure of a knight in full plate armour lying upon a low slab, with hands held up in everlasting prayer, and these figures, oddly enough, were always to be seen if there was any glimmer of light in the church. Their names were lost, but the peasants told of them that they had been fierce and wicked men, marauders by land and sea, who had been the scourge of their time, and had been guilty of deeds so foul that the house they had lived in—the big house, by the way, that had stood on the site of our cottage—had been stricken by lightning and the vengeance of Heaven. But for all that, the gold of their heirs had bought them a place in the church.

Looking at the bad, hard faces reproduced in the marble, this story was easily believed.

The church looked at its best and weirdest on that night, for the shadows of the yew trees fell through the windows upon the floor of the nave and touched the pillars with tattered shade. We sat down together without speaking, and watched the solemn beauty of the old church with some of that awe which inspired its early builders. We walked to the chancel and looked at the sleeping warriors. Then we rested some time on the stone seat in the porch, looking out over the stretch of quiet moonlit meadows, feeling in every fibre of our being the peace of the night and of our happy love; and came away at last with a sense that even scrubbing and black-leading were but small troubles at their worst.

Mrs. Dorman had come back from the village, and I at once invited her to a tête-à-tête.

"Now, Mrs. Dorman," I said, when I had got her into my painting room, "what's all this about your not staying with us?"

"I should be glad to get away, sir, before the end of the month," she answered, with her usual placid dignity.

"Have you any fault to find, Mrs. Dorman?"

"None at all, sir: you and your lady have always been most kind, I'm sure——"

"Well, what is it? Are your wages not high enough?"

"No, sir, I gets quite enough."

"Then why not stay?"

"I'd rather not"—with some hesitation—"my niece is ill."

"But your niece has been ill ever since we came. Can't you stay for another month?"

"No, sir, I'm bound to go by Thursday."

And this was Monday!

"Well, I must say, I think you might have let us know before. There's no time now to get anyone else, and your mistress is not fit to do heavy housework. Can't you stay till next week?"

"I might be able to come back next week."

"But why must you go this week?" I persisted. "Come, out with it."

Mrs. Dorman drew the little shawl, which she always wore, tightly across her bosom, as though she were cold. Then she said, with a sort of effort:

"They say, sir, as this was a big house in Catholic times, and there was a many deeds done here."

The nature of the "deeds" might be vaguely inferred from the inflection of Mrs. Dorman's voice—which was enough to make one's blood run cold. I was glad that Laura was not in the room. She was always nervous, as highly-strung natures are, and I felt that these tales about our house, told by this old peasant woman, with her impressive manner and contagious credulity, might have made our home less dear to my wife.

"Tell me all about it, Mrs. Dorman," I said; "you needn't mind about telling me. I'm not like the young people who make fun of such things."

Which was partly true.

"Well, sir"—she sank her voice—"you may have seen in the church, beside the altar, two shapes."

"You mean the effigies of the knights in armour," I said cheerfully.

"I mean them two bodies, drawed out man-size in marble," she returned, and I had to admit that her description was a thousand times more graphic than mine, to say nothing of a certain weird force and uncanniness about the phrase "drawed out man-size in marble."

"They do say, as on All Saints' Eve them two bodies sits up on their slabs, and gets off of them, and then walks down the aisle, *in their marble*"—(another good phrase, Mrs. Dorman)—"and as the church clock strikes eleven they walks out of the church door, and over the graves, and along the bier-walk, and if it's a wet night there's the marks of their feet in the morning."

"And where do they go?" I asked, rather fascinated.

"They comes back here to their home, sir, and if anyone meets them——"

"Well, what then?" I asked.

But no—not another word could I get from her, save that her niece was ill and she must go.

"Whatever you do, sir, lock the door early on All Saints' Eve, and make the cross-sign over the doorstep and on the windows."

"But has anyone ever seen these things?" I persisted. "Who was here last year?"

"No one, sir; the lady as owned the house only stayed here in summer, and she always went to London a full month afore *the* night. And I'm sorry to inconvenience you and your lady, but my niece is ill and I must go on Thursday."

I could have shaken her for her absurd reiteration of that obvious fiction, after she had told me her real reasons.

I did not tell Laura the legend of the shapes that "walked in their marble," partly because a legend concerning our house might perhaps trouble my wife, and partly, I think, from some more occult reason. This was not quite the same to me as any other story, and I did not want to talk about it till the day was over. I had very soon ceased to think of the legend, however. I was painting a portrait of Laura, against the lattice window, and I could not think of much else. I had got a splendid background of yellow and grey sunset, and was working away with enthusiasm at her face. On Thursday Mrs. Dorman went. She relented, at parting, so far as to say:

"Don't you put yourself about too much, ma'am, and if there's any little thing I can do next week I'm sure I shan't mind."

Thursday passed off pretty well. Friday came. It is about what happened on that Friday that this is written.

I got up early, I remember, and lighted the kitchen fire, and had just achieved a smoky success when my little wife came running down as sunny and sweet as the clear October morning itself. We prepared breakfast together, and found it very good fun. The housework was soon done, and when brushes and brooms and pails were quiet again the house was still indeed. It is wonderful what a difference one makes in a house. We really missed Mrs. Dorman, quite apart from considerations concerning pots and pans. We spent the day in dusting our books and putting them straight, and dined gaily on cold steak and coffee. Laura was, if possible, brighter and gayer and sweeter than usual, and I began to think that a little domestic toil was really good for her. We had never been so merry since we were married, and the walk we had that afternoon was, I think, the happiest time of all my life. When we had watched the deep scarlet clouds slowly pale into leaden grey against a pale green sky and saw the white mists curl up along the hedgerows in the distant marsh we came back to the house hand in hand.

"You are sad, my darling," I said, half-jestingly, as we sat down together in our little parlour. I expected a disclaimer, for my own silence had been the silence of complete happiness. To my surprise she said:

"Yes, I think I am sad, or, rather, I am uneasy. I don't think I'm very well. I have shivered three or four times since we came in; and it is not cold, is it?"

"No," I said, and hoped it was not a chill caught from the treacherous mists that roll up from the marshes in the dying night. No—she said, she did not think so. Then, after a silence, she spoke suddenly:

"Do you ever have presentiments of evil?"

"No," I said, smiling, "and I shouldn't believe in them if I had."

"I do," she went on; "the night my father died I knew it, though he was right away in the North of Scotland." I did not answer in words.

She sat looking at the fire for some time in silence, gently stroking my hand. At last she sprang up, came behind me, and, drawing my head back, kissed me.

"There, it's over now," she said. "What a baby I am! Come,

light the candles, and we'll have some of these new Rubinstein duets."

And we spent a happy hour or two at the piano.

At about half-past ten I began to long for the good-night pipe, but Laura looked so white that I felt it would be brutal of me to fill our sitting-room with the fumes of strong cavendish.

"I'll take my pipe outside," I said.

"Let me come, too."

"No, sweetheart, not to-night; you're much too tired. I shan't be long. Get to bed, or I shall have an invalid to nurse to-morrow as well as the boots to clean."

I kissed her and was turning to go when she flung her arms round my neck and held me as if she would never let me go again. I stroked her hair.

"Come, Pussy, you're over-tired. The housework has been too much for you."

She loosened her clasp a little and drew a deep breath.

"No. We've been very happy to-day, Jack, haven't we? Don't stay out too long."

"I won't, my dearie."

I strolled out of the front door, leaving it unlatched. What a night it was! The jagged masses of heavy dark cloud were rolling at intervals from horizon to horizon, and thin white wreaths covered the stars. Through all the rush of the cloud river the moon swam, breasting the waves and disappearing again in the darkness.

I walked up and down, drinking in the beauty of the quiet earth and the changing sky. The night was absolutely silent. Nothing seemed to be abroad. There was no scurrying of rabbits, or twitter of the half-asleep birds. And though the clouds went sailing across the sky, the wind that drove them never came low enough to rustle the dead leaves in the woodland paths. Across the meadows I could see the church tower standing out black and grey against the sky. I walked there thinking over our three months of happiness.

I heard a bell-beat from the church. Eleven already! I turned to go in, but the night held me. I could not go back into our little warm rooms yet. I would go up to the church.

I looked in at the low window as I went by. Laura was half-lying on her chair in front of the fire. I could not see her face, only her little head showed dark against the pale blue wall. She was quite still. Asleep, no doubt.

I walked slowly along the edge of the wood. A sound broke the stillness of the night, it was a rustling in the wood. I stopped and listened. The sound stopped too. I went on, and now distinctly heard another step than mine answer mine like an echo. It was a poacher or a wood-stealer, most likely, for these were not unknown in our Arcadian neighbourhood. But whoever it was, he was a fool not to step more lightly. I turned into the wood and now the footstep seemed to come from the path I had just left. It must be an echo, I thought. The wood looked perfect in the moonlight. The large dying ferns and the brushwood showed where through thinning foliage the pale light came down. The tree trunks stood up like Gothic columns all around me. They reminded me of the church, and I turned into the bier-walk, and passed through the corpse-gate between the graves to the low porch.

I paused for a moment on the stone seat where Laura and I had watched the fading landscape. Then I noticed that the door of the church was open, and I blamed myself for having left it unlatched the other night. We were the only people who ever cared to come to the church except on Sundays, and I was vexed to think that through our carelessness the damp autumn airs had had a chance of getting in and injuring the old fabric. I went in. It will seem strange, perhaps, that I should have gone half-way up the aisle before I remembered —with a sudden chill, followed by as sudden a rush of self-contempt—that this was the very day and hour when, according to tradition, the "shapes drawed out man-size in marble" began to walk.

Having thus remembered the legend, and remembered it with a shiver, of which I was ashamed, I could not do otherwise than walk up towards the altar, just to look at the figures —as I said to myself; really what I wanted was to assure myself, first, that I did not believe the legend, and, secondly, that it was not true. I was rather glad that I had come. I thought now I could tell Mrs. Dorman how vain her fancies were, and how peacefully the marble figures slept on through the ghastly hour. With my hands in my pockets I passed up the aisle. In the grey dim light the eastern end of the church looked larger than usual, and the arches above the two tombs looked larger too. The moon came out and showed me the reason. I stopped short, my heart gave a leap that nearly choked me, and then sank sickeningly.

The "bodies drawed out man-size" *were gone!* and their marble slabs lay wide and bare in the vague moonlight that slanted through the east window.

Were they really gone, or was I mad? Clenching my nerves, I stooped and passed my hand over the smooth slabs, and felt their flat unbroken surface. Had someone taken the things away? Was it some vile practical joke? I would make sure, anyway. In an instant I had made a torch of a newspaper, which happened to be in my pocket, and, lighting it, held it high above my head. Its yellow glare illumined the dark arches and those slabs. The figures *were* gone. And I was alone in the church; or was I alone?

And then a horror seized me, a horror indefinable and indescribable—an overwhelming certainty of supreme and accomplished calamity. I flung down the torch and tore along the aisle and out through the porch, biting my lips as I ran to keep myself from shrieking aloud. Oh, was I mad—or what was this that possessed me? I leaped the churchyard wall and took the straight cut across the fields, led by the light from our windows. Just as I got over the first stile a dark figure seemed to spring out of the ground. Mad still with that certainty of misfortune, I made for the thing that stood in my path, shouting, "Get out of the way, can't you!"

But my push met with a more vigorous resistance than I had

expected. My arms were caught just above the elbow and held as in a vice, and the raw-boned Irish doctor actually shook me.

"Let me go, you fool," I gasped. "The marble figures have gone from the church; I tell you they've gone."

He broke into a ringing laugh. "I'll have to give ye a draught to-morrow, I see. Ye've bin smoking too much and listening to old wives' tales."

"I tell you, I've seen the bare slabs."

"Well, come back with me. I'm going up to old Palmer's—his daughter's ill; we'll look in at the church and let me see the bare slabs."

"You go, if you like," I said, a little less frantic for his laughter; "I'm going home to my wife."

"Rubbish, man," said he; "d'ye think I'll permit of that? Are ye to go saying all yer life that ye've seen solid marble endowed with vitality, and me to go all me life saying ye were a coward? No, sir—ye shan't do ut."

The night air—a human voice—and I think also the physical contact with this six feet of solid common sense, brought me back a little to my ordinary self, and the word "coward" was a mental shower-bath.

"Come on, then," I said sullenly; "perhaps you're right."

He still held my arm tightly. We got over the stile and back to the church. All was still as death. The place smelt very damp and earthy. We walked up the aisle. I am not ashamed to confess that I shut my eyes: I knew the figures would not be there. I heard Kelly strike a match.

"Here they are, ye see, right enough; ye've been dreaming or drinking, asking yer pardon for the imputation."

I opened my eyes. By Kelly's expiring vesta I saw two shapes lying "in their marble" on their slabs. I drew a deep breath.

"I'm awfully indebted to you," I said. "It must have been some trick of light, or I have been working rather hard, perhaps that's it. I was quite convinced they were gone."

"I'm aware of that," he answered rather grimly; "ye'll have to be careful of that brain of yours, my friend, I assure ye."

He was leaning over and looking at the right-hand figure, whose stony face was the most villainous and deadly in expression.

"By Jove," he said, "something has been afoot here—this hand is broken."

And so it was. I was certain that it had been perfect the last time Laura and I had been there.

"Perhaps someone has *tried* to remove them," said the young doctor.

"Come along," I said, "or my wife will be getting anxious. You'll come in and have a drop of whiskey and drink confusion to ghosts and better sense to me."

"I ought to go up to Palmer's, but it's so late now I'd best leave it till the morning," he replied.

I think he fancied I needed him more than did Palmer's girl, so, discussing how such an illusion could have been possible, and deducing from this experience large generalities concerning ghostly apparitions, we walked up to our cottage. We saw, as we walked up the garden path, that bright light streamed out of the front door, and presently saw that the parlour door was open, too. Had she gone out?

"Come in," I said, and Dr. Kelly followed me into the parlour. It was all ablaze with candles, not only the wax ones, but at least a dozen guttering, glaring tallow dips, stuck in vases and ornaments in unlikely places. Light, I knew, was Laura's remedy for nervousness. Poor child! Why had I left her? Brute that I was.

We glanced round the room, and at first we did not see her. The window was open, and the draught set all the candles flaring one way. Her chair was empty and her handkerchief and book lay on the floor. I turned to the window. There, in the recess of the window, I saw her. Oh, my child, my love, had she gone to that window to watch for me? And what had come into the room behind her? To what had she turned with that look of frantic fear and horror? Oh, my little one, had she thought that it was I whose step she heard, and turned to meet—what?

She had fallen back across a table in the window, and her body lay half on it and half on the window-seat, and her head hung down over the table, the brown hair loosened and fallen to the carpet. Her lips were drawn back, and her eyes wide, wide open. They saw nothing now. What had they seen last?

The doctor moved towards her, but I pushed him aside and sprang to her; caught her in my arms and cried:

"It's all right, Laura! I've got you safe, wifie."

She fell into my arms in a heap. I clasped her and kissed her, and called her by all her pet names, but I think I knew all the time that she was dead. Her hands were tightly clenched. In one of them she held something fast. When I was quite sure that she was dead, and that nothing mattered at all any more, I let him open her hand to see what she held.

It was a grey marble finger.

1862

EVELINE'S VISITANT

by Mrs. Braddon

Mary Elizabeth Braddon had a Victorian passion for hard work. She wrote nearly one hundred published novels and if she had a little free time on her hands tossed off a few plays. Then for relaxation she would write ghost stories, some of the best of the Victorian period. In "Eveline's Visitant" she began to play with an idea that eventually became quite common. It is the theme of the jealous ghost. In the earliest ghost stories the ghost came back because of some discontent in his own soul. He was a shade, perhaps in need of the proper rites so he could enter into the abode of the dead. But by the nineteenth century the ghost was far more sophisticated. When he returned he came back in full possession of human emotions and was often driven to vindictive acts by jealousy and the desire for revenge.

The Victorians derived a particularly delicious entertainment from terror, and found it not only in primitive physical horror, as in "The Gorgon's Head," but with their refined sensibilities felt ethical horror as well. They wrote that there is "a delight that refreshes the human spirit in being shocked." Conventional, prisoners of their overly strong inhibitions, the Victorians protected themselves from being shocked in their social lives, but a story was something else again and sweet Mrs. Braddon shocked them nicely.

It was at a masked ball at the Palais Royal that my fatal quarrel with my first cousin André de Brissac began. The quarrel was about a woman. The women who followed the footsteps of Philip of Orleans were the causes of many such disputes; and there was scarcely one fair head in all that glittering throng which, to a man versed in social histories and mysteries, might not have seemed bedabbled with blood.

I shall not record the name of her for love of whom André de Brissac and I crossed one of the bridges, in the dim August dawn on our way to the waste ground beyond the church of Saint-Germain des Prés.

There were many beautiful vipers in those days, and she was one of them. I can feel the chill breath of that August morning blowing in my face, as I sit in my dismal chamber at my château of Puy Verdun tonight, alone in the stillness, writing the strange story of my life. I can see the white mist rising from the river, the grim outline of the Châtelet, and the square towers of Notre Dame black against the pale-grey sky. Even more vividly can I recall André's fair young face, as he stood opposite to me with his two friends—scoundrels both, and alike eager for that unnatural fray. We were a strange group to be seen in a summer sunrise, all of us fresh from the heat and clamour of the Regent's saloons—André in a quaint hunting-dress copied from a family portrait at Puy Verdun, I costumed as one of Law's Mississippi Indians; the other men in like garish frippery, adorned with broideries the jewels that looked wan in the pale light of dawn.

Our quarrel had been a fierce one—a quarrel which could have but one result, and that the direst. I had struck him; and the welt raised by my open hand was crimson upon his fair, womanish face as he stood opposite to me. The eastern sun shone on the face presently, and dyed the cruel mark with a deeper red; but the sting of my own wrongs was fresh, and I had not yet learned to despise myself for that brutal outrage.

To André de Brissac such an insult was most terrible. He was

These famous duelers are by the nineteenth-century writer and illustrator William Makepeace Thackeray.

the favourite of Fortune, the favourite of women; and I was nothing—a rough soldier who had done my country good service, but in the boudoir of a Parabère a mannerless boor.

We fought, and I wounded him mortally. Life had been very sweet for him; and I think that a frenzy of despair took possession of him when he felt the life-blood ebbing away. He beckoned me to him as he lay on the ground. I went, and knelt at his side.

"Forgive me, André!" I murmured.

He took no more heed of my words than if that piteous entreaty had been the idle ripple of the river near at hand.

"Listen to me, Hector de Brissac," he said. "I am not one who believes that a man has done with earth because his eyes glaze and his jaw stiffens. They will bury me in the old vault at Puy Verdun; and you will be master of the château. Ah, I know how lightly they take things in these days, and how Dubois will laugh when he hears that *Ca* has been killed in a duel. They will bury me, and sing masses for my soul; but you and I have not finished our affair yet, my cousin. I will be with you when you least look to see me—I, with this ugly scar upon the face that women have praised and loved. I will come to you when your life seems brightest. I will come between you and all that you hold fairest and dearest. My ghostly hand shall drop a poison in your cup of joy. My shadowy form shall shut the sunlight from your life. Men with such iron will as mine can do what they please, Hector de Brissac. It is my will to haunt you when I am dead."

All this in short broken sentences he whispered into my ear. I had need to bend my ear close to his dying lips; but the iron will of André de Brissac was strong enough to do battle with Death, and I believe he said all he wished to say before his head fell back upon the velvet cloak they had spread beneath him, never to be lifted again.

As he lay there, you would have fancied him a fragile stripling, too fair and frail for the struggle called life; but there are those who remember the brief manhood of André de Brissac, and who can bear witness to the terrible force of that proud nature.

I stood looking down at the young face with that foul mark upon it, and God knows I was sorry for what I had done.

Of those blasphemous threats which he had whispered in my ear I took no heed. I was a soldier, and a believer. There was nothing absolutely dreadful to me in the thought that I had killed this man. I had killed many men on the battlefield; and this one had done me cruel wrong.

My friends would have had me cross the frontier to escape the consequences of my act; but I was ready to face those consequences, and I remained in France. I kept aloof from the court, and received a hint that I had best confine myself to my own province. Many masses were chanted in the little chapel of Puy Verdun for the soul of my dead cousin, and his coffin filled a niche in the vault of our ancestors.

His death had made me a rich man; and the thought that it was so made my newly acquired wealth very hateful to me. I lived a lonely existence in the old château, where I rarely held converse with any but the servants of the household, all of whom had served my cousin, and none of whom liked me.

It was a hard and bitter life. It galled me, when I rode through the village, to see the peasant children shrink away from me. I have seen old women cross themselves stealthily as I passed them by. Strange reports had gone forth about me; and there were those who whispered that I had given my soul to the Evil One as the price of my cousin's heritage. From my boyhood I had been dark of visage and stern of manner; and hence, perhaps, no woman's love had ever been mine. I remembered my mother's face in all its changes of expression; but I can remember no look of affection that ever shone on me. That other woman, beneath whose feet I laid my heart, was pleased to accept my homage, but she never loved me; and the end was treachery.

I had grown hateful to myself, and had well-nigh begun to hate my fellow-creatures, when a feverish desire seized upon me, and I pined to be back in the press and throng of the busy world once again. I went back to Paris, where I kept myself aloof from the court, and where an angel took compassion upon me.

She was the daughter of an old comrade, a man whose merits had been neglected, whose achievements had been ignored, and who sulked in his shabby lodging like a rat in a hole, while all Paris went mad with the Scotch Financier, and gentlemen and lackeys were trampling one another to death in the Rue Quincampoix. The only child of this little cross-grained old captain of dragoons was an incarnate sunbeam, whose mortal name was Eveline Duchalet.

She loved me. The richest blessings of our lives are often those which cost us least. I wasted the best years of my youth in the worship of a wicked woman, who jilted and cheated me at last. I gave this meek angel but a few courteous words—a little fraternal tenderness—and lo, she loved me. The life which had been so dark and desolate grew bright beneath her influence; and I went back to Puy Verdun with a fair young bride for my companion.

Ah, how sweet a change there was in my life and in my home! The village children no longer shrank appalled as the dark horseman rode by, the village crones no longer crossed themselves; for a woman rode by his side—a woman whose charities had won the love of all those ignorant creatures, and whose companionship had transformed the gloomy lord of the château into a loving husband and a gentle master. The old retainers forgot the untimely fate of my cousin, and served me with cordial willingness, for love of their young mistress.

There are no words which can tell the pure and perfect happiness of that time. I felt like a traveller who had traversed the frozen seas of an arctic region, remote from human love or human companionship, to find himself on a sudden in the bosom of a verdant valley, in the sweet atmosphere of home. The change seemed too bright to be real; and I strove in vain to put away from my mind the vague suspicion that my new life was but some fantastic dream.

So brief were those halcyon hours, that, looking back on them now, it is scarcely strange if I am still half inclined to fancy the first days of my married life could have been no more than a dream.

Neither in my days of gloom nor in my days of happiness had I been troubled by the recollection of André's blasphemous oath. The words which with his last breath he had whispered in my ear were vain and meaningless to me. He had vented his rage in those idle threats, as he might have vented it in idle execrations. That he will haunt the footsteps of his enemy after death is the one revenge which a dying man can promise himself; and if men had power thus to avenge themselves the earth would be peopled with phantoms.

I had lived for three years at Puy Verdun; sitting alone in the solemn midnight by the hearth where he had sat, pacing the corridors that had echoed his footfall; and in all that time my fancy had never so played me false as to shape the shadow of the dead. Is it strange, then, if I had forgotten André's horrible promise?

There was no portrait of my cousin at Puy Verdun. It was the age of boudoir art, and a miniature set in the lid of a gold bonbonnière, or hidden artfully in a massive bracelet, was more fashionable than a clumsy life-size image, fit only to hang on the gloomy walls of a provincial château rarely visited by its owner. My cousin's fair face had adorned more than one bonbonnière, and had been concealed in more than one bracelet; but it was not among the faces that looked down from the panelled walls of Puy Verdun.

In the library I found a picture which awoke painful associations. It was the portrait of a de Brissac, who had flourished in the time of Francis the First; and it was from this picture that my cousin André had copied the quaint hunting-dress he wore at the Regent's ball. The library was a room in which I spent a good deal of my life; and I ordered a curtain to be hung before this picture.

We had been married three months, when Eveline one day asked: "Who is the lord of the château nearest to this?"

I looked at her in astonishment.

"My dearest," I answered, "do you not know that there is no other château within forty miles of Puy Verdun?"

"Indeed!" she said. "That is strange."

I asked her why the fact seemed strange to her; and after much entreaty I obtained from her the reason of her surprise.

In her walks about the park and woods during the last month she had met a man who, by his dress and bearing, was obviously of noble rank. She had imagined that he occupied some château near at hand, and that his estate adjoined ours. I was at a loss to imagine who this stranger could be; for my estate of Puy Verdun lay in the heart of a desolate region, and unless when some traveller's coach went lumbering and jingling through the village, one had little more chance of encountering a gentleman than of meeting a demigod.

"Have you seen this man often, Eveline?" I asked.

She answered, in a tone which had a touch of sadness: "I see him every day."

"Where, dearest?"

"Sometimes in the park, sometimes in the wood. You know the little cascade, Hector, where there is some old neglected rock-work that forms a kind of cavern. I have taken a fancy to that spot, and have spent many mornings there reading. Of late I have seen the stranger there every morning."

"He has never dared to address you?"

"Never. I have looked up from my book, and have seen him standing at a little distance, watching me silently. I have continued reading; and when I have raised my eyes again I have found him gone. He must approach and depart with a stealthy tread, for I never hear his footfall. Sometimes I have almost wished that he would speak to me. It is so terrible to see him standing silently there."

"He is some insolent peasant who seeks to frighten you."

My wife shook her head.

"He is no peasant," she answered. "It is not by his dress alone I judge, for that is strange to me. He has an air of nobility which it is impossible to mistake."

"Is he young or old?"

"He is young and handsome."

I was much disturbed by the idea of this stranger's intrusion on my wife's solitude; and I went straight to the village to enquire if any stranger had been seen there. I could hear of no one. I questioned the servants closely, but without result. Then I determined to accompany my wife in her walks, and to judge for myself of the rank of the stranger.

For a week I devoted all my mornings to rustic rambles with Eveline in the park and woods; and in all that week we saw no one but an occasional peasant in *sabos*, or one of our own household returning from a neighbouring farm.

I was a man of studious habits, and those summer rambles disturbed the even current of my life. My wife perceived this, and entreated me to trouble myself no further.

"I will spend my mornings in the pleasaunce, Hector," she said; "the stranger cannot intrude upon me there."

"I began to think the stranger is only a phantasm of your own romantic brain," I replied, smiling at the earnest face lifted to mine. "A châtelaine who is always reading romances may well meet handsome cavaliers in the woodlands. I dare say I have Mademoiselle Scuderi to thank for this noble stranger, and that he is only the great Cyrus in modern costume."

"Ah, that is the point which mystifies me, Hector," she said. "The stranger's costume is not modern. He looks as an old picture might look if it could descend from its frame."

Her words pained me, for they reminded me of that hidden picture in the library, and the quaint hunting costume of orange and purple, which André de Brissac wore at the Regent's ball.

After this my wife confined her walks to the pleasaunce; and for many weeks I heard no more of the nameless stranger. I dismissed all thought of him from my mind, for a graver and heavier care had come upon me. My wife's health began to droop. The change in her was so gradual as to be almost imperceptible to those who watched her day by day. It was only when she put on a rich gala dress which she had not worn for months that I saw how wasted the form must be on which the embroidered bodice hung so loosely, and how wan and dim were the eyes which had once been brilliant as the jewels she wore in her hair.

I sent a messenger to Paris to summon one of the court physicians; but I knew that many days must needs elapse before he could arrive at Puy Verdun.

In the interval I watched my wife with unutterable fear.

It was not her health only that had declined. The change was more painful to behold than any physical alteration. The bright and sunny spirit had vanished, and in the place of my joyous young bride I beheld a woman weighed down by rooted melancholy. In vain I sought to fathom the cause of my darling's sadness. She assured me that she had no reason for sorrow or discontent, and that if she seemed sad without a motive, I must forgive her sadness, and consider it as a misfortune rather than a fault.

I told her that the court physician would speedily find some cure for her despondency, which must needs arise from physical causes, since she had no real ground for sorrow. But although she said nothing, I could see she had no hope or belief in the healing powers of medicine.

One day, when I wished to beguile her from that pensive silence in which she was wont to sit an hour at a time, I told her, laughing, that she appeared to have forgotten her mysterious cavalier of the wood, and it seemed also as if he had forgotten her.

To my wonderment, her pale face became a sudden crimson; and from crimson changed to pale again in a breath.

"You have never seen him since you deserted your woodland grotto?" I said.

She turned to me with a heart-rending look.

"Hector," she cried, "I see him every day; and it is that which is killing me."

She burst into a passion of tears when she had said this. I took her in my arms as if she had been a frightened child, and tried to comfort her.

"My darling, this is madness," I said. "You know that no stranger can come to you in the pleasaunce. The moat is ten feet wide and always full of water, and the gates are kept locked day and night by old Massou. The châtelaine of a medieval fortress need fear no intruder in her antique garden."

My wife shook her head sadly.

"I see him every day," she said.

On this I believed that my wife was mad. I shrank from questioning her more closely concerning her mysterious visitant.

It would be ill, I thought, to give a form and substance to the shadow that tormented her by too close inquiry about its looks and manner, its coming and going.

I took care to assure myself that no stranger to the household could by any possibility penetrate to the pleasaunce. Having done this, I was fain to await the coming of the physician.

He came at last. I revealed to him the conviction which was my misery. I told him that I believed my wife to be mad. He saw her—spent an hour alone with her, and then came to me. To my unspeakable relief he assured me of her sanity.

"It is just possible that she may be affected by one delusion," he said; "but she is so reasonable upon all other points that I can scarcely bring myself to believe her the subject of a monomania. I am rather inclined to think that she really sees the person of whom she speaks. She described him to me with a perfect minuteness. The descriptions of scenes or individuals given by patients afflicted with monomania are always more or less disjointed; but your wife spoke to me as clearly and calmly as I am now speaking to you. Are you sure there is no one who can approach her in that garden where she walks?"

"I am quite sure."

"Is there any kinsman of your steward, or hanger-on of your household—a young man with a fair, womanish face, very pale and rendered remarkable by a crimson scar, which looks like the mark of a blow?"

"My God!" I cried, as the light broke in upon me all at once. "And the dress—the strange, old-fashioned dress?"

"The man wears a hunting costume of purple and orange," answered the doctor.

I knew then that André de Brissac had kept his word, and that in the hour when my life was brightest his shadow had come between me and happiness.

I showed my wife the picture in the library, for I would fain assure myself that there was some error in my fancy about my cousin. She shook like a leaf when she behold it, and clung to me convulsively.

"This is witchcraft, Hector," she said. "The dress in that picture is the dress of the man I see in the pleasaunce; but the face is not his."

Then she described to me the face of the stranger; and it was my cousin's face line for line—André de Brissac, whom she had never seen in the flesh. Most vividly of all did she describe the cruel mark upon his face, the trace of a fierce blow from an open hand.

After this I carried my wife away from Puy Verdun. We wandered far—through the southern provinces, and into the very heart of Switzerland. I thought to distance the ghastly phantom, and I fondly hoped that change of scene would bring peace to my wife.

It was not so. Go where we would, the ghost of André de Brissac followed us. To my eyes that fatal shadow never revealed itself. *That* would have been too poor a vengeance. It was my wife's innocent heart which André made the instrument of his revenge. The unholy presence destroyed her life. My constant companionship could not shield her from the horrible intruder. In vain did I watch her; in vain did I strive to comfort her.

"He will not let me be at peace," she said. "He comes between us, Hector. He is standing between us now. I can see his face with the red mark upon it plainer than I see yours."

One fair moonlight night, when we were together in a mountain village in the Tyrol, my wife cast herself at my feet, and told me she was the worst and vilest of women. "I have confessed all to my Director," she said; "from the first I have not hidden my sin from heaven. But I feel that death is near me; and before I die I would fain reveal my sin to you."

"What sin, my sweet one?"

"When first the stranger came to me in the forest, his

presence bewildered and distressed me, and I shrank from him as from something strange and terrible. He came again and again; by and by I found myself thinking of him, and watching for his coming. His image haunted me perpetually; I strove in vain to shut his face out of my mind. Then followed an interval in which I did not see him; and, to my shame and anguish, I found that life seemed dreary and desolate without him. After that came the time in which he haunted the pleasaunce; and—oh, Hector, kill me if you will, for I deserve no mercy at your hands!—I grew in those days to count the hours that must elapse before his coming, to take no pleasure save in the sight of that pale face with the red brand upon it. He plucked all old familiar joys out of my heart, and left in it but one weird, unholy pleasure—the delight of his presence. For a year I have lived but to see him. And now curse me, Hector; for this is my sin. Whether it comes of the baseness of my own heart, or is the work of witchcraft, I know not; but I know that I have striven against this wickedness in vain."

I took my wife to my breast, and forgave her. In sooth, what had I to forgive? Was the fatality that overshadowed us any work of hers? On the next night she died, with her hand in mine; and at the very last she told me, sobbing and affrighted, that *he* was by her side.

Charlotte Perkins Gilman

1896

THE YELLOW WALL PAPER

by Charlotte Perkins Gilman

Toward the end of the nineteenth century the horror story began to take a new turn. When ghosts were portrayed as real ghosts and werewolves still terrified the credulous, the horror story had a kind of outside reality to it that later disappeared. There were new ideas afloat: perhaps some of the horrors were in our own minds, not in the outside world at all. This idea gave birth to the psychological horror story, and "The Yellow Wall Paper" by Charlotte Perkins Gilman shows she was a mistress of the art.

Mrs. Gilman needed no legends to cull a great story. She needed no walking ghosts, no monster, no werewolf. She was a woman of her time, very active in the movement for women's rights, and she was also sensitive to the undercurrents of psychology that had come to the fore by the end of the last century and the beginning of the twentieth. She knew with remarkable insight that the real horrors are not the things, as the Scots used to say, that go "bump" in the night. She knew that there is a strange night place in all of us—as you can see, most tales of horror seem to take place in darkness—and that those dark sides of our minds give us our own ghosts, our own fears. In this story she delves into a new kind of terror, a terror that was to be explored extensively in the twentieth century, the terror described by Dorothy Sayers as "the nightmare country between sanity and madness; the pressure of mind upon living mind and the lonely horror of the dark places of the soul."

It is very seldom that mere ordinary people like John and myself secure ancestral halls for the summer.

A colonial mansion, a hereditary estate, I would say a haunted house, and reach the height of romantic felicity—but that would be asking too much of fate!

Still I will proudly declare that there is something queer about it.

Else, why should it be let so cheaply? And why have stood so long untenanted?

John laughs at me, of course, but one expects that in marriage.

John is practical in the extreme. He has no patience with faith, an intense horror of superstition, and he scoffs openly at any talk of things not to be felt and seen and put down in figures.

John is a physician, and *perhaps*—(I would not say it to a living soul, of course, but this is a dead paper and a great relief to my mind)—*perhaps* that is one reason I do not get well faster.

You see, he does not believe I am sick!

And what can one do?

If a physician of high standing, and one's own husband, assures friends and relatives that there is really nothing the matter with one but temporary nervous depression,—a slight hysterical tendency,—what is one to do?

My brother is also a physician, and also of high standing, and he says the same thing.

So I take phosphates or phosphites,—whichever it is,—and tonics, and journeys, and air, and exercise and am absolutely forbidden to "work" until I am well again.

Personally I disagree with their ideas.

Personally I believe that congenial work, with excitement

and change, would do me good.

But what is one to do?

I did write for a while in spite of them; but it *does* exhaust me a good deal—having to be so sly about it, or else meet with heavy opposition.

I sometimes fancy that in my condition if I had less opposition and more society and stimulus—but John says the very worst thing I can do is to think about my condition, and I confess it always makes me feel bad.

So I will let it alone and talk about the house.

The most beautiful place! It is quite alone, standing well back from the road, quite three miles from the village. It makes me think of English places that you read about, for there are hedges, and walls and gates that lock, and lots of separate little houses for the gardeners and people.

There is a *delicious* garden! I never saw such a garden—large and shady, full of box-border paths, and lined with long grape-covered arbors with seats under them.

There were greenhouses, too, but they are all broken now.

There was some legal trouble, I believe, something about the heirs and co-heirs; anyhow, the place has been empty for years.

That spoils my ghostliness, I am afraid; but I don't care—there is something strange about the house—I can feel it.

I even said so to John one moonlight evening, but he said what I felt was a *draught*, and shut the window.

I get unreasonably angry with John sometimes. I'm sure I never used to be so sensitive. I think it is due to this nervous condition.

But John says if I feel so I shall neglect proper self-control; so I take pains to control myself—before him, at least, and that makes me very tired.

I don't like our room a bit. I wanted one downstairs that opened on the piazza and had roses all over the window, and such pretty, old-fashioned chintz hangings! but John would not hear of it.

He said there was only one window and not room for two

beds, and no near room for him if he took another.

He is very careful and loving, and hardly lets me stir without special direction.

I have a schedule prescription for each hour in the day; he takes all care from me, and I feel so basely ungrateful not to value it more.

He said we came here solely on my account, that I was to have perfect rest and all the air I could get. "Your exercise depends on your strength, my dear," said he, "and your food somewhat on your appetite; but air you can absorb all the time." So we took the nursery, at the top of the house.

It is a big, airy room, the whole floor nearly, with windows that look all ways, and air and sunshine galore. It was nursery first and then playground and gymnasium, I should judge; for the windows are barred for little children, and there are rings and things in the walls.

The paint and paper look as if a boys' school had used it. It is stripped off—the paper—in great patches all around the head of my bed, about as far as I can reach, and in a great place on the other side of the roof low down. I never saw a worse paper in my life.

One of those sprawling flamboyant patterns committing every artistic sin.

It is dull enough to confuse the eye in following, pronounced enough to constantly irritate, and provoke study, and when you follow the lame, uncertain curves for a little distance they suddenly commit suicide—plunge off at outrageous angles, destroy themselves in unheard-of contradictions.

The color is repellent, almost revolting; a smoldering, unclean yellow, strangely faded by the slow-turning sunlight.

It is a dull yet lurid orange in some places, a sickly sulphur tint in others.

No wonder the children hated it! I should hate it myself if I had to live in this room long.

There comes John, and I must put this away—he hates to have me write a word.

We have been here two weeks, and I haven't felt like writing before, since that first day.

I am sitting by the window now, up in this atrocious nursery, and there is nothing to hinder my writing as much as I please, save lack of strength.

John is away all day, and even some nights when his cases are serious.

I am glad my case is not serious!

But these nervous troubles are dreadfully depressing.

John does not know how much I really suffer. He knows there is no *reason* to suffer, and that satisfies him.

Of course it is only nervousness. It does weigh on me so not to do my duty in any way!

I meant to be such a help to John, such a real rest and comfort, and here I am a comparative burden already!

Nobody would believe what an effort it is to do what little I am able—to dress and entertain, and order things.

It is fortunate Mary is so good with the baby. Such a dear baby!

And yet I *cannot* be with him, it makes me so nervous.

I suppose John never was nervous in his life. He laughs at me so about this wall paper!

At first he meant to repaper the room, but afterward he said that I was letting it get the better of me, and that nothing was worse for a nervous patient than to give way to such fancies.

He said that after the wall paper was changed it would be the heavy bedstead, and then the barred windows, and then that gate at the head of the stairs, and so on.

"You know the place is doing you good," he said, "and really, dear, I don't care to renovate the house just for a three months' rental."

"Then do let us go downstairs," I said, "there are such pretty rooms there."

Then he took me in his arms and called me a blessed little goose, and said he would go down cellar if I wished, and would have it whitewashed into the bargain.

But he is right enough about the beds and windows and things.

It is as airy and comfortable a room as any one need wish, and of course, I would not be so silly as to make him uncomfortable just for a whim.

I'm really getting quite fond of the big room, all but that horrid paper.

Out of one window I can see the garden, those mysterious deep-shaded arbors, the riotous old-fashioned flowers, and bushes and gnarly trees.

Out of another I get a lovely view of the bay and a little private wharf belonging to the estate. There is a beautiful shaded lane that runs down there from the house. I always fancy I see people walking in these numerous paths and arbors, but John has cautioned me not to give way to fancy in the least. He says that with my imaginative power and habit of story-making a nervous weakness like mine is sure to lead to all manner of excited fancies, and that I ought to use my will and good sense to check the tendency. So I try.

I think sometimes that if I were only well enough to write a little it would relieve the press of ideas and rest me.

But I find I get pretty tired when I try.

It is so discouraging not to have any advice and companionship about my work. When I get really well John says we will ask Cousin Henry and Julia down for a long visit; but he says he would as soon put fire-works in my pillow-case as to let me have those stimulating people about now.

I wish I could get well faster.

But I must not think about that. This paper looks to me as if it *knew* what a vicious influence it had!

There is a recurrent spot where the pattern lolls like a broken neck and two bulbous eyes stare at you upsidedown.

I get positively angry with the impertinence of it and the everlastingness. Up and down and sideways they crawl, and those absurd, unblinking eyes are everywhere. There is one place where two breadths didn't match, and the eyes go all up and down the line, one a little higher than the other.

I never saw so much expression in an inanimate thing before, and we all know how much expression they have!

I used to lie awake as a child and get more entertainment and terror out of blank walls and plain furniture than most children could find in a toy-store.

I remember what a kindly wink the knobs of our big old bureau used to have, and there was one chair that always seemed like a strong friend.

I used to feel that if any of the other things looked too fierce I could always hop into that chair and be safe.

The furniture in this room is no worse than inharmonious, however, for we had to bring it all from downstairs. I suppose when this was used as a playroom they had to take the nursery things out, and no wonder! I never saw such ravages as the children have made here.

The wall paper, as I said before, is torn off in spots, and it sticketh closer than a brother—they must have had perseverance as well as hatred.

Then the floor is scratched and gouged and splintered, the plaster itself is dug out here and there, and this great heavy bed, which is all we found in the room, looks as if it had been through the wars.

But I don't mind it a bit—only the paper.

There comes John's sister. Such a dear girl as she is, and so careful of me! I must not let her find me writing.

She is a perfect, an enthusiastic housekeeper, and hopes for no better profession. I verily believe she thinks it is the writing which made me sick!

But I can write when she is out, and see her a long way off from these windows.

There is one that commands the road, a lovely, shaded winding road, and one that just looks off over the country. A lovely country, too, full of great elms and velvet meadows.

This wall paper has a kind of sub-pattern in a different shade, a particularly irritating one, for you can only see it in certain lights, and not clearly then.

But in the places where it isn't faded, and where the sun is just so, I can see a strange, provoking, formless sort of figure, that seems to sulk about that silly and conspicuous front design.

There's sister on the stairs.

Well, the Fourth of July is over! The people are all gone and I am tired out. John thought it might do me good to see a little company, so we just had mother and Nellie and the children down for a week.

Of course I didn't do a thing, Jennie sees to everything now.

But it tired me all the same.

John says if I don't pick up faster he shall send me to Weir Mitchell in the fall.

But I don't want to go there at all. I had a friend who was in his hands once, and she says he is just like John and my brother, only more so!

Besides, it is such an undertaking to go so far.

I don't feel as if it was worth while to turn my hand over for anything, and I'm getting dreadfully fretful and querulous.

I cry at nothing, and cry most of the time.

Of course I don't when John is here, or anybody else, but when I am alone.

And I am alone a good deal just now. John is kept in town very often by serious cases, and Jennie is good and lets me alone when I want her to.

So I walk a little in the garden or down that lovely lane, sit on the porch under the roses, and lie down up here a good deal.

I'm getting really fond of the room in spite of the wall paper. Perhaps *because* of the wall paper.

It dwells in my mind so!

I lie here on this great immovable bed—it is nailed down, I believe—and follow that pattern about by the hour. It is as good as gymnastics, I assure you. I start, we'll say at the bottom, down in the corner over there where it has not been touched, and I determine for the thousandth time that I *will* follow that pointless pattern to some sort of a conclusion.

I know a little of the principles of design, and I know this thing was not arranged on any laws of radiation, or alternation, or repetition, or symmetry, or anything else that I ever heard of.

It is repeated, of course, by the breadths, but not otherwise.

Looked at in one way, each breadth stands alone, the bloated curves and flourishes—a kind of "debased Romanesque" with *delirium tremens*—go waddling up and down in isolated columns of fatuity.

But, on the other hand, they connect diagonally, and the sprawling outlines run off in great slanting waves of optic horror, like a lot of wallowing seaweeds in full chase.

The whole thing goes horizontally, too, at least it seems so, and I exhaust myself in trying to distinguish the order of its going in that direction.

They have used a horizontal breadth for a frieze, and that adds wonderfully to the confusion.

There is one end of the room where it is almost intact, and there, when the close-lights fade and the low sun shines directly upon it, I can almost fancy radiation, after all—the interminable grotesques seem to form around a common center and rush off in headlong plunges of equal distraction.

It makes me tired to follow it. I will take a nap, I guess.

I don't know why I should write this.

I don't want to.

I don't feel able.

And I know John would think it absurd. But I *must* say what I feel and think in some way—it is such a relief!

But the effort is getting to be greater than the relief.

Half the time now I am awfully lazy, and lie down ever so much.

John says I mustn't lose my strength, and has me take cod-liver oil and lots of tonics and things, to say nothing of ale and wine and rare meat.

Dear John! He loves me very dearly, and hates to have me sick. I tried to have a real earnest reasonable talk with him the other day, and tell him how I wished he would let me go and make a visit to Cousin Henry and Julia.

But he said I wasn't able to go, nor able to stand it after I got there; and I did not make out a very good case for myself, for I was crying before I had finished.

It is getting to be a great effort for me to think straight. Just this nervous weakness, I suppose.

And dear John gathered me up in his arms, and just carried me upstairs and laid me on the bed, and sat by me and read to me till he tired my head.

He said I was his darling and his comfort and all he had, and that I must take care of myself for his sake, and keep well.

He says no one but myself can help me out of it, that I must use my will and self-control and not let my silly fancies run away with me.

There's one comfort, the baby is well and happy, and does not have to occupy this nursery with the horrid wall paper.

If we had not used it that blessed child would have! What a fortunate escape! Why, I wouldn't have a child of mine, an impressionable little thing, live in such a room for worlds.

I never thought of it before, but it is lucky that John kept me here, after all. I can stand it so much easier than a baby, you see.

Of course I never mention it to them any more,—I am too wise,—but I keep watch of it all the same.

There are things in that paper that nobody knows but me, or ever will.

Behind that outside pattern the dim shapes get clearer every day.

It is always the same shape, only very numerous.

And it is like a woman stooping down and creeping about

behind that pattern. I don't like it a bit. I wonder—I begin to think—I wish John would take me away from here!

It is so hard to talk with John about my case, because he is so wise, and because he loves me so.

But I tried it last night.

It was moonlight. The moon shines in all around, just as the sun does.

I hate to see it sometimes, it creeps so slowly, and always comes in by one window or another.

John was asleep and I hated to waken him, so I kept still and watched the moonlight on that undulating wall paper till I felt creepy.

The faint figure behind seemed to shake the pattern, just as if she wanted to get out.

I got up softly and went to feel and see if the paper *did* move, and when I came back John was awake.

"What is it, little girl?" he said. "Don't go walking about like that—you'll get cold."

I thought it was a good time to talk, so I told him that I really was not gaining here, and that I wished he would take me away.

"Why, darling!" said he, "our lease will be up in three weeks, and I can't see how to leave before.

"The repairs are not done at home, and I cannot possibly leave town just now. Of course if you were in any danger I could and would, but you really are better, dear, whether you can see it or not, I am a doctor, dear, and I know. You are gaining flesh and color, your appetite is better. I feel really much easier about you."

"I don't weigh a bit more," said I, "nor as much; and my appetite may be better in the evening, when you are here, but it is worse in the morning, when you are away."

"Bless her little heart!" said he with a big hug; "she shall be as sick as she pleases. But now let's improve the shining hours, by going to sleep, and talk about it in the morning."

"And you won't go away?" I asked gloomily.

"Why, how can I, dear? It is only three weeks more and then we will take a nice little trip of a few days while Jennie is getting the house ready. Really, dear, you are better!"

"Better in body, perhaps—" I began, and stopped short, for he sat up straight and looked at me with such a stern, reproachful look that I could not say another word.

"My darling," said he, "I beg of you, for my sake and for our child's sake, as well as for your own, that you will never for one instant let that idea enter your mind! There is nothing so dangerous, so fascinating, to a temperament like yours. It is a false and foolish fancy. Can you not trust me as a physician when I tell you so?"

So of course I said no more on that score, and we went to sleep before long. He thought I was asleep first, but I wasn't—I lay there for hours trying to decide whether that front pattern and the back pattern really did move together or separately.

On a pattern like this, by daylight, there is a lack of sequence, a defiance of law, that is a constant irritant to a normal mind.

The color is hideous enough, and unreliable enough, and infuriating enough, but the pattern is torturing.

You think you have mastered it, but just as you get well under way in following, it turns a back somersault, and there you are. It slaps you in the face, knocks you down, and tramples upon you. It is like a bad dream.

The outside pattern is a florid arabesque, reminding one of a fungus. If you can imagine a toadstool in joints, an interminable string of toadstools, budding and sprouting in endless convolutions,—why, that is something like it.

That is, sometimes!

There is one marked peculiarity about this paper, a thing nobody seems to notice but myself, and that is that it changes as the light changes.

When the sun shoots in through the east window—I always

watch for that first long, straight ray—it changes so quickly that I never can quite believe it.

That is why I watch it always.

By moonlight—the moon shines in all night when there is a moon—I wouldn't know it was the same paper.

At night in any kind of light, in twilight, candlelight, lamplight, and worst of all by moonlight, it becomes bars! The outside pattern, I mean, and the woman behind it is as plain as can be.

I didn't realize for a long time what the thing was that showed behind,—that dim sub-pattern,—but now I am quite sure it is a woman.

By daylight she is subdued, quiet. I fancy it is the pattern that keeps her so still. It is so puzzling. It keeps me quiet by the hour.

I lie down ever so much now. John says it is good for me, and to sleep all I can.

Indeed, he started the habit by making me lie down for an hour after each meal.

It is a very bad habit, I am convinced, for, you see, I don't sleep.

And that cultivates deceit, for I don't tell them I'm awake,—oh, no!

The fact is, I am getting a little afraid of John.

He seems very queer sometimes, and even Jennie has an inexplicable look.

It strikes me occasionally, just as a scientific hypothesis, that perhaps it is the paper!

I have watched John when he did not know I was looking, and come into the room suddenly on the most innocent excuses, and I've caught him several times *looking at the paper!* And Jennie too. I caught Jennie with her hand on it once.

She didn't know I was in the room, and when I asked her in a quiet, a very quiet voice, with the most restrained manner possible, what she was doing with the paper she turned around as if she had been caught stealing, and looked quite angry—asked me why I should frighten her so!

Then she said that the paper stained everything it touched, and that she had found yellow smooches on all my clothes and John's, and she wished we would be more careful!

Did not that sound innocent? But I know she was studying that pattern, and I am determined that nobody shall find it out but myself!

Life is very much more exciting now than it used to be. You see I have something more to expect, to look forward to, to watch. I really do eat better, and am more quiet than I was.

John is so pleased to see me improve! He laughed a little the other day, and said I seemed to be flourishing in spite of my wall paper.

I turned it off with a laugh. I had no intention of telling him that it was *because* of the wall paper—he would make fun of me. He might even want to take me away.

I don't want to leave now until I have found it out. There is a week more, and I think that will be enough.

I'm feeling ever so much better! I don't sleep much at night, for it is so interesting to watch developments; but I sleep a good deal in the daytime.

In the daytime it is tiresome and perplexing.

There are always new shoots on the fungus, and new shades of yellow all over it. I cannot keep count of them, though I have tried conscientiously.

It is the strangest yellow, that wall paper! It makes me think of all the yellow things I ever saw—not beautiful ones like buttercups, but old foul, bad yellow things.

But there is something else about that paper—the smell! I noticed it the moment we came into the room, but with so much air and sun it was not bad! Now we have had a week of fog and rain, and whether the windows are open or not the smell is here.

It creeps all over the house.

I find it hovering in the dining-room, skulking in the parlor, hiding in the hall, lying in wait for me on the stairs.

It gets into my hair.

Even when I go to ride, if I turn my head suddenly and surprise it—there is that smell!

Such a peculiar odor, too! I have spent hours in trying to analyze it, to find what it smelled like.

It is not bad—at first, and very gentle, but quite the subtlest, most enduring odor I ever met.

In this damp weather it is awful. I wake up in the night and find it hanging over me.

It used to disturb me at first. I thought seriously of burning the house—to reach the smell.

But now I am used to it. The only thing I can think of that it is like is the *color* of the paper—a yellow smell.

There is a very funny mark on this wall, low down, near the mopboard. A streak that runs around the room. It goes behind every piece of furniture, except the bed, a long, straight, even *smooch,* as if it had been rubbed over and over.

I wonder how it was done and who did it, and what they did it for. Round and round and round—round and round and round—it makes me dizzy!

I really have discovered something at last.

Through watching so much at night, when it changes so, I have finally found out.

The front pattern *does* move—and no wonder! The woman behind shakes it!

Sometimes I think there are a great many women behind, and sometimes only one, and she crawls around fast, and her crawling shakes it all over.

Then in the very bright spots she keeps still, and in very shady spots she just takes hold of the bars and shakes them hard.

And she is all the time trying to climb through. But nobody could climb through that pattern—it strangles so; I think that is why it has so many heads.

They get through, and the pattern strangles them off and turns them upside-down, and makes their eyes white!

If those heads were covered or taken off it would not be half so bad.

I think that woman gets out in the daytime!

And I'll tell you why—privately—I've seen her!

I can see her out of every one of my windows!

It is the same woman. I know, for she is always creeping, and most women do not creep by daylight.

I see her in that long shaded lane, creeping up and down. I see her in those dark grape arbors, creeping all around the garden.

I see her on that long road under the trees, creeping along, and when a carriage comes she hides under the blackberry vines.

I don't blame her a bit. It must be very humiliating to be caught creeping by daylight!

I always lock the door when I creep by daylight. I can't do it at night, for I know John would suspect something at once.

And John is so queer, now, that I don't want to irritate him. I wish he would take another room! Besides, I don't want anybody to get that woman out at night but myself.

I often wonder if I could see her out of all the windows at one time.

And though I always see her she *may* be able to creep faster than I can turn!

I have watched her sometimes away off in the open country, creeping as fast as a cloud shadow in a high wind.

If only that top pattern could be gotten off from the under one! I mean to try it, little by little.

I have found out another funny thing, but I sha'n't tell it this time! It does not do to trust people too much.

There are only two more days to get this paper off, and I believe John is beginning to notice. I don't like the look in his eyes.

And I heard him ask Jennie a lot of professional questions about me. She had a very good report to give.

She said I slept a good deal in the daytime.

John knows I don't sleep very well at night, for all I'm so quiet!

He asked me all sorts of questions, too, and pretended to be very loving and kind.

As if I couldn't see through him!

It only interests me, but I feel sure John and Jennie are secretly affected by it.

Hurrah! This is the last day, but it is enough, John is to stay in town over night, and won't be out until this evening.

Jennie wanted to sleep with me—the sly thing! but I told her I should undoubtedly rest better for a night all alone.

That was clever, for really I wasn't alone a bit! As soon as it was moonlight, and that poor thing began to crawl and shake the pattern, I got up and ran to help her.

I pulled and she shook, I shook and she pulled, and before morning we had peeled off yards of that paper.

A strip about as high as my head and half around the room.

And then when the sun came and that awful pattern began to laugh at me I declared I would finish it today!

We go away tomorrow, and they are moving all my furniture down again to leave things as they were before.

Jennie looked at the wall in amazement, but I told her merrily that I did it out of pure spite at the vicious thing.

She laughed and said she wouldn't mind doing it herself, but I must not get tired.

How she betrayed herself that time!

But I am here, and no person touches this paper but me—not *alive!*

She tried to get me out of the room—it was too patent! But

I said it was so quiet and empty and clean now that I believed I would lie down again and sleep all I could; and not to wake me even for dinner—I would call when I woke.

So now she is gone, and the servants are gone, and the things are gone, and there is nothing left but that great bed-stead nailed down, with the canvas mattress we found on it.

We shall sleep downstairs tonight, and take the boat home tomorrow.

I quite enjoy the room, now it is bare again.

How those children did tear about here!

This bedstead is fairly gnawed!

But I must get to work.

I have locked the door and thrown the key down into the front path.

I don't want to go out, and I don't want to have anybody come in, till John comes.

I want to astonish him.

I've got a rope up here that even Jennie did not find. If that woman does get out, and tries to get away, I can tie her!

But I forgot I can not reach far without anything to stand on!

This bed will *not* move!

I tried to lift and push it until I was lame, and then I got so angry I bit off a little piece at one corner—but it hurt my teeth.

Then I peeled off all the paper I could reach standing on the floor. It sticks horribly and the pattern just enjoys it! All those strangled heads and bulbous eyes and waddling fungus growths just shriek with derision!

I am getting angry enough to do something desperate. To jump out of the window would be admirable exercise, but the bars are too strong even to try.

Besides, I wouldn't do it. Of course not. I know well enough that a step like that is improper and might be misconstrued.

I don't like to *look* out of the windows even—there are so many of those creeping women, and they creep so fast.

I wonder if they all come out of that wall paper, as I did?

But I am securely fastened now by my well-hidden rope—you don't get *me* out in the road there!

I suppose I shall have to get back behind the pattern when it comes night, and that is hard!

It is so pleasant to be out in this great room and creep around as I please!

I don't want to go outside. I won't, even if Jennie asks me to.

For outside you have to creep on the ground, and everything is green instead of yellow.

But here I can creep smoothly on the floor, and my shoulder just fits in that long smooch around the wall, so I cannot lose my way.

Why, there's John at the door!

It is no use, young man, you can't open it!

How he does call and pound!

Now he's crying for an ax.

It would be a shame to break down that beautiful door!

"John, dear!" said I in the gentlest voice, "the key is down by the front steps, under a plantain leaf!"

That silenced him for a few moments.

Then he said—very quietly indeed, "Open the door, my darling!"

"I can't," said I. "The key is down by the front door, under a plantain leaf!"

And then I said it again, several times, very gently and slowly, and said it so often that he had to go and see, and he got it, of course, and came in. He stopped short by the door.

"What is the matter?" he cried. "For God's sake, what are you doing?"

I kept on creeping just the same, but I looked at him over my shoulder.

"I've got out at last," said I, "in spite of you and Jennie! And I've pulled off most of the paper, so you can't put me back!"

Now why should that man have fainted? But he did, and right across my path by the wall, so that I had to creep over him every time!

By the beginning of the twentieth century, lady writers had taken to that invaluable machine, the typewriter. This is the daughter of the inventor of the first practical typewriter.

Twentieth Century

Specialists in this type of fiction like to say that the ghost story disappeared when electric light began to illuminate our lives. While ghosts die hard, it is true that the ghost novel is a rarity today. Today real horror stalks our lives—wars, bombs, the destruction of our environment, the possibility of annihilation. But with all the knowledge of reality that science has brought us in the twentieth century, there are some things we can neither understand nor explain. Some of the best writers of this century so far have been women who have probed the possibilities of other dimensions in time and human consciousness. The seven superbly written selections that follow are the work of seven highly original minds.

1952

HAND IN GLOVE

by Elizabeth Bowen

The literature of Ireland is pervaded by supernatural and macabre themes. The ghostly happening has always had a certain amount of easy acceptance with the Irish. Even their fairies were often considered the spirits of the dead, and when William Butler Yeats, the great collector of such tales, traveled the Irish countryside in search of fairy lore he would often ask, "Have you ever seen a fairy or ghost or such like?" "Amn't I annoyed with them," said one old lady. Another old gentlewoman said that she intensely disliked seeing them because they always brought bad weather. Many women writers in Ireland have been great exponents of the story of terror. Lady Wilde collected such supernatural tales as she walked up and down Ireland; Lady Augusta Gregory was responsible for some of the great folklore collections that captured the essence of Irish ghosts and fairy tales; other women writers have collected and explored strange areas of human experience.

Elizabeth Bowen, one of the greatest contemporary Irish writers, gives us here one of the best horror stories of the twentieth century, with an apparently gentle theme—two sisters desire simply to be the belles of their day and need the clothes to go with it, including a pair of gloves.

Elizabeth Bowen

Jasmine Lodge was favourably set on a residential, prettily-wooded hillside in the south of Ireland, overlooking a river and, still better, the roofs of a lively garrison town. Around 1904, which was the flowering period of the Miss Trevors, girls could not have had a more auspicious home—the neighbourhood spun merrily round the military. Ethel and Elsie, a spirited pair, garnered the full advantage—no ball, hop, picnic, lawn tennis, croquet or boating party was complete without them; in winter, though they could not afford to hunt, they trimly bicycled to all meets, and on frosty evenings, with their guitars, set off to soirées, snug inside their cab in their fur-tipped capes.

They possessed an aunt, a Mrs. Varley de Grey, *née* Elysia Trevor, a formerly notable local belle, who, drawn back again in her widowhood to what had been the scene of her early triumphs, occupied a back bedroom in Jasmine Lodge. Mrs. Varley de Grey had had no luck: her splashing match, in its time the talk of two kingdoms, had ended up in disaster—the well-born captain in a cavalry regiment having gone so far as to blow out his brains in India, leaving behind him nothing but her and debts. Mrs. Varley de Grey had returned from India with nothing but seven large trunks crammed with recent finery; and she also had been impaired by shock. This had taken place while Ethel and Elsie, whose father had married late, were still unborn—so it was that, for as long as the girls recalled, their aunt had been the sole drawback to Jasmine Lodge. Their parents had orphaned them, somewhat thoughtlessly, by simultaneously dying of scarlet fever when Ethel was just out and Elsie soon to be—they were therefore left lacking a chaperone and, with their gift for putting everything to some use, propped the aunt up in order that she might play that role. Only when her peculiarities became too marked did they feel it necessary to withdraw her: by that time, however, all the surrounding ladies could be said to compete for the honour of taking into society the sought-after Miss Trevors. From then on, no more was seen or heard of Mrs. Varley de Grey. ("Oh, just a trifle unwell, but nothing much!") She remained upstairs, at the back; when the girls were giving one of their little parties, or a couple of officers came to call, the key of her room would be turned in the outer lock.

The girls hung Chinese lanterns from the creepered verandah, and would sit lightly strumming on their guitars. Not less fascinating was their badinage, accompanied by a daring flash of the eyes. They were known as the clever Miss Trevors, not because of any taint of dogmatism or book-learning—no, when a gentleman cried "Those girls have brains!" he meant it wholly in admiration—but because of their accomplishments, ingenuity, and agility. They took leading parts in theatricals, lent spirit to numbers of drawingroom games, were naughty mimics, and sang duets. Nor did their fingers lag behind their wits—they constructed lampshades, crêpe paper flowers and picturesque hats; and, above all, varied their dresses marvellously—no one could beat them for ideas, snipping, slashing or fitting. Once more allowing nothing to go to waste, they had remodelled the

In the nineteenth and early twentieth centuries, fashionable ladies were required to wear long white gloves for evening dress, like these in a drawing from Godey's Lady's Book. *Manners might be forgotten, as in Elizabeth Bowen's superb story, but gloves—never!*

trousseau out of their aunt's trunks, causing sad old tulles and tarlatans, satins and *moiré* taffetas to appear to have come from Paris only to-day. They re-stitched spangles, pressed ruffles crisp, and revived many a corsage of squashed silk roses. They went somewhat softly about that task, for the trunks were all stored in the attic immediately over the back room.

They wore their clothes well. "A pin on either of those two would look smart!" declared other girls. All that they were short of was evening gloves—they had two pairs each, which they had been compelled to buy. *What* could have become of Mrs. Varley de Grey's presumably sumptuous numbers of this item, they were unable to fathom, and it was too bad. Had gloves been overlooked in her rush from India?—or, were they here, in that *one* trunk the Trevors could not get at? All other locks had yielded to pulls or pickings, or the sisters found keys to fit them, or they had used the tool-box; but this last stronghold defied them. In that sad little soiled silk sack, always on her person, Mrs. Varley de Grey, they became convinced, hoarded the operative keys, along with some frippery and brooches—all true emeralds, pearls and diamonds having been long ago, as they knew, sold. Such contrariety on their aunt's part irked them—meanwhile, gaieties bore hard on their existing gloves. Last thing at nights when they came in, last thing in the evenings before they went out, they would manfully dab away at the fingertips. So, it must be admitted that a long whiff of benzine pursued them as they whirled round the ballroom floor.

They were tall and handsome—nothing so soft as pretty, but in those days it was a vocation to be a handsome girl; many of the best marriages had been made by such. They carried themselves imposingly, had good busts and shoulders, waists firm under the whalebone, and straight backs. Their features were striking, their colouring high; low on their foreheads bounced dark mops of curls. Ethel was, perhaps, the dominant one, but both girls were pronounced to be full of character.

Whom, and still more when, did they mean to marry? They

had already seen regiments out and in; for quite a number of years, it began to seem, bets in the neighbourhood had been running high. Sympathetic spy-glasses were trained on the conspicuous gateway to Jasmine Lodge; each new cavalier was noted. The only trouble might be, their promoters claimed, that the clever Trevors were always so surrounded that they had not a moment in which to turn or choose. Or otherwise, could it possibly be that the admiration aroused by Ethel and Elsie, and their now institutional place in the local scene, scared out more tender feeling from the masculine breast? It came to be felt, and perhaps by the girls themselves, that, having lingered so long and so puzzlingly, it was up to them to bring off (like their aunt) a *coup*. Society around this garrison town had long plumed itself upon its romantic record; summer and winter, Cupid shot his darts. Lush scenery, the oblivion of all things else bred by the steamy climate, and perpetual gallivanting—all were conducive. Ethel's and Elsie's names, it could be presumed, were by now murmured wherever the Union Jack flew. Nevertheless, it was time they should decide.

Ethel's decision took place late one spring. She set her cap, in a manner worthy of her, at the second son of an English marquess. Lord Fred had come on a visit, for the fishing, to a mansion some miles down the river from Jasmine Lodge. He first made his appearance, with the rest of the house-party, at one of the more resplendent military balls, and was understood to be a man-about-town. The civilian glint of his *pince-nez*, at once serene and superb, instantaneously wrought, with his great name, on Ethel's heart. She beheld him, and the assembled audience, with approbation, looked on at the moment so big with fate. The truth, it appeared in a flash, was that Ethel, though so condescending with her charms, had not from the first been destined to love a soldier; and that here, after long attrition, her answer was. Lord Fred was, by all at once signed over to her. For his part, he responded to her attentions quite gladly, though in a somewhat dazed way. If he did not so often dance with her—indeed, how could he, for she was much besought?—he could at least be perceived to gaze. At a swiftly-organised river picnic, the next evening, he by consent fell to Ethel's lot—she had spent the foregoing morning snipping and tacking at a remaining muslin of Mrs. Varley de Grey's, a very fresh forget-me-not-dotted pattern. The muslin did not survive the evening out, for when the moon should have risen, rain poured into the boats. Ethel's good-humoured drollery carried all before it, and Lord Fred wrapped his blazer around her form.

Next day, more rain; and all felt flat. At Jasmine Lodge the expectant deck chairs had to be hurried in from the garden, and the small close rooms, with their greeneried windows and plentiful bric-à-brac, gave out a stuffy, resentful, indoor smell. The maid was out; Elsie was lying down with a migraine; so it devolved on Ethel to carry up Mrs. Varley de Grey's tea—the invalid set very great store by tea, and her manifestations by door-rattlings, sobs and mutters were apt to become disturbing if it did not appear. Ethel, with the not particularly dainty tray, accordingly entered the back room, this afternoon rendered dark by its outlook into a dripping uphill wood. The aunt, her visage draped in a cobweb shawl, was as usual sitting up in bed. "Aha!" she at once cried, screwing one eye up and glittering round at Ethel with the other, "so what's all this in the wind to-day?"

Ethel, as she lodged the meal on the bed, shrugged her shoulders, saying, "I'm in a hurry."

"No doubt you are. The question is, will you get him?"

"Oh, drink your tea!" snapped Ethel, her colour rising.

The old wretch responded by popping a lump of sugar into her cheek and sucking at it while she fixed her wink on her niece. She then observed: "*I* could tell you a thing or two!"

"We've had enough of *your* fabrications, Auntie."

"Fabrications!" croaked Mrs. Varley de Grey. "And who's been the fabricator, I'd like to ask? Who's so nifty with the scissors and needle? Who's been going a-hunting in my clothes?"

"Oh, what a fib!" exclaimed Ethel, turning her eyes up. "Those old musty miserable bundles of things of yours—would Elsie or I consider laying a finger on them?"

Mrs. Varley de Grey replied, as she sometimes did, by heaving up and throwing the tray at Ethel. Nought, therefore, but cast-off kitchen china nowadays was ever exposed to risk; and the young woman, not trying to gather the debris up, statuesquely, thoughtfully stood with her arms folded, watching tea-steam rise from the carpet. To-day, the effort seemed to have been too much for Aunt Elysia, who collapsed on her pillows, faintly blue in the face. "Rats in the attic," she muttered. "*I've* heard them, rats in the attic! Now where's my tea?"

"You've had it," said Ethel, turning to leave the room. However, she paused to study a photograph in a tarnished, elaborate silver frame. "Really quite an Adonis, poor Uncle Harry. From the first glance, you say, he never looked back?"

"My lovely tea," said the widow, beginning to sob.

As Ethel slowly put down the photograph, her eyes could be seen to calculate, her mouth hardened and a reflective cast came over her brow. Step by step, once more she approached the bed, and, as she did so, altered her tune. She suggested, in a beguiling tone: "You said you could tell me a thing or two . . . ?"

Time went on; Lord Fred, though forever promising, still failed to come within Ethel's grasp. Ground gained one hour seemed to be lost the next—it seemed, for example, that things went better for Ethel in the afternoons, in the open air, than at the dressier evening functions. It was when she swept down on him in full plumage that Lord Fred seemed to contract. Could it be that he feared his passions?—she hardly thought so. Or did her complexion not light up well? When there was a question of dancing, he came so late that her programme already was black with other names, whereupon he would heave a gallant sigh. When they did take the floor together, he held her so far at arm's length, and with his face turned so far away, that when she wished to address him she had to shout—she told herself this must be the London style, but it piqued her, naturally. Next morning, all was as it was before, with nobody so completely assiduous as Lord Fred—but, through it all, he still never came to the point. And worse, the days of his visit were running out; he would soon be back in the heart of the London season. "Will you ever get him, Ethel, now, do you think?" Elsie asked, with trying solicitude, and no doubt the neighbourhood wondered also.

She conjured up all her fascinations. But was something further needed, to do the trick?

It was now that she began to frequent her aunt.

In that dank little back room looking into the hill, proud Ethel humbled herself, to prise out the secret. Sessions were close and long. Elsie, in mystification outside the door, heard the dotty voice of their relative rising, falling, with, now and then, blood-curdling little knowing laughs. Mrs. Varley de Grey was back in the golden days. Always, though, of a sudden it would break off, drop back into pleas, whimpers and jagged breathing. No doctor, though she constantly asked for one, had for years been allowed to visit Mrs. Varley de Grey—the girls saw no reason for that expense, or for the interference which might follow. Aunt's affliction, they swore, was confined to the head; all she required was quiet, and that she got. Knowing, however, how gossip spreads, they would let no servant near her for more than a minute or two, and then with one of themselves on watch at the door. They had much to bear from the foetid state of her room.

"You don't think you'll kill her, Ethel?" the out-of-it Elsie asked. "Forever sitting on top of her, as you now do. Can it be healthy, egging her on to talk? What's this attraction, all of a sudden?—whatever's this which has sprung up between you two? She and you are becoming quite hand-in-glove."

Elsie merely remarked this, and soon forgot: she had her own fish to fry. It was Ethel who had cause to recall the words—for, the afternoon of the very day they were spoken, Aunt Elysia whizzed off on another track, screamed for what was impossible and, upon being thwarted, went into a seizure unknown before. The worst of it was, at the outset her mind cleared—she pushed her shawl back, reared up her unkempt grey head and looked at Ethel, unblinkingly studied Ethel, with a lucid accumulation of years of hate. "You fool of a gawk," she said, and with such contempt! "Coming running to me to know how to trap a man. Could *you* learn, if it was from Venus herself? Wait till I show you beauty. Bring down those trunks!"

"Oh, Auntie."

"Bring them down, I say. I'm about to dress myself up."

"Oh but I cannot; they're heavy; I'm single-handed."

"Heavy?—they came here heavy. But there've been rats in the attic. *I* saw you, swishing downstairs in my *eau-de-nil.*"

"Oh, you dreamed that!"

"Through the crack of the door.—Let me up, then. Let us go where they are, and look—we shall soon see!" Aunt Elysia threw back the bedclothes and began to get up. "Let's take a look," she said "at the rats' work." She set out to totter towards the door.

"Oh, but you're not fit!" Ethel protested.

"And when did a doctor say so?" There was a swaying; Ethel caught her in time and, not gently, lugged her back to the bed —and Ethel's mind the whole of this time was whirling, for to-night was the night upon which all hung. Lord Fred's last local appearance was to be, like his first, at a ball: to-morrow he left for London. So it must be to-night, at this ball, or never! How was it that Ethel felt so strangely, wildly confident of the outcome? It was time to begin on her coiffure, lay out her dress. Oh, to-night she would shine as never before! She flung back the bedclothes over the helpless form, heard a clock strike, and hastily turned to go.

"I will be quits with you," said the voice behind her.

Ethel, in a kimono, hair half done, was in her own room, in front of the open glove-drawer, when Elsie came in—home from a tennis party. Elsie acted oddly—she went at once to the drawer and buried her nose in it. "Oh my goodness," she cried, "it's all too true, and it's awful!"

"What is?" Ethel carelessly asked.

"Ethel dear, would you ever face it out if I were to tell you a certain rumour I heard to-day at the party as to Lord Fred?"

Ethel turned from her sister, took up the heated tongs and applied more crimps to her natural curliness. She said: "Certainly; spit it out."

"Since childhood, he's recoiled from the breath of benzine. He wilts away when it enters the very room!"

"Who says that's so?"

"He confided it to his hostess, who is now spitefully putting it around the country."

Ethel bit her lip and put down the tongs, while Elsie sorrowfully concluded: "And your gloves stink, Ethel, as I'm sure do mine." Elsie then thought it wiser to slip away.

In a minute more, however, she was back, and this time with still more peculiar air. She demanded: "In what state did you leave Auntie? She was sounding so very quiet that I peeped in, and *I* don't care for the looks of her now at all!" Ethel swore, but consented to take a look. She stayed in there in the back room, with Elsie biting her thumb-nail outside the door, for what seemed an ominous length of time; when she did emerge, she looked greenish, but held her head high. The sisters' eyes met. Ethel said, stonily, "Dozing."

"You're certain she's *not* . . . ? She *couldn't* ever be—you know?"

"Dozing, I tell you." Ethel stared Elsie out.

"If she *was* gone," quavered the frailer sister, "just think of it—why, we'd never get to the ball!—And a ball that everything hangs on," she ended, with a scared but conspiratorial glance at Ethel.

"Reassure yourself. Didn't you hear me say?"

As she spoke Ethel, chiefly from habit, locked her late Aunt's door on the outside. The act caused a sort of secret jingle to be heard from inside her fist, and Elsie asked: "What's that you've got hold of, now?" "Just a few little keys and trinkets she made me keep," replied Ethel, disclosing the small bag she had found where she'd looked for it, under the dead one's pillow. "Scurry on now, Elsie, or you'll never be dressed. Care to make use of my tongs, while they're so splendidly hot?"

Alone at last, Ethel drew in a breath, and, with a gesture of resolution, re-tied her kimono-sash tightly over her corset. She took the key from the bag and regarded it, murmuring, "Providential!," then gave a glance upward, towards where the attics were. The late spring sun had set, but an apricot afterglow, not unlike the light cast by a Chinese lantern, crept through the upper storey of Jasmine Lodge. The cessation of all those rustlings, tappings, whimpers and moans from inside Mrs. Varley de Grey's room had set up an unfamiliar, somewhat unnerving hush. Not till a whiff of singeing hair announced that Elsie was well employed did Ethel set out on the quest which held all her hopes. Success was imperative—she *must* have gloves. Gloves, gloves . . .

Soundlessly, she set foot on the attic stairs.

Under the skylight she had to suppress a shriek, for a rat—yes, of all things!—leaped at her out of an empty hatbox: and the rodent gave her a wink before it darted away. Now Ethel and Elsie knew for a certain fact that there never *had* been rats in Jasmine Lodge. However, she continued to steel her nerves, and to push her way to the one inviolate trunk.

All Mrs. Varley de Grey's other Indian luggage gaped and yawned at Ethel, void, showing its linings, on end or toppling, forming a barricade around the object of her search. She pushed, pitched and pulled, scowling as the dust flew into her hair. But the last trunk, when it came into view and reach, still had something select and bridal about it: on top, the initials E. V. de G. stared out, quite luminous in a frightening way—for indeed how dusky the attic was! Shadows not only multiplied in the corners but seemed to finger their way up the sloping roof. Silence pierced up through the floor from that room below—and, worst, Ethel had the sensation of being watched by that pair of fixed eyes she had not stayed to close. She glanced this way, that way, backward over her shoulder. But, Lord Fred was at stake!—she knelt down and got to work with the key.

This trunk had two neat brass locks, one left, one right, along the front of the lid. Ethel, after fumbling, opened the first—then, so great was her hurry to know what might be within that she could not wait but slipped her hand in under the lifted corner. She pulled out one pricelessly lacy tip of what must be a bride-veil, and gave a quick laugh—must not this be an omen? She pulled again, but the stuff resisted, almost as though it were being grasped from inside the trunk—she let go, and either her eyes deceived her or the lace began to be drawn back slowly, in again, inch by inch. What was odder was, that the spotless finger-tip of a white kid glove appeared for a moment, as though exploring its way out, then withdrew.

Ethel's heart stood still—but she turned to the other lock. Was a giddy attack overcoming her?—for, as she gazed, the entire lid of the trunk seemed to bulge upward, heave and strain, so that the E. V. de G. upon it rippled.

Untouched by the key in her trembling hand, the second lock tore itself open.

She recoiled, while the lid slowly rose—of its own accord.

She should have fled. But oh, how she craved what lay there exposed!—layer upon layer, wrapped in transparent paper, of elbow-length, magnolia-pure white gloves, bedded on the inert folds of the veil. "Lord Fred," thought Ethel, "now you're within my grasp!"

That was her last thought, nor was the grasp to be hers. Down on her knees again, breathless with lust and joy, Ethel flung herself forward on to that sea of kid, scrabbling and seizing. The glove she had seen before was now, however, readier for its purpose. As first it merely pounced after Ethel's fingers, as though making mock of their greedy course; but the hand within it was all the time filling out. . . . With one snowy flash through the dusk, the glove clutched Ethel's front hair, tangled itself in her black curls and dragged her head down. She began to choke among the sachets and tissue—then the glove let go, hurled her back, and made its leap at her throat.

It was a marvel that anything so dainty should be so strong. So great, so convulsive was the swell of the force that, during the strangling of Ethel, the seams of the glove split.

In any case, the glove would have been too small for her.

The shrieks of Elsie, upon the attic threshold, began only when all other sounds had died down. . . . The ultimate spark of the once-famous cleverness of the Miss Trevors appeared in Elsie's extrication of herself from this awkward mess—for, who was to credit how Ethel came by her end? The sisters' reputation for warmth of heart was to stand the survivor in good stead—for, could those affections nursed in Jasmine Lodge, extending so freely even to the unwell aunt, have culminated in Elsie's setting on Ethel? No. In the end, the matter was hushed up—which is to say, is still talked about even now. Ethel Trevor and Mrs. Varley de Grey were interred in the same grave, as everyone understood that they would have wished. What conversation took place under the earth one does not know.

1952

WHITEWASH

by Rose Macaulay

Just as Gertrude Bacon in her travels in the nineteenth century found the materials for her story "The Gorgon's Head" in an old Greek legend, so Rose Macaulay in the twentieth found the basis of "Whitewash" in ancient Roman history. Often a visitor to the Isle of Capri, she was familiar with the local legends about the intense cruelty of the Emperor Tiberius, who had retired there.

Tiberius was the emperor of Rome from A.D. 14 to 37. His was a particularly tempestuous reign. Tiberius himself had a highly suspicious nature: he instituted a wide practice of political espionage that resulted in a rule of tyranny. Always vindictive, he was, said most of the contemporary historians, given to excesses of cruelty. Tiberius grew so unpopular in Rome —he had put to death many well-respected Roman senators on the charge of treason—that he decided to leave the city and live in the countryside. In the year 27 A.D., he took up residence on the island of Capri, a short distance from the Campanian coast of Italy. There his reputation grew into that of a monster.

In the early twentieth century some historians and writers began to re-examine the character of Tiberius. Believing that he had been maligned, they began to "whitewash" his reputation. One of these writers was Rose Macaulay's friend Norman

An early photograph of Rose Macaulay

Douglas, who implied in his writings that tales of the wickedness of Tiberius were overdone. In this extraordinary "time" tale the past and present converge to tell us otherwise.

The sea as it swung gently against the rocks was jade green, like the evening sky. I was reclining on thymy turf, reading *The Story of San Michele.* Six feet down in the sea my aunt was scrambling among broken marble wreckage that had been once an imperial bath. When she surfaced I looked up from Dr. Axel Münthe and said, "It's nice to know what an excellent man Tiberius actually was, after all one was brought up to think of him."

My aunt coughed up water and turned on her back to float. "I know nothing of the sort," she said. "I would rather believe his contemporaries than these modern whitewashers. And I have the islanders with me, to a man, woman and child."

"Naturally," I agreed. "Timberio is their local industry. If he lost his wickedness, he would have nothing but a few ruined villas and baths and a rock up there by the Faro from which no one was ever thrown. What use would visitors have for a beneficent old gentleman who retired here to flee the corrupt world and commune with his soul? Suetonius and Tacitus and all the legend-makers since are the local Bible. But they are wrong. Timberio has been cleared, and I am delighted that all these villas and baths were used by so saintly an emperor."

"One after another," said my aunt, "they take them from us. Nero. Tiberius. The Borgias. King John, Richard III. Are we to be deprived of all the monsters of the past? Are they all to be of the present? And how long will it be before our contemporary monsters have the whitewash buckets poured over them and emerge saints, or victims of circumstance, more sinned against than sinning? Most of us are more sinning than sinned against; why should monsters be exceptions?"

I made no effort to convert my aunt on this subject. She required monsters, and, so far as I was concerned, could have them.

"I shall go exploring some of the caves," I said. "Will you come?"

"Not I," said my aunt. "When one thinks what went on in them," she added, primly, as she climbed out of the sea. "I am going back to the villa. Dinner at nine."

Capri is a rocky island whose coast is sharply marked by cave openings and other rock formations. Some of the ruins of the twelve villas built there by Tiberius are still preserved.

"I'll be back," I said.

My aunt draped herself in her scarlet bernous and set off up the steep rock stairway that would conduct her in the end to the villa. I dropped into the warm twilight sea again, and swam round the next jut of rock. Above me the island sloped down to the sea, smelling of pine and thyme and cistus and the stored heat of the August day. Below me lay Roman villas and baths that had slipped long since into the waves and got drowned. I had explored these remains often enough; what I now wanted was a cave. There was one a little further on. I swam into it; it was a deep cave, thrusting far back into the rock. Round it, just above sea level, ran a broad ledge, slippery and green with seaweed. I hoisted myself on to it and walked along it. It was almost dark inside the cave. But, after walking a few yards, I felt a draught on my right, and saw a good-sized round opening in the rock. I remembered tales told by the locals of passages that climbed up from caves to one or another of Timberio's villas. Perhaps this one did so. I entered it, meaning to explore it for a little way. It sloped gently up, and was about the height of my shoulders. But I did not get far; a cold wind suddenly came against me like a hand on my chest, pushing me back. It struck me that I would rather explore that passage by day, and that I was inexplicably shivering, and had better get out of the cave and go home. In a few moments I was back on the slippery ledge; the little waves were lapping against the rock with a sound like whispering voices—or was it sharp, frightened gasps? A frightened crowd, it sounded like; a collection of people scared out of their wits. I slipped down into the water, which had become colder, and swam towards the cave's mouth. Outside was the green evening sky, the green evening sea. At the entrance I felt, oddly, as if a strong tide were running against me; I swam, but made no progress; in fact, I was being pushed back. But there was no tide, and the sea was calm. I struck out harder, and was pushed back further. I began to panic. What current was driving with such force into the cave that I could not swim against it? I remembered nightmare battles with Cornish tides that, swim as I would, carried me out to sea, the landmarks slipping from me in a losing race. I had been rescued by boats. There was no boat now, and I could not get out. I was growing tired; I was not a strong swimmer. Suppose I had to spend the night on that slippery, slimy ledge, among that whispering, frightened chatter? And would the sea rise? The Mediterranean is not quite tideless. I went on struggling; for a moment it seemed to me that I made headway. Then, looking up, I saw a dark shape, floating quietly just outside the cave's mouth; it was just under the surface but for a sharp, sail-shaped fin; it seemed to wait, rolling to and fro, in no hurry, but just waiting. That decided me; I retreated into the cave and climbed on to the ledge. I was shaking so much that I could scarcely make it. If the shark should enter the cave, I would climb into the passage.

I sat on the cold ledge, huddled up, my arms round my knees. It seemed to me that the chattering and whispering of the sea slapping against the rocky wall was louder, quicker, more verbal. The atmosphere in the cave was tense; it was sheer terror. It caught me like a wave, drowning me in cold panic. I have never known fear so intense, such submerging anguish.

Then, above the whispered clamour, rose a soft, jeering voice from the passage behind me. It said, "*Veni, cete, veni.*" The next moment the cave mouth darkened; the great shark drove in with a noise of rushing water. I saw its white belly and its row of terrible teeth. I did not wait; I plunged head first into the passage in the rock.

Then something more than a wind drove against me; it was as if some other strength met mine, pushing me back. I gripped a jut of rock with both hands; my feet were tensed against the side wall of the passage. I looked into the darkness of the corridor that wound ahead; suddenly on it there hung palely, as in phosphorescent light, a head and face I knew: I had seen it on coins, in busts, in reliefs. A handsome, sneering face, its lips curled now in a sensual smile. From them came a rich, pleased chuckling. And from the cave behind me came a snapping of jaws and a thin screaming, and splash after splash, as if things were being dragged down from the ledge into the water. At each splash came the low chuckling.

I was being pushed, but half-heartedly, as if the pusher's attention were concentrated elsewhere; or as if there were no real bodily contact. I held on to my position with hands and feet; I was not really much afraid of losing it, for I was alive, and the pusher had been dead for close on two thousand years, and what physical force can the dead and the living exert over one another? My terror was of the scene behind me; the thin screams, the snapping jaws, the splashing. . . . And of the leering phosphorescent face hanging in the dark rock corridor in front of me; and of that enjoying chuckle. I shut my eyes, but could not stop my ears.

I do not know how long the ghastly scene lasted. But before very long I realised that there was silence in the cave, but for a heavy, gorged, wallowing sound. Then the drawling voice said "*Abi, cete, abi hinc*"; and the heavy shape seemed to flounder through the water, out of the cave into the sea beyond.

I opened my eyes. The face was gone. I seemed quite alone; the soft slap-slap of water against rock was no longer like whispering voices. I slithered down on to the ledge, staring in horror at the deep green water below me, now silvered by the first long shafts of a rising moon. I don't know what I feared to see in it—mangled limbs, ripples running red . . . but there was only green sea water touched with silver. All the same I did not get into it; I followed the ledge round to the cave's mouth, and peered warily out. No dark shape was in sight; no fin. I knew I was alone.

I slipped into the moon-struck sea and swam round the jut of rock to the place where we had bathed among the ruins of the Roman bath. My bathing wrap lay there. Putting it over my shivering body, I was back in the twentieth century. The tension slackened; I lay limply on the rocks and was sick.

What time it was I had no idea. Getting up, I saw *The Story of San Michele* lying open where I had put it down; I picked it up and climbed the path up the hill.

I came in through the open French window; my aunt lay smoking in a long chair.

"So there you are at last," she said. "I've kept your dinner for you. Do you know," she added, reflectively, "I was beginning to fear that Timberio had got you after all."

"I began to think so too," I told her. "And you will be glad to know that Suetonius and Tacitus and the locals are all perfectly right about him, and that Dr. Münthe and Norman and the other whitewashers are perfectly wrong; they haven't the faintest idea what they are talking about."

"No," my aunt tranquilly agreed. "Whitewashers never have. Evil does exist, and monsters have always been monsters. Nero, Tiberius, the Borgias, Richard III, John, our contemporary tyrants . . . I believe in them all."

"Or," I asked myself presently, when warmed and clothed and fed, "can I have had some kind of a fit? I shall tell Norman about it to-morrow, and ask what he thinks."

I met Norman in his favourite piazza café next morning. Though the most patriotic of islanders, he told me that I had been the victim of an erroneous mass mythology. For Timberio had been a most excellent man, kind of heart and temperate of habit.

"Only," he added, re-filling his three glasses, "you've hardly begun yet. Timberio, according to the Capraeans, could do much better than that. You must try some of the other caves."

1952

THE BIRDS

by Daphne du Maurier

It is interesting that while the ghost story which enthralled the nineteenth-century reader has been losing its power, in the twentieth century natural phenomena have inspired stories of terror. Here the great suspense writer Daphne du Maurier takes a look at the world of birds.

Birds have always had a curious magic in the history of supernatural lore. In the days before men could fly, these flying creatures inspired awe. The Greeks and Romans tried to read the future from the way the birds flew or the pattern of their flight. Some birds were particularly sacred—the swallow, the wren, the robin. Old stories of the significance of birds persist. The cock, for example, when it cries at dawn is thought to make all ghosts and spirits disappear; the wren carried even today by Manx fishermen is believed to protect those who go to sea. Some birds were evil; to see a magpie always meant trouble. In Scotland, for example, they used to say a magpie had a drop of the devil's blood under its tongue, and you had to protect yourself against it by saying "Devil, devil, I defy thee." To hear the shriek of an owl is still a bad omen in many country places, and a crow on a roof is a sign of death.

Daphne du Maurier's story is a very contemporary tale of terror. It was made into a movie, but you'll find here that the pen is mightier than the camera.

Daphne du Maurier

On December the third the wind changed overnight and it was winter. Until then the autumn had been mellow, soft. The earth was rich where the plow had turned it.

Nat Hocken, because of a wartime disability, had a pension and did not work full time at the farm. He worked three days a week, and they gave him the lighter jobs. Although he was married, with children, his was a solitary disposition; he liked best to work alone.

It pleased him when he was given a bank to build up, or a gate to mend, at the far end of the peninsula, where the sea surrounded the farmland on either side. Then, at midday, he would pause and eat the meat pie his wife had baked for him and, sitting on the cliff's edge, watch the birds.

In autumn great flocks of them came to the peninsula, restless, uneasy, spending themselves in motion; now wheeling, circling in the sky; now settling to feed on the rich, new-turned soil; but even when they fed, it was as though they did so without hunger, without desire.

Restlessness drove them to the skies again. Crying, whistling, calling, they skimmed the placid sea and left the shore.

Make haste, make speed, hurry and begone; yet where, and to what purpose? The restless urge of autumn, unsatisfying, sad, had put a spell upon them, and they must spill themselves of motion before winter came.

Perhaps, thought Nat, a message comes to the birds in autumn, like a warning. Winter is coming. Many of them will perish. And like people who, apprehensive of death before their time, drive themselves to work or folly, the birds do likewise; tomorrow we shall die.

The birds had been more restless than ever this fall of the year. Their agitation more remarked because the days were still.

As Mr. Trigg's tractor traced its path up and down the western hills, and Nat, hedging, saw it dip and turn, the whole machine and the man upon it were momentarily lost in the great cloud of wheeling, crying birds.

Nat remarked upon them to Mr. Trigg when the work was finished for the day.

"Yes," said the farmer, "there are more birds about than usual. I have a notion the weather will change. It will be a hard winter. That's why the birds are restless."

The farmer was right. That night the weather turned.

The bedroom in the cottage faced east. Nat woke just after two and heard the east wind, cold and dry. It sounded hollow in the chimney, and a loose slate rattled on the roof. Nat listened, and he could hear the sea roaring in the bay. He drew the blanket round him, leaned closer to the back of his wife, deep in sleep. Then he heard the tapping on the windowpane. It continued until, irritated by the sound, Nat got out of bed and went to the window. He opened it; and as he did so something brushed his hand, jabbing at his knuckles, grazing the skin. Then he saw the flutter of wings and the thing was gone again, over the roof, behind the cottage.

It was a bird. What kind of bird he could not tell. The wind must have driven it to shelter on the sill.

He shut the window and went back to bed, but feeling his knuckles wet, put his mouth to the scratch. The bird had drawn blood.

Frightened, he supposed, bewildered, seeking shelter, the

bird had stabbed at him in the darkness. Once more he settled himself to sleep.

Presently the tapping came again—this time more forceful, more insistent. And now his wife woke at the sound, and turning in the bed, said to him, "See to the window, Nat; it's rattling."

"I've already been to it," he told her. "There's some bird there, trying to get in."

"Send it away," she said. "I can't sleep with that noise."

He went to the window for the second time, and now when he opened it, there was not one bird on the sill but half a dozen; they flew straight into his face.

He shouted, striking out at them with his arms, scattering them; like the first one, they flew over the roof and disappeared.

He let the window fall and latched it.

Suddenly a frightened cry came from the room across the passage where the children slept.

"It's Jill," said his wife, roused at the sound.

There came a second cry, this time from both children. Stumbling into their room, Nat felt the beating of wings about him in the darkness. The window was wide open. Through it came the birds, hitting first the ceiling and the walls, then swerving in midflight and turning to the children in their beds.

"It's all right. I'm here," shouted Nat, and the children flung themselves, screaming, upon him, while in the darkness the birds rose, and dived, and came for him again.

"What is it, Nat? What's happened?" his wife called. Swiftly he pushed the children through the door to the passage and shut it upon them, so that he was alone in their bedroom with the birds.

He seized a blanket from the nearest bed, and using it as a weapon, flung it to right and left about him.

He felt the thud of bodies, heard the fluttering of wings; but the birds were not yet defeated, for again and again they returned to the assault, jabbing his hands, his head, their little stabbing beaks sharp as pointed forks.

The blanket became a weapon of defense. He wound it about his head, and then in greater darkness, beat at the birds with his bare hands. He dared not stumble to the door and open it lest the birds follow him.

How long he fought with them in the darkness he could not tell; but at last the beating of the wings about him lessened, withdrew; and through the dense blanket he was aware of light.

He waited, listened; there was no sound except the fretful crying of one of the children from the bedroom beyond.

He took the blanket from his head and stared about him. The cold gray morning light exposed the room.

Dawn and the open window had called the living birds; the dead lay on the floor.

Sickened, Nat went to the window and stared out across his patch of garden to the fields.

It was bitter cold, and the ground had all the hard, black look of the frost that the east wind brings. The sea, fiercer now with turning tide, whitecapped and steep, broke harshly in the bay. Of the birds there was no sign.

Nat shut the window and the door of the small bedroom and went back across the passage to his own room.

His wife sat up in bed, one child asleep beside her; the smaller one in her arms, his face bandaged.

"He's sleeping now," she whispered. "Something must have cut him; there was blood at the corners of his eyes. Jill said it was the birds. She said she woke up and the birds were in the room."

His wife looked up at Nat, searching his face for confirmation. She looked terrified, bewildered. He did not want her to know that he also was shaken, dazed almost, by the events of the past few hours.

"There are birds in there," he said. "Dead birds, nearly fifty of them." He sat down on the bed beside his wife.

"It's the hard weather," he said. "It must be that; it's the hard weather. They aren't the birds, maybe, from around here.

They've been driven down from upcountry."

"But Nat," whispered his wife, "it's only this night that the weather turned. They can't be hungry yet. There's food for them out there in the fields."

"It's the weather," repeated Nat. "I tell you, it's the weather."

His face, too, was drawn and tired, like hers. They stared at one another for a while without speaking.

Nat went to the window and looked out. The sky was hard and leaden, and the brown hills that had gleamed in the sun the day before looked dark and bare. Black winter had descended in a single night.

The children were awake now. Jill was chattering, and young Johnny was crying once again. Nat heard his wife's voice, soothing, comforting them as he went downstairs.

Presently they came down. He had breakfast ready for them.

"Did you drive away the birds?" asked Jill.

"Yes, they've all gone now," Nat said. "It was the east wind brought them in."

"I hope they won't come again," said Jill.

"I'll walk with you to the bus," Nat said to her.

Jill seemed to have forgotten her experience of the night before. She danced ahead of him, chasing the leaves, her face rosy under her pixy hood.

All the while Nat searched the hedgerows for the birds, glanced over them to the fields beyond, looked to the small wood above the farm where the rooks and jackdaws gathered; he saw none. Soon the bus came ambling up the hill.

Nat saw Jill onto the bus, then turned and walked back toward the farm. It was not his day for work, but he wanted to satisfy himself that all was well. He went to the back door of the farmhouse; he heard Mrs. Trigg singing, the wireless making a background for her song.

"Are you there, missus?" Nat called.

She came to the door, beaming, broad, a good-tempered woman.

"Hullo, Mr. Hocken," she said. "Can you tell me where this

cold is coming from? Is it Russia? I've never seen such a change. And it's going on, the wireless says. Something to do with the Arctic Circle."

"We didn't turn on the wireless this morning," said Nat. "Fact is, we had trouble in the night."

"Kiddies poorly?"

"No." He hardly knew how to explain. Now, in daylight, the battle of the birds would sound absurd.

He tried to tell Mrs. Trigg what had happened, but he could see from her eyes that she thought his story was the result of nightmare following a heavy meal.

"Sure they were real birds?" she said, smiling.

"Mrs. Trigg," he said, "there are fifty dead birds—robins, wrens, and such—lying now on the floor of the children's bedroom. They went for me; they tried to go for young Johnny's eyes."

Mrs. Trigg stared at him doubtfully. "Well, now," she answered. "I suppose the weather brought them; once in the bedroom they wouldn't know where they were. Foreign birds maybe, from that Arctic Circle."

"No," said Nat. "They were the birds you see about here every day."

"Funny thing," said Mrs. Trigg. "No explaining it, really. You ought to write up and ask the *Guardian*. They'd have some answer for it. Well, I must be getting on."

Nat walked back along the lane to his cottage. He found his wife in the kitchen with young Johnny.

"See anyone?" she asked.

"Mrs. Trigg," he answered. "I don't think she believed me. Anyway, nothing wrong up there."

"You might take the birds away," she said. "I daren't go into the room to make the beds until you do. I'm scared."

"Nothing to scare you now," said Nat. "They're dead, aren't they?"

He went up with a sack and dropped the stiff bodies into it, one by one. Yes, there were fifty of them all told. Just the ordinary, common birds of the hedgerow; nothing as large even as a thrush. It must have been fright that made them act the way they did.

He took the sack out into the garden and was faced with a fresh problem. The ground was frozen solid, yet no snow had fallen; nothing had happened in the past hours but the coming of the east wind. It was unnatural, queer. He could see the whitecapped seas breaking in the bay. He decided to take the birds to the shore and bury them.

When he reached the beach below the headland, he could scarcely stand, the force of the east wind was so strong. It was low tide; he crunched his way over the shingle to the softer sand and then, his back to the wind, opened up his sack.

He ground a pit in the sand with his heel, meaning to drop the birds into it; but as he did so, the force of the wind lifted them as though in flight again, and they were blown away from him along the beach, tossed like feathers, spread and scattered.

The tide will take them when it turns, he said to himself.

He looked out to sea and watched the crested breakers, combing green. They rose stiffly, curled, and broke again; and because it was ebb tide, the roar was distant, more remote, lacking the sound and thunder of the flood.

Then he saw them. The gulls. Out there, riding the seas.

What he had thought at first were the whitecaps of the waves were gulls. Hundreds, thousands, ten of thousands.

They rose and fell in the troughs of the seas, heads to the wind, like a mighty fleet at anchor, waiting on the tide.

Nat turned; leaving the beach, he climbed the steep path home.

Someone should know of this. Someone should be told. Something was happening, because of the east wind and the weather, that he did not understand.

As he drew near the cottage, his wife came to meet him at the door. She called to him, excited. "Nat," she said, "it's on the wireless. They've just read out a special news bulletin. It's not only here, it's everywhere. In London, all over the country. Something has happened to the birds. Come listen; they're repeating it."

Together they went into the kitchen to listen to the announcement.

"Statement from the Home Office, at eleven A.M. this morning. Reports from all over the country are coming in hourly about the vast quantity of birds flocking above towns, villages, and outlying districts, causing obstruction and damage and even attacking individuals. It is thought that the Artic air stream at present covering The British Isles is causing birds to migrate south in immense numbers, and that intense hunger may drive these birds to attack human beings. Householders are warned to see to their windows, doors, and chimneys, and to take reasonable precautions for the safety of their children. A further statement will be issued later."

A kind of excitement seized Nat. He looked at his wife in triumph. "There you are," he said. "I've been telling myself all morning there's something wrong. And just now, down on the beach, I looked out to sea and there were gulls, thousands of them, riding on the sea, waiting."

"What are they waiting for, Nat?" she asked.

He stared at her. "I don't know," he said slowly.

He went over to the drawer where he kept his hammer and other tools.

"What are you going to do, Nat?"

"See to the windows and the chimneys, like they tell you to."

"You think they would break in with the windows shut? Those wrens and robins and such? Why, how could they?"

He did not answer. He was not thinking of the robins and the wrens. He was thinking of the gulls.

He went upstairs and worked there the rest of the morning, boarding the windows of the bedrooms, filling up the chimney bases.

"Dinner's ready." His wife called him from the kitchen.

"All right. Coming down."

When dinner was over and his wife was washing up, Nat switched on the one o'clock news. The same announcement was repeated, but the news bulletin enlarged upon it. "The flocks of birds have caused dislocation in all areas," said the announcer, "and in London the mass was so dense at ten o'clock this morning that it seemed like a vast black cloud. The birds settled on rooftops, on window ledges, and on chimneys. The species included blackbird, thrush, the common house sparrow, and as might be expected in the metropolis, a vast quantity of pigeons, starlings, and that frequenter of the London river, the blackheaded gull. The sight was so unusual that traffic came to a standstill in many thoroughfares, work was abandoned in shops and offices, and the streets and pavements were crowded with people standing about to watch the birds."

The announcer's voice was smooth and suave; Nat had the impression that he treated the whole business as he would an elaborate joke. There would be others like him, hundreds of them, who did not know what it was to struggle in darkness with a flock of birds.

Nat switched off the wireless. He got up and started work on the kitchen windows. His wife watched him, young Johnny at her heels.

"What they ought to do," she said, "is to call the Army out and shoot the birds."

"Let them try," said Nat. "How'd they set about it?"

"I don't know. But something should be done. They ought to do something."

Nat thought to himself that "they" were no doubt considering the problem at that very moment, but whatever "they" decided to do in London and the big cities would not help them here, nearly three hundred miles away.

"How are we off for food?" he asked.

"It's shopping day tomorrow, you know that. I don't keep uncooked food about. Butcher doesn't call till the day after. But I can bring back something when I go in tomorrow."

Nat did not want to scare her. He looked in the larder for himself and in the cupboard where she kept her tins.

They could hold out for a couple of days.

He went on hammering the boards across the kitchen windows. Candles. They were low on candles. That must be another thing she meant to buy tomorrow. Well, they must go early to bed tonight. That was, if—

He got up and went out the back door and stood in the garden, looking down toward the sea.

There had been no sun all day, and now, at barely three o'clock, a kind of darkness had already come; the sky was sullen, heavy, colorless like salt. He could hear the vicious sea drumming on the rocks.

He walked down the path halfway to the beach. And then he stopped. He could see the tide had turned. The gulls had risen. They were circling, hundreds of them, thousands of them, lifting their wings against the wind.

It was the gulls that made the darkening of the sky.

And they were silent. They just went on soaring and circling, rising, falling, trying their strength against the wind. Nat turned. He ran up the path back to the cottage.

"I'm going for Jill," he said to his wife.

"What's the matter?" she asked. "You've gone quite white."

"Keep Johnny inside," he said. "Keep the door shut. Light up now and draw the curtains."

"It's only gone three," she said.

"Never mind. Do what I tell you."

He looked inside the tool shed and took the hoe.

He started walking up the lane to the bus stop. Now and again he glanced back over his shoulder; and he could see the gulls had risen higher now, their circles were broader, they were spreading out in huge formation across the sky.

He hurried on. Although he knew the bus would not come before four o'clock, he had to hurry.

He waited at the top of the hill. There was half an hour still to go.

The east wind came whipping across the fields from the higher ground. In the distance he could see the clay hills, white and clean against the heavy pallor of the sky.

Something black rose from behind them, like a smudge at first, then widening, becoming deeper. The smudge became a cloud; and the cloud divided again into five other clouds, spreading north, east, south, and west; and then they were not clouds at all but birds.

He watched them travel across the sky, within two or three hundred feet of him. He knew, from their speed, that they were bound inland; they had no business with the people here on the peninsula. They were rooks, crows, jackdaws, magpies, jays, all birds that usually preyed upon the smaller species, but bound this afternoon on some other mission.

He went to the telephone call box, stepped inside, lifted the receiver. The exchange would pass the message on. "I'm speaking from the highway," he said, "by the bus stop. I want to report large formations of birds traveling upcountry. The gulls are also forming in the bay."

"All right," answered the voice, laconic, weary.

"You'll be sure and pass this message on to the proper quarter?"

"Yes. Yes." Impatient now, fed up. The buzzing note resumed.

She's another, thought Nat. She doesn't care.

The bus came lumbering up the hill. Jill climbed out.

"What's the hoe for, Dad?"

"I just brought it along," he said. "Come on now, let's get home. It's cold; no hanging about. See how fast you can run."

He could see the gulls now, still silent, circling the fields, coming in toward the land.

"Look, Dad; look over there. Look at all the gulls."

"Yes. Hurry now."

"Where are they flying to? Where are they going?"

"Upcountry, I dare say. Where it's warmer."

He seized her hand and dragged her after him along the lane.

"Don't go so fast. I can't keep up."

The gulls were copying the rooks and the crows. They were spreading out, in formation, across the sky. They headed, in bands of thousands, to the four compass points.

"Dad, what is it? What are the gulls doing?"

They were not intent upon their flight, as the crows, as the jackdaws, had been. They still circled overhead. Nor did they fly so high. It was as though they waited upon some signal; as though some decision had yet to be given.

"I wish the gulls would go away." Jill was crying. "I don't like them. They're coming closer to the lane."

He started running, swinging Jill after him. As they went past the farm turning, he saw the farmer backing his car into the garage. Nat called to him.

"Can you give us a lift?" he said.

Mr. Trigg turned in the driver's seat and stared at them. Then a smile came to his cheerful, rubicund face. "It looks as though we're in for some fun," he said. "Have you seen the gulls? Jim and I are going to take a crack at them. Everyone's gone bird crazy, talking of nothing else. I hear you were troubled in the night. Want a gun?"

Nat shook his head.

The small car was packed, but there was room for Jill on the back seat.

"I don't want a gun," said Nat, "but I'd be obliged if you'd run Jill home. She's scared of the birds."

"Okay," said the farmer. "I'll take her home. Why don't you stop behind and join the shooting match? We'll make the feathers fly."

Jill climbed in, and turning the car, the driver sped up the lane. Nat followed after. Trigg must be crazy. What use was a gun against a sky of birds?

They were coming in now toward the farm, circling lower in the sky. The farm, then, was their target. Nat increased his pace toward his own cottage. He saw the farmer's car turn and come back along the lane. It drew up beside him with a jerk.

"The kid has run inside," said the farmer. "Your wife was watching for her. Well, what do you make of it? They're saying in town the Russians have done it. The Russians have poisoned the birds."

"How could they do that?" asked Nat.

"Don't ask me. You know how stories get around."

"Have you boarded your windows?" asked Nat.

"No. Lot of nonsense. I've had more to do today than to go round boarding up my windows."

"I'd board them now if I were you."

"Garn. You're windy. Like to come to our place to sleep?"

"No, thanks all the same."

"All right. See you in the morning. Give you a gull breakfast."

The farmer grinned and turned his car to the farm entrance. Nat hurried on. Past the little wood, past the old barn, and then across the stile to the remaining field. As he jumped the stile, he heard the whir of wings. A black-backed gull dived down at him from the sky. It missed, swerved in flight, and rose to dive again. In a moment it was joined by others—six, seven, a dozen.

Nat dropped his hoe. The hoe was useless. Covering his head with his arms, he ran toward the cottage.

They kept coming at him from the air—noiseless, silent, save for the beating wings. The terrible, fluttering wings. He could feel the blood on his hands, his wrists, upon his neck. If only he could keep them from his eyes. Nothing else mattered.

With each dive, with each attack, they became bolder. And they had no thought for themselves. When they dived low and missed, they crashed, bruised and broken, on the ground.

As Nat ran he stumbled, kicking their spent bodies in front of him.

He found the door and hammered upon it with his bleeding

hands. "Let me in," he shouted. "It's Nat. Let me in."

Then he saw the gannet, poised for the dive, above him in the sky.

The gulls circled, retired, soared, one with another, against the wind.

Only the gannet remained. One single gannet, above him in the sky. Its wings folded suddenly to its body. It dropped like a stone.

Nat screamed; and the door opened.

He stumbled across the threshold, and his wife threw her weight against the door.

They heard the thud of the gannet as it fell.

His wife dressed his wounds. They were not deep. The backs of his hands had suffered most, and his wrists. Had he not worn a cap, the birds would have reached his head. As for the gannet—the gannet could have split his skull.

The children were crying, of course. They had seen the blood on their father's hands.

"It's all right now," he told them. "I'm not hurt."

His wife was ashen. "I saw them overhead," she whispered. "They began collecting just as Jill ran in with Mr. Trigg. I shut the door fast, and it jammed. That's why I couldn't open it at once when you came."

"Thank God the birds waited for me," he said. "Jill would have fallen at once. They're flying inland, thousands of them. Rooks, crows, all the bigger birds. I saw them from the bus stop. They're making for the towns."

"But what can they do, Nat?"

"They'll attack. Go for everyone out in the streets. Then they'll try the windows, the chimneys."

"Why don't the authorities do something? Why don't they get the Army, get machine guns?"

"There's been no time. Nobody's prepared. We'll hear what they have to say on the six o'clock news."

"I can hear the birds," Jill said. "Listen, Dad."

Nat listened. Muffled sounds came from the windows, from the door. Wings brushing the surface, sliding, scraping, seeking a way of entry. The sound of many bodies pressed together, shuffling on the sills. Now and again came a thud, a crash, as some bird dived and fell.

Some of them will kill themselves that way, he thought, but not enough. Never enough.

"All right," he said aloud. "I've got boards over the windows, Jill. The birds can't get in."

He went and examined all the windows. He found wedges—pieces of old tin, strips of wood and metal—and fastened them at the sides of the windows to reinforce the boards.

His hammering helped to deafen the sound of the birds, the shuffling, the tapping, and—more ominous—the splinter of breaking glass.

"Turn on the wireless," he said.

He went upstairs to the bedrooms and reinforced the windows there. Now he could hear the birds on the roof—the scraping of claws, a sliding, jostling sound.

He decided the whole family must sleep in the kitchen and keep up the fire. He was afraid of the bedroom chimneys. The boards he had placed at their bases might give way. In the kitchen they would be safe because of the fire.

He would have to make a joke of it. Pretend to the children they were playing camp. If the worst happened and the birds forced an entry by way of the bedroom chimneys, it would be hours, days perhaps, before they could break down the doors. The birds would be imprisoned in the bedrooms. They could do no harm there. Crowded together, they would stifle and die. He began to bring the mattresses downstairs.

At sight of them, his wife's eyes widened in apprehension.

"All right," he said cheerfully. "We'll all sleep together in the kitchen tonight. More cozy, here by the fire. Then we won't be worried by those silly old birds tapping at the windows."

He made the children help him rearrange the furniture, and

he took the precaution of moving the dresser against the windows.

We're safe enough now, he thought. We're snug and tight. We can hold out. It's just the food that worries me. Food and coal for the fire. We've enough for two or three days, not more. By that time—

No use thinking ahead as far as that. And they'd be given directions on the wireless.

And now, in the midst of many problems, he realized that only dance music was coming over the air. He knew the reason. The usual programs had been abandoned; this only happened at exceptional times.

At six o'clock the records ceased. The time signal was given. There was a pause, and then the announcer spoke. His voice was solemn, grave. Quite different from midday.

"This is London," he said. "A national emergency was proclaimed at four o'clock this afternoon. Measures are being taken to safeguard the lives and property of the population, but it must be understood that these are not easy to effect immediately, owing to the unforeseen and unparalleled nature of the present crisis. Every householder must take precautions about his own building. Where several people live together, as in flats and hotels, they must unite to do the utmost that they can to prevent entry. It is absolutely imperative that every individual stay indoors tonight.

"The birds, in vast numbers, are attacking anyone on sight, and have already begun an assault upon buildings; but these, with due care, should be impenetrable.

"The population is asked to remain calm.

"Owing to the exceptional nature of the emergency, there will be no further transmission from any broadcasting station until seven A.M. tomorrow."

They played "God Save the Queen." Nothing more happened.

Nat switched off the set. He looked at his wife. She stared back at him.

"We'll have supper early," suggested Nat. "Something for a treat—toasted cheese, eh? Something we all like."

He winked and nodded at his wife. He wanted the look of dread, of apprehension, to leave her face.

He helped with the supper, whistling, singing, making as much clatter as he could. It seemed to him that the shuffling and the tapping were not so intense as they had been at first, and presently he went up to the bedrooms and listened. He no longer heard the jostling for place upon the roof.

They've got reasoning powers, he thought. They know it's hard to break in here. They'll try elsewhere.

Supper passed without incident. Then, when they were clearing away, they heard a new sound, a familiar droning.

His wife looked up at him, her face alight.

"It's planes," she said. "They're sending out planes after the birds. That will get them. Isn't that gunfire? Can't you hear guns?"

It might be gunfire, out at sea. Nat could not tell. Big naval guns might have some effect upon the gulls out at sea, but the gulls were inland now. The guns couldn't shell the shore because of the population.

"It's good, isn't it," said his wife, "to hear the planes?"

Catching her enthusiasm, Jill jumped up and down with Johnny. "The planes will get the birds."

Just then they heard a crash about two miles distant. Followed by a second, then a third. The droning became more distant, passed away out to sea.

"What was that?" asked his wife.

"I don't know," answered Nat. He did not want to tell her that the sound they had heard was the crashing of aircraft.

It was, he had no doubt, a gamble on the part of the authorities to send out reconnaissance forces, but they might have known the gamble was suicidal. What could aircraft do against birds that flung themselves to death against propeller and fuselage but hurtle to the ground themselves?

"Where have the planes gone, Dad?" asked Jill.

"Back to base," he said. "Come on now, time to tuck down for bed."

There was no further drone of aircraft, and the naval guns had ceased. Waste of life and effort, Nat said to himself. We can't destroy enough of them that way. Cost too heavy. There's always gas. Maybe they'll try spraying with gas, mustard gas. We'll be warned first, of course, if they do. There's one thing, the best brains of the country will be on it tonight.

Upstairs in the bedrooms all was quiet. No more scraping and stabbing at the windows. A lull in battle. The wind hadn't dropped, though. Nat could still hear it roaring in the chimneys. And the sea breaking down on the shore.

Then he remembered the tide. The tide would be on the turn. Maybe the lull in battle was because of the tide. There was some law the birds obeyed, and it had to do with the east wind and the tide

He glanced at his watch. Nearly eight o'clock. It must have gone high water an hour ago. That explained the lull. The birds attacked with the flood tide.

He reckoned the time limit in his head. They had six hours to go without attack. When the tide turned again, around 1:20 in the morning, the birds would come back.

He called softly to his wife and whispered to her that he would go out and see how they were faring at the farm, see if the telephone was still working there so that they might get news from the exchange.

"You're not to go," she said at once, "and leave me alone with the children. I can't stand it."

"All right," he said, "all right. I'll wait till morning. And we can get the wireless bulletin then, too, at seven. But when the tide ebbs again, I'll try for the farm; they may let us have bread and potatoes."

His mind was busy again, planning against emergency. They would not have milked, of course, this evening. The cows would be standing by the gate, waiting; the household would be inside, battened behind boards as they were here at the cottage.

That is, if they had had time to take precautions.

Softly, stealthily, he opened the back door and looked outside.

It was pitch-dark. The wind was blowing harder than ever, coming in steady gusts, icy, from the sea.

He kicked at the step. It was heaped with birds. These were the suicides, the divers, the ones with broken necks. Wherever he looked, he saw dead birds. The living had flown seaward with the turn of the tide. The gulls would be riding the seas now, as they had done in the forenoon.

In the far distance on the hill, something was burning. One of the aircraft that had crashed; the fire, fanned by the wind, had set light to a stack.

He looked at the bodies of the birds. He had a notion that if he stacked them, one upon the other, on the window sills, they would be added protection against the next attack.

Not much, perhaps, but something. The bodies would have to be clawed at, pecked and dragged aside before the living birds gained purchase on the sills and attacked the panes.

He set to work in the darkness. It was queer. He hated touching the dead birds, but he went on with his work. He noticed grimly that every windowpane was shattered. Only the boards had kept the birds from breaking in.

He stuffed the cracked panes with the bleeding bodies of the birds and felt his stomach turn. When he had finished, he went back into the cottage and barricaded the kitchen door, making it doubly secure.

His wife had made him cocoa; he drank it thirstily. He was very tired. "All right," he said, smiling, "don't worry. We'll get through."

He lay down on his mattress and closed his eyes.

He dreamed uneasily because, through his dreams, ran the dread of something forgotten. Some piece of work that he should have done. It was connected, in some way, with the burning aircraft.

It was his wife, shaking his shoulder, who awoke him finally.

"They've begun," she sobbed. "They've started this last hour. I can't listen to it any longer alone. There's something smells bad too, something burning."

Then he remembered. He had forgotten to make up the fire.

The fire was smoldering, nearly out. He got up swiftly and lighted the lamp.

The hammering had started at the windows and the door, but it was not that he minded now. It was the smell of singed feathers.

The smell filled the kitchen. He knew what it was at once. The birds were coming down the chimney, squeezing their way down to the kitchen range.

He got sticks and paper and put them on the embers, then reached for the can of kerosene.

"Stand back," he shouted to his wife. He threw some of the kerosene onto the fire.

The flame roared up the pipe, and down into the fire fell the scorched, blackened bodies of the birds.

The children waked, crying. "What is it?" asked Jill. "What's happened?"

Nat had no time to answer her. He was raking the bodies from the chimney, clawing them out onto the floor.

The flames would drive away the living birds from the chimney top. The lower joint was the difficulty though. It was choked with the smoldering, helpless bodies of the birds caught by fire.

He scarcely heeded the attack on the windows and the door. Let them beat their wings, break their backs, lose their lives, in the desperate attempt to force an entry into his home. They would not break in.

"Stop crying," he called to the children. "There's nothing to be afraid of. Stop crying."

He went on raking out the burning smoldering bodies as they fell into the fire.

This'll fetch them, he said to himself. The draft and the flames together. We're all right as long as the chimney doesn't catch.

Amid the tearing at the window boards came the sudden homely striking of the kitchen clock. Three o'clock.

A little more than four hours to go. He could not be sure of the exact time of high water. He reckoned the tide would not turn much before half past seven.

He waited by the range. The flames were dying. But no more blackened bodies fell from the chimney. He thrust his poker up as far as it could go and found nothing.

The danger of the chimney's being choked up was over. It could not happen again, not if the fire was kept burning day and night.

I'll have to get more fuel from the farm tomorrow, he thought. I can do all that with the ebb tide. It can be worked; we can fetch what we need when the tide's turned. We've just got to adapt ourselves, that's all.

They drank tea and cocoa, ate slices of bread. Only half a loaf left, Nat noticed. Never mind, though; they'd get by.

If they could hang on like this until seven, when the first news bulletin came through, they would not have done too badly.

"Give us a smoke," he said to his wife. "It will clear away the smell of the scorched feathers."

"There's only two left in the packet," she said. "I was going to buy you some."

"I'll have one," he said.

He sat with one arm around his wife and one around Jill, with Johnny on his lap, the blankets heaped about them on the mattress.

"You can't help admiring the beggars," he said. "They've got persistency. You'd think they'd tire of the game, but not a bit of it."

Admiration was hard to sustain. The tapping went on and

on; and a new, rasping note struck Nat's ear, as though a sharper beak than any hitherto had come to take over from its fellows.

He tried to remember the names of birds; he tried to think which species would go for this particular job.

It was not the tap of the woodpecker. That would be light and frequent. This was more serious; if it continued long, the wood would splinter as the glass had done.

Then he remembered the hawks. Could the hawks have taken over from the gulls? Were there buzzards now upon the sills, using talons as well as beaks? Hawks, buzzards, kestrels, falcons; he had forgotten the birds of prey. He had forgotten the gripping power of the birds of prey. Three hours to go; and while they waited, the sound of the splintering wood, the talons tearing at the wood.

Nat looked about him, seeing what furniture he could destroy to fortify the door.

The windows were safe because of the dresser. He was not certain of the door. He went upstairs; but when he reached the landing, he paused and listened.

There was a soft patter on the floor of the children's bedroom. The birds had broken through.

The other bedroom was still clear. He brought out the furniture to pile at the head of the stairs should the door of the children's bedroom go.

"Come down, Nat. What are you doing?" called his wife.

"I won't be long," he shouted. "I'm just making everything shipshape up here."

He did not want her to come. He did not want her to hear the pattering in the children's bedroom, the brushing of those wings against the door.

After he suggested breakfast, he found himself watching the clock, gazing at the hands that went so slowly around the dial. If his theory was not correct, if the attack did not cease with the turn of the tide, he knew they were beaten. They could not continue through the long day without air, without rest, without fuel.

A crackling in his ears drove away the sudden, desperate desire for sleep.

"What is it? What now?" he said sharply.

"The wireless," said his wife. "I've been watching the clock. It's nearly seven."

The comfortable crackling of the wireless brought new life.

They waited. The kitchen clock struck seven.

The crackling continued. Nothing else. No chimes. No music.

They waited until a quarter past. No news bulletin came through.

"We heard wrong," he said. "They won't be broadcasting until eight o'clock."

They left the wireless switched on. Nat thought of the battery, wondered how much power was left in the battery. If it failed, they would not hear the instructions.

"It's getting light," whispered his wife. "I can't see it but I can feel it. And listen! The birds aren't hammering so loud now."

She was right. The rasping, tearing sound grew fainter every moment. So did the shuffling, the jostling for place upon the step, upon the sills. The tide was on the turn.

By eight there was no sound at all. Only the wind. And the crackling of the wireless. The children, lulled at last by the stillness, fell asleep.

At half past eight Nat switched the wireless off.

"We'll miss the news," said his wife.

"There isn't going to be any news," said Nat. "We've got to depend upon ourselves."

He went to the door and slowly pulled away the barricades. He drew the bolts, and kicking the broken bodies from the step outside the door, breathed the cold air.

He had six working hours before him, and he knew he must reserve his strength to the utmost, not waste it in any way.

Food and light and fuel; these were the most necessary things. If he could get them, they could endure another night.

He stepped into the garden; and as he did so, he saw the

living birds. The gulls had gone to ride the sea, as they had done before. They sought sea food and the buoyancy of the tide before they returned to the attack.

Not so the land birds. They waited, and watched.

Nat saw them on the hedgerows, on the soil, crowded in the trees, outside in the field—line upon line of birds, still, doing nothing. He went to the end of his small garden.

The birds did not move. They merely watched him.

I've got to get food, Nat said to himself. I've got to go to the farm to get food.

He went back to the cottage. He saw to the windows and the door.

"I'm going to the farm," he said.

His wife clung to him. She had seen the living birds from the open door.

"Take us with you," she begged. "We can't stay here alone. I'd rather die than stay here alone."

"Come on, then," he said. "Bring baskets and Johnny's pram. We can load up the pram."

They dressed against the biting wind. His wife put Johnny in the pram, and Nat took Jill's hand.

"The birds," Jill whimpered. "They're all out there in the fields."

"They won't hurt us," he said. "Not in the light."

They started walking across the field toward the stile, and the birds did not move. They waited, their heads turned to the wind.

When they reached the turning to the farm, Nat stopped and told his wife to wait in the shelter of the hedge with the two children. "But I want to see Mrs. Trigg," she protested. "There are lots of things we can borrow if they went to market yesterday, and—"

"Wait here," Nat interrupted. "I'll be back in a moment."

The cows were lowing, moving restlessly in the yard, and he could see a gap in the fence where the sheep had knocked their way through to roam unchecked in the front garden before the farmhouse.

No smoke came from the chimneys. Nat was filled with misgiving. He did not want his wife or the children to go down to the farm.

He went down alone, pushing his way through the herd of lowing cows, who turned this way and that, distressed, their udders full.

He saw the car standing by the gate. Not put away in the garage.

All the windows of the farmhouse were smashed. There were many dead gulls lying in the yard and around the house.

The living birds perched on the group of trees behind the farm and on the roof of the house. They were quite still. They watched him. Jim's body lay in the yard. What was left of it. His gun was beside him.

The door of the house was shut and bolted, but it was easy to push up a smashed window and climb through.

Trigg's body was close to the telephone. He must have been trying to get through to the exchange when the birds got him. The receiver was off the hook, and the instrument was torn from the wall.

No sign of Mrs. Trigg. She would be upstairs. Was it any use going up? Sickened, Nat knew what he would find there.

Thank God, he said to himself, there were no children.

He forced himself to climb the stairs, but halfway up he turned and descended again. He could see Mrs. Trigg's legs protruding from the open bedroom door. Beside her were the bodies of black-backed gulls and an umbrella, broken. It's no use doing anything, Nat thought. I've only got five hours; less than that. The Triggs would understand. I must load up with what I can find.

He tramped back to his wife and children.

"I'm going to fill up the car with stuff," he said. "We'll take it home and return for a fresh load."

"What about the Triggs?" asked his wife.

"They must have gone to friends," he said.

"Shall I come and help you then?"

"No, there's a mess down there. Cows and sheep all over the place. Wait; I'll get the car. You can sit in the car."

Her eyes watched his all the time he was talking. He believed she understood. Otherwise she certainly would have insisted on helping him find the bread and groceries.

They made three journeys altogether, to and from the farm, before he was satisfied they had everything they needed. It was surprising, once he started thinking, how many things were necessary. Almost the most important of all was planking for the windows. He had to go around searching for timber. He wanted to renew the boards on all the windows at the cottage.

On the final journey he drove the car to the bus stop and got out and went to the telephone box.

He waited a few minutes, jangling the hook. No good, though. The line was dead. He climbed onto a bank and looked over the countryside, but there was no sign of life at all, nothing in the fields but the waiting, watching birds.

Some of them slept; he could see their beaks tucked into their feathers.

You'd think they'd be feeding, he said to himself, not just standing that way.

Then he remembered. They were gorged with food. They had eaten their fill during the night. That was why they did not move this morning.

He lifted his face to the sky. It was colorless, gray. The bare trees looked bent and blackened by the east wind.

The cold did not affect the living birds, waiting out there in the fields.

This is the time they ought to get them, Nat said to himself. They're a sitting target now. They must be doing this all over the country. Why don't our aircraft take off now and spray them with mustard gas? What are all our chaps doing? They must know; they must see for themselves.

He went back to the car and got into the driver's seat.

"Go quickly past that second gate," whispered his wife. "The postman's lying there. I don't want Jill to see."

It was a quarter to one by the time they reached the cottage. Only an hour to go.

"Better have dinner," said Nat. "Hot up something for yourself and the children, some of that soup. I've no time to eat now. I've got to unload all this stuff from the car."

He got everything inside the cottage. It could be sorted later. Give them all something to do during the long hours ahead.

First he must see to the windows and the door.

He went around the cottage methodically, testing every window and the door. He climbed onto the roof also, and fixed boards across every chimney except the kitchen's.

The cold was so intense he could hardly bear it, but the job had to be done. Now and again he looked up, searching the sky for aircraft. None came. As he worked, he cursed the inefficiency of the authorities.

He paused, his work on the bedroom chimney finished, and looked out to sea. Something was moving out there. Something gray and white among the breakers.

"Good old Navy," he said. "They never let us down. They're coming down channel; they're turning into the bay."

He waited, straining his eyes toward the sea. He was wrong, though. The Navy was not there. It was the gulls rising from the sea. And the massed flocks in the fields, with ruffled feathers, rose in formation from the ground and, wing to wing, soared upward to the sky.

The tide had turned again.

Nat climbed down the ladder and went inside the cottage. The family were at dinner. It was a little after two.

He bolted the door, put up the barricade, and lighted the lamp.

"It's nighttime," said young Johnny.

His wife had switched on the wireless once again. The crackling sound came, but nothing else.

"I've been all round the dial," she said, "foreign stations and all. I can't get anything but the crackling."

"Maybe they have the same trouble," he said. "Maybe it's the same right through Europe."

They ate in silence.

The tapping began at the windows, at the door, the rustling, the jostling, the pushing for position on the sills. The first thud of the suicide gulls upon the step.

When he had finished dinner, Nat planned, he would put the supplies away, stack them neatly, get everything shipshape. The boards were strong against the windows and across the chimneys. The cottage was filled with stores, with fuel, with all they needed for the next few days.

His wife could help him, and the children too. They'd tire themselves out between now and a quarter to nine, when the tide would ebb; then he'd tuck them down on their mattresses, see that they slept good and sound until three in the morning.

He had a new scheme for the windows, which was to fix barbed wire in front of the boards. He had brought a great roll of it from the farm. The nuisance was, he'd have to work at this in the dark, when the lull came between nine and three. Pity he had not thought of it before. Still, as long as the wife and kids slept—that was the main thing.

The smaller birds were at the windows now. He recognized the light tap-tapping of their beaks and the soft brush of their wings.

The hawks ignored the windows. They concentrated their attack upon the door.

Nat listened to the tearing sound of splintering wood, and wondered how many million years of memory were stored in those little brains, behind the stabbing beaks, the piercing eyes, now giving them this instinct to destroy mankind with all the deft precision of machines.

"I'll smoke that last cigarette," he said to his wife. "Stupid of me. It was the one thing I forgot to bring back from the farm."

He reached for it, switched on the crackling wireless.

He threw the empty jacket onto the fire and watched it burn.

1950

THE TREE'S WIFE

by Mary Elizabeth Counselman

Two sections of our country have been particularly rich in the development of the ghost story. One is New England, where Mary Wilkins Freeman found her ghost. The other section, of course, is the South, where the folklore and folktales of the countryside have always been particularly rich with spectral beings, ghosts in lonely houses, and macabre mysteries in magnolia gardens.

In this seemingly simple, folktale-like story of the South, Mary Elizabeth Counselman invests a tree with supernatural life. In ancient days trees were closely associated with the gods; the Egyptians worshiped the sacred sycamore, the cyprus was the sacred tree of Persia, the ancient Chaldeans thought of the cedar as the source of the god Ea. To Athena belonged the sacred olive tree, and the ancient coins of Greece were always stamped with an olive branch. Even today a banyan tree, three thousand years old, is never touched in India because they say there is a god concealed in its foliage.

Not only gods, but lesser spirits haunted the forests. Sometimes they are portrayed as nymphs who occasionally marry mortals, only to die when their tree form is cut down. Sometimes the wood spirit is particularly vindictive. To strike at it invites an attack of sudden weakness; to some who approach it with an ax it brings instant death.

These old legends come from very ancient agricultural cus-

Mary Elizabeth Counselman

toms when man and the plant and animal life around him were mutually interdependent. Today, when the despoilers of our land are cutting down our forests and ruining our environment, a story such as "The Tree's Wife" seems particularly pertinent in its portrayal of a primitive belief reawakened in modern times.

I smiled at my companion, Hettie Morrison, County Welfare investigator for the Bald Mountain district. When I dropped into her office that morning, mostly to dig up nostalgic old memories of our college days at the University of Virginia, I found her arguing over the telephone with a local mechanic. "But I have to make a field trip this morning! . . . WHY can't you get the parts? Take them out of somebody else's car! . . . Oh, the devil with what you think wouldn't be right! This family may be starving. . . . !"

Hettie had hung up, still sputtering, a gaunt severe-looking old maid with a heart as big as the Blue Ridge Mountains. She glanced up then, to see me grinning at her, jingling the car-keys of my new club-coupe by way of an invitation. We were such close friends, no words were needed—Hettie merely jerked a nod, slammed on her hat, and started out the door with me in tow.

"You'll be sorry," she warned me. "The road I have to take is an old Indian trail—and if they had to get back and forth on *that*, no wonder they're called the Vanishing Americans! You'll break a spring."

I looked so dismayed, pausing to unlock my first new car in ten years, that she closed one eye in a crafty look I knew so well, from days at college when she was about to ask the loan of my best hose.

"It's a dull trip, just routine field work. Of course you wouldn't be interested," she drawled casually, "in Florella Dabney—the girl who married a tree. We pass right by the Dabney place. No, no, dear; you're liable to scratch up that nice blue paint. And Holy Creek crosses the road four times; we'd have to drive through it, hub-deep. I always get stuck and have to—"

I scowled at my old friend, familiar with all her clever tricks of getting her way, but still unable to cope with them.

"*Tree?*" I demanded. "Did you say—? Married a —?"

"That's right," Hettie nodded with a smug grin. "It's a strange case—almost a legend up around Bald Mountain. Although," she added, blatantly climbing into my car, "it's not without precedent, in the old Greek legends. Zeus was forever turning some girl into a spring or a flower, or some inanimate object, so his wife Hera wouldn't find out about his goings on. Even as late as the fifteenth century, there were proxy weddings, where some queen or other married her knight's sword because he was off at war. Then, there's an African tribe in which the men are married, at puberty, to some tree."

I grimaced impatiently, climbed into the coupe, and started it with a jerk. Hettie had aroused my interest, and well she knew it. She would get her ride over the wild, bushy crest of Bald Mountain—or I would never find out about that girl who married a tree.

A man or a woman being turned into a tree was a recurring theme in ancient Greek and Roman legends. This Italian print from the year 1500 shows the goddess Daphne being turned into a laurel tree to escape the god Apollo.

An hour later, bouncing over a rocky trail pressed closely on both sides by scrub pine and mountain laurel, she began to tell me about Florella Dabney—and the bloody feud that, a trained psychiatrist might explain, had left her a mental case with a strange delusion.

The Dabneys (Hettie related) had built their cabin and begun to wrest a living out of the side of Bald Mountain about the time of Daniel Boone. Six generations of underfed, overworked mountaineers had lived therein, planting a little, hunting a little, and raising a batch of children as wild as the foxes that made inroads on their chicken supply. Florella was the youngest daughter, a shy willowy child of fifteen, with flowing dark hair and big luminous dark eyes like a fawn. Barefoot, clad in the simple gingham shift that all mountain girls wore, she could be seen running down the steep side of Old Baldy, as nimbly as a city child might run along a sidewalk. Her older brothers and sisters married and moved away, her mother died, and Florella lived with her father now on the sparse farm.

On the other side of the mountains lived another such family of "old settlers," the Jenningses. As far back as anyone could remember, there had been bad blood between the two, starting with a free-for-all over a load of cordwood, which had sent two Dabneys to the hospital and three Jenningses to jail. Both attended the little mountain church perched on the ridge that divided their farms, but no Jennings ever spoke to a Dabney, even at all-day singings, when everyone was pleasantly full of food and "home-brew." No Dabney would sit left of the aisle; and any baptizing that was done in Holy Creek, after a rousing revival meeting, had to be arranged with Jenningses and Dabneys immersed on alternate days. Reverend Posy Adkins, the lay preacher, recognized this as a regrettable but inevitable condition. And that was the law on Bald Mountain—up until the spring evening when Joe Ed Jennings and Florella Dabney "run off together."

When and how they had ever seen enough of each other to

fall in love, neither family could imagine. Joe Ed was a stocky blond boy who could play a guitar and shoot the eye out of a possum at fifty yards—but not much else. What astonished everyone was Florella's regard for such a do-little, since she was halfway promised to a boy from Owl's Hollow. It was assumed, when a party of hunters saw them streaking through the woods one night, that Florella had been carried off by force, much against her will. She had gone out after one of the hogs, which had strayed. At midnight, when she had not returned, her pa, Lafe Dabney, went out to search for her, ran into the hunting party—and promptly stalked back to his cabin for his rifle.

He was starting out again, with murder in his close-set, mean little eyes, when a pair of frightened young people suddenly walked through the sagging front gate. With them was Preacher Adkins, dressed either for a buryin' or a marryin', with the Good Book clutched in a hand that trembled. But he spoke steadily.

"Lafe, these two young'nes has sinned. But the Lord's likely done forgave 'em already. Now they aim to marry, so don't try an' stop it!"

Without preamble, he motioned for Florella and Joe Ed to stand under a big whiteoak that grew in the front yard, towering over the rough cabin and silhouetted darkly against the moonlit sky. High up on the trunk, if Lafe had noticed, was cut a heart with the initials J.E.J. and F.D.

Solemnly, the old preacher began to intone the marriage ceremony, while Florella's pa stood there staring at them, his lean face growing darker with fury, his tight mouth working. Hardly had the immortal words, "Do you take this man—?" been spoken, when he whipped the rifle to his shoulder and fired at Joe Ed, pointblank. The boy was dead as he crumpled up at his bride's small bare feet.

"I'll larn you to go sparkin' our girl behind my back!" Lafe roared. "You triflin' no-account!"

He never finished, for a second shot rang out in the quiet night. Lafe Dabney pitched forward on his face, crawled across the body of his prospective son-in-law, and fired twice toward the powder flash in the woods beyond the cabin. A moment later, all hell broke loose. It seems that Reverend Adkins had expected just such a blow-up. Someone had carried the news to Joe Ed's pa. Clem Jennings had also hastened to the spot, to stop the wedding. The old preacher, fearing this, had notified "the law." The sheriff, with a hastily gathered posse, had showed up at the moment when Lafe and Clem fired at each other, over the body of young Joe Ed and the prostrate sobbing form of his near-bride.

In a matter of minutes, the posse had both fathers handcuffed and hauled off to jail. But, behind them, they left a tragic tableau—little Florella weeping over the body of her lost lover, with old Reverend Adkins standing dumbly in the background. Two of the posse had stayed behind to help with Joe Ed's body, which the weeping girl had begged the preacher to bury, then and there, "under our tree." It was there Joe Ed had first caught her and kissed her, holding his hand over her mouth and laughing, with Lafe not ten yards away. It was there, in the night, that she had first told him she loved him—and promised to slip away with him, into the deep silent woods of Old Baldy, for a lover's tryst forbidden by both their families. It was there, months later, terrified and ashamed, that she had sobbed out to him that she was with child. She knew there was nothing left but to kill herself. Her lover was a Jennings, and she had expected no more from him than a few moments of wild secret ecstasy.

But Joe Ed had surprised her. Fiercely protective and loyal, he had announced that, the following night, he would stand with her under the tree in the Dabneys' yard, and have Preacher Adkins marry them—right in front of old Lafe. His child must bear his name, the boy said proudly and tenderly, and he hoped it would be a fawn-eyed little girl exactly like Florella.

All this old Preacher Adkins related to the two members of the posse, while they took turns digging a grave for Joe Ed Jennings—at the foot of the big whiteoak under which he was to have been married. Florella stood numbly by, watching and no longer crying, like a trapped animal at last resigned to its bitter fate.

But, regarding her, the old lay-preacher suddenly remembered a story from his school days, a myth, a legend. Walking over to the girl, he took her hand quietly and led her over to the tree, where the two pitying neighbors were just patting the last spadeful of dirt over Joe Ed's crude grave.

"Daughter," the old preacher said, "I've heard tell of queens in the old days marryin' a sword that belonged to some feller that'd been killt in battle. Now, Joe Ed, he'd want you should go ahead and take his name—so I'm goin' t' make out like this-here tree is Joe Ed, him bein' buried underneath it. I want you two men," he faced the gravediggers solemnly, "to witness this-here marryin'—of Joe Ed Jennings and Florella Dabney." He raised his eyes humbly. "If hit's a wrong thing I'm doin', punish me, Lord. If hit's right, bless this-here ceremony!"

There in the moonlit night, the old preacher proceeded with that strange proxy wedding of a girl to a tree. The two members of the posse stood by, wide-eyed and amazed, as they heard Reverend Adkins repeat the familiar words of the marriage ceremony. Heard Florella's sobbing replies. And then heard—was it only wind in the great tree towering above them? Or was it—? Both men later swore that what they heard sounded like a whispering voice. A man's voice, Joe Ed's, coming from the depths of those thick green branches. But (as Hettie remarked dryly) it had been a hysterical night, and hysteria can play weird tricks on the human senses numerous times.

"Well? That isn't *all?*" I demanded as my car lurched madly into Holy Creek's third crossing and plunged wetly out again. "What happened to the girl? With her father in prison, who looked after her while—? Was the child all right?"

"Slow down, you idiot!" Hettie snapped at me pleasantly, clinging to the car door on her side. "Yes, of course, the child was all right. A little girl. I had Welfare send a doctor out here, when we got the message that Florella was in labor. She had been living on in her father's cabin, quite alone—for the simple reason that all her relatives and all of Joe Ed's were afraid to come near the place!"

I frowned, puzzled. "Why?"

"Because of the tree," Hettie said, blandly. "Word got around that it was haunted. That Joe Ed had 'gone into that oak' and —well, that it was alive. Sentient, that is. That it—didn't behave like a tree any more. I must say—look out for that rock, you goose! Want to wreck this thing?—I must say some of the things that happened were—odd, to say the least!"

I slowed down obediently, picking my way over the rocky road. Anything to keep Hettie on the story that had so captured my imagination!

"What things?" I demanded. "Anybody can hear voices in the wind. Leaves rustling. Branches rubbing together."

"But," Hettie drawled, "just anybody can't see a tree catch a live rabbit, or a dove that has lit on a branch of it. Just anybody can't—"

"*What?*" I gaped at her. "I never heard of anything so ridiculous!" My attempted laugh sounded flat, however, even to my own ears. "How on earth could—?"

"Don't ask me," Hettie said cheerfully. "All I know is, the lower branch of that big whiteoak kept Florella supplied with meat. Rabbits, doves, once a possum. They—they got choked, someway. Got their necks caught in the twigs. She'd find them there, all ready to be cooked and eaten. The way any good mountaineer might trap to feed his family. So she got to believing—that *he* caught them. Joe Ed had quite a reputation as a hunter and trapper."

"Good Lord!" I tried to laugh again. "You're not hinting—? The poor kid," I broke off pityingly. "But an experience like that would naturally affect her mind. Living there all alone, too, with a baby!"

"Then," Hettie went on pleasantly, "there was the fall day,

real cold, when a neighbor woman dropped in. Nosy old sister. Just wanted to say something spiteful to Florella about the baby. When she was leaving, though—well," Hettie chuckled, "it seems her coat got tangled in a tree branch that dipped down over the gate. It yanked the coat right off her back, the way she told it. She lit out of there, screaming bloody-murder, and told everybody that Joe Ed took her coat for Florella! When the girl tried to return it to her, she wouldn't touch it. Said it wasn't her best coat, anyhow, and she wasn't going to argue with a tree!"

"Oh no!" I shook my head, laughing—but still trying to ignore a small shiver that kept running down my spine. "These mountain people are awfully superstitious, aren't they? Naturally, it was just the woman's fear that made her think—"

"Maybe," Hettie said dryly, "but it wasn't fear that snatched my new hat off last spring, when I happened to walk under that tree. Checking up on Florella—she's a hardship case, of course. Yessir," she said in a queer tone. "Big limb swooped down and snatched that bonnet right off my head. I couldn't reach it, and Florella couldn't climb up and get it. Too soon after the baby's arrival; poor girl was still kind of weak. But the way she giggled, and started talking to that tree like it was a person! Honestly, it made my flesh crawl, she was so matter of fact about it! 'Joe Ed, you rascal,' she said, 'give Miss Hettie back her bonnet, now! I don't need no fancy clothes. Me and the baby's doin' just fine.' " Hettie peered at me, sheepishly. "Way she said it made me feel like—like a selfish old turkey-gobbler! Besides, a hat like that was too pretty for an old hatchet-face like me. But it did give me a turn, I'll have to admit! When—" she gulped slightly, "when I told Florella she could have the hat, it—it immediately fell out of the tree. Plop! Right smack on that girl's head! I must say," she added crossly, "it was very becoming. Probably the first one she ever owned, poor little thing! Lafe was a stingy old coot; Florella's mother never had a rag she didn't weave herself!"

I turned the steering wheel sharply to avoid a raccoon ambling across the trail. Then I peered at Hettie.

"Go on," I said grimly. "Tell me how the tree shed its wood in stacks, so Florella wouldn't have to chop any!"

Hettie chuckled. "Oh, no. Mountain men take it for granted that their wives must work like mules. All they do is feed 'em, shelter 'em, and protect 'em—with an occasional pretty thrown in when they feel in a generous mood. That's what Florella expected from her tree-husband, and that's what she got. Though I suppose a psychologist would say her delusion gave her a sense of security that merely made her able to fend for herself. Lots of people need a crutch for their self-confidence—if it's only a lucky coin they carry around. Coincidence and superstition, hm?"

"Well," my friend smiled, "I *am* obliged to you for the lift. We had a message that Kirby Marsh, a farmer who lives near the Dabney place, got in a fight with somebody and crawled home, pretty banged up. His wife is bedridden, so they'll need help if he's seriously injured. You were a life-saver to bring me. This is the turn"; she broke off abruptly, grinning at me with a sly twinkle in her eye. "The Dabney farm is just around this bend."

I slowed down, feeling again that cold shiver run down my spine as we rounded the curve. An old cabin of square-hewn logs perched on the mountainside a few yards above the road, with the usual well in the yard and the usual small truck-garden in back. A huge whiteoak towered over the gate of a sagging rail fence. Its sturdy trunk leaned a bit toward the house in a curiously protective manner, shading the worn front stoop with its thick dark-green foliage.

I braked the car outside the gate, and Hettie grinned at my expression.

"There it is," she announced dryly. "There's where the girl lives who married a tree. And that's the tree. That's *him*."

I got out of the coupe and walked warily to the gate. Hettie climbed out stiffly, and called, in her pleasantly harsh voice:

"Hello? Hello the house?" in traditional mountain style.

There was no answer, but all at once I saw a quilt pallet spread under the oak Hettie had indicated as "*him.*" A fair-haired baby girl was sprawled on the folded quilt, gurgling and cooing. She looked to be about two years old, with the sturdy good health of most mountain children, despite their skimpy diet and constant exposure to the elements.

I stood watching her for a moment, charmed by the picture she made. Then I frowned.

"She's too young to be left alone," I muttered. "Where's her mother?"

"Oh, out picking blackberries, I guess." Hettie shrugged. "Josie's all right, though. Her father's minding her," she added with another impish grin at my expression. "Hello!" she called again. "Florella!"

At that moment a lovely slender girl came running around the house, her feet bare, her dark hair flying. There was a sprig of laurel over her ear, and blackberry stains on her brown fingers. I stared at her, thinking how like a dryad she looked—wild, free, and happily unafraid.

"Oh! Howdy, Miss Hettie!" she greeted my friend warmly. "Come in and set. Who's that with ye? Kinfolk?"

Hettie introduced me as a school chum, with no mention of the fact that I wrote stories of the supernatural for my bread and butter. We entered the gate, and Hettie stooped over to pat the baby, proffering a peppermint from the endless supply she always seems to carry around. I fidgeted beside her, at a loss for conversation with this pretty, normal-looking young mother who, from all Hettie had told me, was as crazy as a coot. Once, nervously, I started as a limb of the great tree under which we stood brushed my shoulder, plucking at my scarf. On impulse, I took it off and gave it to the girl, who beamed and thanked me shyly, then tied it proudly around her own neck. I caught Hettie's eye at that moment—and flushed as she grinned, winked, and glanced up at the giant tree.

Then she turned to Florella, lovelier than ever in my blue

chiffon scarf—and with no more madness in her face than in mine.

"I got word that Kirby Marsh was hurt in a fight," my friend said conversationally. "Anybody over there looking after his wife and kids? Heard the doctor came, and took Kirby to the hospital with concussion and a sprained shoulder. Must have been some fight, to have—"

Hettie broke off, noticing the girl's sudden expression of regret beyond the politeness expected of a neighbor. Florella ducked her head suddenly, with a rueful little smile.

"Yes, ma'am," she said simply. "He come over here to our place late last night, and went to pesterin' me. Oh, not that Kirby ain't a real nice feller," she apologized for her neighbor gently, "exceptin' when he's likkered up. I told him to leave go o' me," she added with wifely dignity. "Told him Joe Ed wouldn't like it. But he wouldn't listen. So I run out to Joe Ed, with it a-stormin' awful. He'd been a'bangin' on the roof, to warn Kirby, but he likely thought 'twas only the wind."

I gulped, racked with pity, and threw a glance at my friend.

"Then—?" Hettie prompted softly, in an odd tone. "You ran out into the yard? Kirby ran after you, and—?"

"And Joe Ed, he whanged him over the head," the girl finished, half apologetic, half proud, as any other woman might speak of a husband who had stoutly defended her honor. "He like to busted Kirby's skull wide open. But he hadn't ought to've tried to kiss me," she defended primly. "Ought he, Miss Hettie? And me a married woman with a young'ne!"

"No, dear," Hettie answered, in the gentlest voice I have ever heard her use. "No—Joe Ed did the right thing. I don't think Kirby was badly injured, but somebody has to look after his folks while he's in the hospital. Did you go over and see his wife today?"

"Yes ma'am," the girl said quietly. "But they wouldn't let me in. I reckon, on account they was scared. I mean, of Joe Ed. But he wouldn't hurt nobody less'n they was botherin' me or the baby! He's real good-hearted."

"Yes," my friend said softly. "I understand. Well—don't worry about it, dear. Next time Kirby will know better! I rather imagine," she chuckled, "that this experience will keep him sober for some time!"

The girl nodded shyly, and bent to pick up the child. But small Josie toddled away from her and ran around the great tree to where a low limb dipped almost to the ground.

"Pa!" she chirped suddenly, holding up her chubby arms to the giant oak. "Fing baby! Fing *high*, Pa!"

Florella laughed, shaking her head mildly and calling: "No! *No*, now, Joe Ed—you're liable to drop that young'un! Don't ye—"

But as I stared, that low limb dipped down as under unseen pressure. The child, Josie, seized it and, as I gasped at the spectacle, was tossed ten feet off the ground, as if a gust of wind had blown the branch skyward, it had scooped up the baby, swinging her high above us. Then, as gently, it let her down again, while the young mother shook her head again in laughing reproof. My scalp crawled at her matter-of-fact, unself-conscious manner.

"Joe Ed's always a-doin' that," she said pleasantly. "She loves it. Why, Miss Hettie!" she broke off, pouting as I sidled pointedly back toward the gate, "I thought you-all would stay for dinner! Joe Ed caught me a rabbit, and I was just fixin' to fry it real nice and brown. Cain't ye stay?"

But I was out the gate and climbing into my car by that time, shaking my head covertly and beckoning for Hettie to come away. For some reason—which I will always firmly deny—my teeth were clicking like castanets. And I kept glancing up nervously at that tall spreading oak tree, brooding over the little mountain cabin, and the woman and child who lived there alone.

Alone—?

"Pitiful case, isn't it?" Hettie murmured cheerfully, as she climbed into the car and waved goodbye to Florella Dabney—or "Mrs. Joe Edward Jennings," as she was listed in the Welfare files. "I mean," my friend expanded, "the way that poor girl lives, with her baby. From hand to mouth, and the prey of —well, men like Kirby. She'd be so lonely and frightened if it weren't for that pathetic delusion of hers. And she's got the child to believing it now! Guess you noticed her swinging on that tree—she called it *'Pa!'* Stout branch, to pick up a child that heavy, wasn't it?" She drawled carelessly. "Wind blew it, I guess—like the other night, when it whacked Kirby Marsh over the head. Awful windy up here on Old Baldy." She peeked at me slyly, lips twitching.

I glared at her and stepped on the gas, aware of the cold perspiration that had sprung out on my forehead. Because it was not windy. It was close and very still—and beside me, Hettie was chuckling softly as I glanced back at the barren little farm. Except for one low limb of that giant oak tree—again tossing that happy child playfully into the air while its mother looked on; lifting it gently, like a man's strong protective arms—not a leaf was stirring as far as we could see over the rugged mountainside.

1959

MOONLIGHT–STARLIGHT

by Virginia Layefsky

In the calendar of the supernatural one night stands out above all others. It is, of course, Halloween, the eve of All Hallows' Day. This is the time, according to ancient tradition, "of a universal walking abroad of spirits." It is a time of a curious meeting of the visible and invisible worlds. In the old books they used to say that "corporeal tenements did then wander abroad through the realms of space"—or, to put it bluntly, it was a time of ghosts.

A Halloween party is a time of festivity, but the festivity has a special quality. A traditional Halloween party game is ducking for apples. A nineteenth-century book tells us to "set the apples afloat in a tub of water into which the juveniles by turns duck their heads with the view of catching an apple. Great fun goes on in watching the attempts of the youngster in the pursuit of the swimming fruit, which wriggles from side to side of the tub, and evades all attempts to capture it; whilst the disappointed aspirant is obliged to abandon the chase in favor of another whose turn has now arrived."

Ducking for apples is a hallowed custom, but there are "unhallowed" customs, strange customs akin to witchcraft. You can, for example, on Halloween determine the person you will marry from the apple seeds in the apple. You can sow hemp seed to make your future lover appear before you. Or if you are one of those remarkable people born on Halloween, you will always be able to see and speak with supernatural beings.

But it is a time for parties, blindfolds, masks, costumes, and gaiety; no one can resist its appeal. Certainly not a child, and particularly not the two children Virginia Layefsky tells about in "Moonlight—Starlight."

The genesis of the idea for the party was in an old Halloween costume Anne Carey found packed in a box in the attic. It had been made thirty years ago for a seven-year-old Anne by her mother. She had been a woman who threw nothing away.

After Anne inherited the large Victorian spaces her mother had swept and garnished most of her life, she often came upon pieces of her own life—up until her marriage at least—neatly labeled and stored here or there. She was apt to find them on those first days of her husband's occasional absences when she used house cleaning as a balm for initial loneliness.

The costume she found that day was so beautifully sewn and carefully packed that its state of preservation was remarkable. When she shook out its folds, the coins which her mother had sewn individually on the bodice long ago clinked with a special sound that set up a painful little echo of disappointment in her forgetful heart. Though she remembered clearly then the smell of chrysanthemums and sewing-machine oil in her mother's room the day the costume was fitted, she could not have said why the sound of the coins oppressed her with such a profound sense of loss.

It had to do with the party she had lost, of course. It was to have been her very own. The games had been planned and the decorations made. Invitations had already been sent when, due to the death by drowning of two small cousins in upstate New York, the party was canceled. The accident had happened the day before they were to leave to visit Anne. She had been broken-hearted, not for the cousins whom she had never seen but for the party which was canceled. In time she was able to forget everything about it but the sense of loss, which persisted unacknowledged up to today when she opened the box to find the costume still waiting there.

And that was the reason why Halloween became the occasion for the only really large children's party Anne Carey ever gave. She made a costume, less carefully done, for her nine-year-old son and dressed her daughter in the gypsy outfit she herself was to have worn long ago.

The party was a resounding success. Children, remembering it, asked her for months afterwards to give another, but she never did. Nor did she tell the reasons why it became the last children's party of any kind that she ever gave. . . .

The arrangements seemed so simple at first. She told her son Bobby he could invite the entire fourth grade with all its younger brothers and sisters.

Games and refreshments were no problem. Now that Anne thought of it, she remembered the entire program of the beautiful party planned long ago. The bobbing for apples, followed by pin-the-tail-on-the-donkey and musical chairs, marched through her mind in a succession almost as orderly and magical now as then. There would be none of the professional entertainment that had figured recently in some of the more ambitious neighborhood parties. What she wanted was a real, old-fashioned Halloween party.

It was something she was to repeat often during the week to the friends who called her with warnings and advice.

Had she a first-aid kit? She would probably need one. And be sure to omit the booby prizes—children who won them were apt to weep, considering them a disgrace.

The warnings began to include, unpleasantly often, the names of the Usher children. Everyone hoped they had not been invited, although on being questioned no one seemed able to tell Anne more than that they were considered strange, the rather menacing unknown quantity in the local algebra of human relationships. They were not much liked by other children.

And then, everyone knew how strange the parents were, living off by themselves as they did, never associating with anyone.

Had she seen the father's work? Gruesome decadent stuff that no one who hadn't a morbid streak would think of painting. And according to rumors, it was just as well they did keep to themselves. It seemed Usher had a sense of humor that, to say the least, was sardonic. It could be, they had heard, very ugly at times.

By that time, however, it was too late. The older child—the girl—was in the fourth grade. She and her brother had been invited along with the rest.

On Halloween Anne with her two children stood in the golden porch light welcoming their guests. The children, in various disguises, began to come shortly after dark. They all seemed to arrive at the same time, coming out of the gloomy, old-fashioned lane like a small army of faceless grotesques. Every child was masked.

For an instant Anne felt invaded by a force of nameless, not necessarily friendly strangers. Only the shadows of parents coming from the obscurity into familiarity assured her that beneath the grinning skull or monstrous face was a dimple or a freckled nose she knew.

The party had become a reality at last. Each adult whispered instructions of various sorts to each small mystery at his side before setting it free to join its wriggling, hopping contemporaries. As they took leave of Anne with compliments and thanks, there was an unmistakable look of relief on most of their departing faces. She had said she could manage alone, even with her husband absent on business for his firm.

By eight o'clock, when the party hats had been passed out, and the last parent had gone, almost everyone who had been invited was there.

The party began in good order. They all pinned the tail on the donkey. Waiting patiently, good-children-all-in-a-line, each child was blindfolded and sent with cardboard tail in hand towards the donkey on the wall. Only one very young black cat —anonymous to Anne—cried because it had pinned its particular tail to the donkey's nose. It was quite easily comforted.

The second game passed gaily, even hilariously. The children unmasked as they went to the big tin washbowl full of apples floating on top of the water that filled it. At the sight of laughter on small faces freed so recently from the horrors which had hidden them from sight, Anne was charmed with a sudden feeling of felicity.

The children, hands held behind their backs, bobbed for the apples. She watched them, holding to her moment with the sweet satisfaction of fulfillment.

Down to the last detail, from the sound of the children's shrill, excited voices to the orange-and-black crepe paper and balloons, the festive smell of candle wax heating the pulpy pumpkins, she had her party at last.

It was well that she held to the moment, listening to the laughter, seeing the children's warm cheeks and tender, perspiring necks, her own daughter's thrilled awareness of her multicolored petticoats. For shortly after that the party began to change.

It started during the next game, which was musical chairs, and at first it was almost imperceptible. Perhaps because it was the third rather strenuous game of the evening, Anne noticed some of the children showing signs of being overtired. Some of the smaller ones' cheeks were too flushed or pale.

They had put the chairs in a row themselves, working rather wildly with some petty wrangling. There were quarrels in the air before they even started. And at the same time, something else, an odd feeling of restlessness and distraction as though their minds were somewhere else.

Watching them march around the chairs, and the way each scrambled for a place once the music stopped, Anne decided she never had liked the game. It demanded a ruthlessness in the end that she found unpleasant, disliking the ultimate winner.

She was glad when it was over and she had settled the children to making funny men and animals out of the marshmallows, gumdrops and toothpicks she had set out on card tables.

A drooping rabbit's ear, a cat's tail hanging from its owner down the back of a chair, a worn sneaker sticking out beneath a ghost's shroud seemed charming to her still. And yet, she felt less delighted than before.

The room became quiet enough for her to hear the children's labored breathing as they concentrated on their efforts. As they reached for the colored candies to fit them awkwardly on the toothpicks, Anne was not able to get rid of the slight depression settling over her. There was that furtive, restless quality creeping about the room as though all the small figures bending over their nonsense were less intent than they pretended to be. There was a sense of shifting, of lifting the head to listen, though no child did these things.

In the near silence she heard the wind rising outside. It was then, too, that she heard the front gate creak as it opened.

No child looked up. As Anne listened for the footsteps which should have sounded on the porch afterward, each child seemed to concentrate more obliviously than before.

When Anne crossed the room to the entrance hall, she felt she was being watched. It was such a strong feeling she turned to look back. No one had even seen her go.

Nothing but the wind, rushing into the hall like some belated guest, met her at the open door. Behind it, in darkness that crept away from the porch light, she could see no one.

It was when her eyes searched the old garden at the side of the house that she saw them. They were standing by a small stone sundial Anne's grandfather had set there years ago. A boy and a girl, hand in hand, they stood looking at her, motionless as it was.

Not until she called to them inviting them inside did they move forward. As they came through the dark, up the porch steps, Anne felt at last how truly starless the night was, how like these particular parents to send them out alone.

They passed in silence through the door she held open for

them. Once inside the hall, they waited, making no move towards the living room, standing always together in their peculiar stillness. Anne, for some reason unknown, not only closed but bolted the door.

They were staring wordlessly up at her when she turned back to them. She found herself struggling with a feeling of aversion for them, since now that they had arrived she realized how relieved she had been earlier at their absence.

The girl was a head taller than her brother, though both were identically costumed. Neither of them was masked, yet it was only one face that both turned to her, the boy's being simply a smaller version of the girl's.

To Anne they had the look of having been drawn by their father instead of procreated in the usual way. She thought she even recognized Usher's personal style in the deliberate exaggeration of line and the faintly corrupt, half-graceful proportions of that face with its twofold glance.

The eyes, in particular, were as overly large as the ones he painted. They were a flat, tobacco brown. It was to the expression in them that she owed her feeling of aversion. For both pairs held a fixed, impersonal intentness that was less unchildlike, she thought, than inhuman.

Still, they were only children, just come to a strange house. Anne, feeling slightly guilty, pointed the way to the living room.

They walked ahead of her, docilely enough, not seeming to notice when Anne, following them, suddenly stopped still. She had noticed at last what they were wearing. She felt a sense of affront, of somehow being publicly insulted. If friends had called Usher's humor unpleasant and sardonic, she had not known up until then what those words could mean. For even to Anne, no authority on such matters, it was obvious he had sent them dressed in costumes representing the grave clothes of children of a past generation. Both wore on their heads wreaths of stiff formal leaves, and were dressed in folds of white cloth from shoulder to foot. The costumes were draped delicately and, from a distance at least, looked as beautifully sewn as her own child's dress. That each detail had the stamp of conscious artistic effect only added to the cynical horror of the idea.

Though the other children looked up as they entered the room, they remained sitting at their tables. Anne, sensing the general withdrawal on their part, came closer to her new guests, intending to reassure them. Close enough to the boy, in fact, to feel she had seen the worst, ultimate point of the joke. For the material of their costumes had the limp suppleness of age. The hand-sewn lace on them was yellow.

After their initial drawing back the children began to speak again, to laugh, get up from the tables and show her what they had made.

They began a game of blindman's bluff. It was not one of the games planned for the evening, but Anne took advantage of it to go away to privacy for a few moments.

She stood alone in the gaily decorated dining room with its rows of shining, waiting plates. She frowned, moving her lips slightly like a child over a mathematics problem, wondering uneasily how the children of such a father might be expected to behave. A need to see what was happening, as urgent as the need for privacy had been a few minutes before, sent her to the door of the room.

What she saw reassured her. The two children, along with the others, crouched, hiding from the blindfolded child who groped after them with outstretched hands. She saw the boy shrink away in his turn from the blindman, giggling softly. His eyes were shining childishly. She reproached herself.

Yet the party was changed. The mood of it began to resemble more nearly the wild "play-outs" of her childhood's summer nights, when the long, soft dusk encouraged a feeling of lawlessness, of perilous emotions, a sort of childish debauch. There was a feverish, tense look on some of their faces.

Anne had gone to the kitchen before the party went out of control. The children had begun to choose their own games by that time, and had been playing a comparatively quiet one when she left the room. It was an ancient game, a sort of ritual she remembered having played herself, known as old witch.

> "I'm going downtown to smoke my pipe
> And I won't be back till Saturday night
> And if you dare let the old witch in
> I'll beat you red—white—and blue!"

A small voice chanted the words behind her as she entered the kitchen. For a time she busied herself pouring cider, warming plates, mentally counting heads, as she concentrated on her own activities.

Until the lights went out.

The entire house was suddenly dark. Someone, she knew, had pulled a switch. When she called out anxiously she was answered by her son's cheerful voice.

They had decided, he called, to play moonlight-starlight.

The name, heard aloud, made a chill run over Anne. She hadn't thought of it for years. As a child it had been the only game she had feared and hated. She felt intolerable anxiety as she wondered, while knowing at once, who had suggested it. The party was out of hand.

She groped across the kitchen to the drawer that held her husband's flashlight, disguising her unreasonable fear with irritation at her son for pulling the switch without permission.

Someone had taken and forgotten to return the flashlight. As she turned away, trying to think where she had put candles, she was remembering against her will the way the game was played.

For moonlight-starlight was an outdoor game, another part of the summer nights. Children played it only after dark.

Anne remembered it well. The child who was "it," the ghost, hid in some dark and secret place. Each child, separate and alone, had to wander in search of it. On finding it they, too, became ghosts. Until at last only one child was left to wander alone, watched by all the secret ghosts, who would, in the end, pounce upon it.

There were no candles. She set out in darkness.

The switch box was located across the living room in an alcove which had been built as a small conservatory with french doors opening into the garden. Even in the blackness of the hall, Anne knew exactly where it was.

The house, except for small sounds and sudden scamperings, was silent. It seemed to take a long time to walk the length of the hall. In darkness the house grew larger, as large as she had thought it as a child. And now, more nearly child than adult, she walked forward with dread.

At any time now "it," changed from the familiar playmate to some nameless horror, could jump suddenly upon her from its hiding place. For, like it or not, she, too, was a player now.

Her hand touched the living-room wall and she groped forward, angry with herself for the way she shrank against it. She had reached the doors leading to the conservatory before she heard the whispering. It came from inside the room and there was a quality in it that froze her motionless, hardly breathing.

For a few seconds her faculties were turned inward on her own pounding heart. It was only gradually, as she realized she had not been noticed, that she calmed somewhat. She found she was able to see dimly the three small figures standing inside. The white garments of two of them even shone slightly, though so little light came from the night which waited outside in the garden.

When she was able to hear something besides her own pulse she listened to the phrase the two in white whispered again and again, distinguishing, at last, the words.

"Come out . . . come out into the dark . . . come with us. . . ."

They whispered it together, excited, persuasive, with an urgent, secret sibilance that held an increasing seductiveness at each repetition.

The third child, so enticed, whimpered once and stood quiet between them after that. It had been the small sound of an animal so full of fear as to be beyond outcry.

It released Anne from the fear that held her. For the voice had been her daughter's.

Though she leaped forward she made no attempt to reach her child. Her urge was the primitive, overwhelming one for light to chase away the darkness. The hands that had fumbled so often before moved with the speed and sureness of fear which is beyond panic.

And the taller of the two, the girl, swayed gently towards her with smiling teeth at the same second lights blazed throughout the house and her own child was in her arms.

They stood alone in the glass-enclosed room. Other players who had been wandering about downstairs blinked their eyes in the sudden light, calling reproachful questions.

Every child had come back into the living-room before Anne, with trembling hands, shut the french doors which had been swinging open in the wind from the garden. No child asked where two of the guests had gone.

No one mentioned them at all through the final stages of the party. Anne, having had to choose between illness and anger, chose rightly. It was anger that sustained her through the refreshments, the collecting of coats and the arrival, thanks and good-byes of parents.

It was faithful through the night. She went to bed angry and it was with her when she woke the next morning. She guarded it carefully as she planned the call she would make to Usher that day, since if she lost it she feared what might take its place.

In the end, it was Mrs. Usher who called Anne first. She had a pleasant voice, crisp and courteous though rather impersonal sounding.

She called, she said, to explain why her children had not been able to attend the party. They had had fever all day and she believed it might be developing into a light case of chicken pox. Both she, and they, had been so disappointed. She had made their costumes herself; they were to have gone as a cat and a mouse.

The voice seemed to fade out on the next few sentences. At the first words Anne heard there had been a slight, sickening wrench somewhere inside her. It was a relatively mild one, considering that it was the displacement of whatever held her being secure in its particular place in the universe.

The voice wanted to know if most of the other children had been able to make it. Some of them, it knew, had had to come a long way.

The invitations had been on orange paper. She remembered them. Her mother had let her cut out and address them herself, guiding her hand as it made fat wavering letters on the envelopes. She had been so proud that they were to go all the way to upstate New York.

Anne's voice, when she answered, was steadier than the room, still wheeling crazily around herself and the telephone.

Yes, she said, some of the children had had to come a very long way.

Children would do almost anything not to miss a party, the voice said.

Yes, Anne said. All the children had come.

1952

THE LOVELY HOUSE

by Shirley Jackson

Some houses, particularly old houses, have an aura of other lives, other times. Many writers have been fascinated by what they call "the spirit of place." It obsessed the writers of the nineteenth century; it is less current in our mobile society today when most of us have more shallow roots in our communities. But even now you will pass some house with a history, a house with a quaint horror about it, a house with a strange story. Shirley Jackson tells such a story about a "lovely house."

This is a story of the fourth dimension, that area where there is a curious welding of space and time. Although writers of the nineteenth century vaguely felt and used this concept, it was not until Einstein formulated the concept of relativity that the fourth-dimension story took on full significance.

In the twentieth century, time is still one of the most important concepts to be explored. Yesterday, today, tomorrow? Are they all separate or is there a kind of "melting" that permits us to glide back and forth in ordinary space and time? The studies of Freud in particular made it clear in the twentieth century that the unconscious, that dark part of our minds which is not easily accessible to most of us, has no sense of time; the past and the future are always companion to the present. The greatest contemporary writer of such stories was undoubtedly Shirley Jackson whose story "The Lovely House" has secured a place for itself in great literature.

Shirley Jackson

The house in itself was, even before anything had happened there, as lovely a thing as she had ever seen. Set among its lavish grounds, with a park and a river and a wooded hill surrounding it, and carefully planned and tended gardens close upon all sides, it lay upon the hills as though it were something too precious to be seen by everyone; Margaret's very coming there had been a product of such elaborate arrangement, and such letters to and fro, and such meetings and hopings and wishings, that when she alighted with Carla Montague at the doorway of Carla's home, she felt that she too had come home, to a place striven for and earned. Carla stopped before the doorway and stood for a minute, looking first behind her, at the vast reaching gardens and the green lawn going down to the river, and the soft hills beyond, and then at the perfect grace of the house, showing so clearly the long-boned structure within, the curving staircases and the arched doorways and the tall thin lines of steadying beams, all of it resting back against the hills, and up, past rows of windows and the flying lines of the roof, on, to the tower—Carla stopped, and looked, and smiled, and then turned and said, "Welcome, Margaret."

"It's a lovely house," Margaret said, and felt that she had much better have said nothing.

The doors were opened and Margaret, touching as she went the warm head of a stone faun beside her, passed inside. Carla, following, greeted the servants by name, and was welcomed with reserved pleasure; they stood for a minute on the rose and white tiled floor. "Again, welcome, Margaret," Carla said.

Far ahead of them the great stairway soared upward, held to the hall where they stood by only the slimmest of carved ballustrades; on Margaret's left hand a tapestry moved softly as the door behind was closed. She could see the fine threads of the weave, and the light colors, but she could not have told the picture unless she went far away, perhaps as far away as the staircase, and looked at it from there; perhaps, she thought, from halfway up the stairway this great hall, and perhaps the whole house, is visible, as a complete body of story together, all joined and in sequence. Or perhaps I shall be allowed to move slowly from one thing to another, observing each, or would that take all the time of my visit?

"I never saw anything so lovely," she said to Carla, and Carla smiled.

"Come and meet my mama," Carla said.

They went through doors at the right, and Margaret, before she could see the light room she went into, was stricken with fear at meeting the owners of the house and the park and the river, and as she went beside Carla she kept her eyes down.

"Mama," said Carla, "this is Margaret, from school."

"Margaret," said Carla's mother, and smiled at Margaret kindly. "We are very glad you were able to come."

She was a tall lady wearing pale green and pale blue, and Margaret said as gracefully as she could, "Thank you, Mrs. Montague; I am very grateful for having been invited."

"Surely," said Mrs. Montague softly, "surely my daughter's friend Margaret from school should be welcome here; surely we should be grateful that she has come."

"Thank you, Mrs. Montague," Margaret said, not knowing how she was answering, but knowing that she was grateful.

When Mrs. Montague turned her kind eyes on her daughter, Margaret was at last able to look at the room where she stood next to her friend; it was a pale green and a pale blue long room with tall windows that looked out onto the lawn and the sky, and thin colored china ornaments on the mantel. Mrs. Montague had left her needlepoint when they came in and from where Margaret stood she could see the pale sweet pattern from the underside; all soft colors it was, melting into one another endlessly, and not finished. On the table nearby were books, and one large book of sketches that were most certainly Carla's; Carla's harp stood next to the windows, and beyond one window were marble steps outside, going shallowly down to a fountain, where water moved in the sunlight. Margaret thought of her own embroidery—a pair of slippers she was working for her friend—and knew that she should never be able to bring it into this room, where Mrs. Montague's long white hands rested on the needlepoint frame, soft as dust on the pale colors.

"Come," said Carla, taking Margaret's hand in her own. "Mama has said that I might show you some of the house."

They went out again into the hall, across the rose and white tiles which made a pattern too large to be seen from the floor, and through a doorway where tiny bronze fauns grinned at them from the carving. The first room that they went into was all gold, with gilt on the window frames and on the legs of the chairs and tables, and the small chairs standing on the yellow carpet were made of gold brocade with small gilded backs, and on the wall were more tapestries showing the house as it looked in the sunlight with even the trees around it shining, and these tapestries were let into the wall and edged with thin gilded frames.

"There is so much tapestry," Margaret said.

"In every room," Carla agreed. "Mama has emboidered all the hangings for her own room, the room where she writes her letters. The other tapestries were done by my grandmamas and my great-grandmamas and my great-great-grandmamas."

The next room was silver, and the small chairs were of silver brocade with narrow silvered backs, and the tapestries on the walls of this room were edged with silver frames and showed the house in moonlight, with the white light shining on the stones and the windows glittering.

"Who uses these rooms?" Margaret asked.

"No one," Carla said.

They passed then into a room where everything grew smaller as they looked at it: the mirrors on both sides of the room showed the door opening and Margaret and Carla coming through, and then, reflected, a smaller door opening and a small Margaret and a smaller Carla coming through, and then, reflected again, a still smaller door and Margaret and Carla, and so on, endlessly, Margaret and Carla diminishing and reflecting. There was a table here and nesting under it another lesser table, and under that another one, and another under that one, and on the greatest table lay a carved wooden bowl holding within it another carved wooden bowl, and another within that, and another within that one. The tapestries in this room were of the house reflected in the lake, and the tapestries themselves were reflected, in and out, among the mirrors on the wall, with the house in the tapestries reflected in the lake.

This room frightened Margaret rather, because it was so difficult for her to tell what was in it and what was not, and how far in any direction she might easily move, and she backed out hastily, pushing Carla behind her. They turned from here into another doorway which led them out again into the great hall under the soaring staircase, and Carla said, "We had better go upstairs and see your room; we can see more of the house another time. We have *plenty* of time, after all," and she squeezed Margaret's hand joyfully.

They climbed the great staircase, and passed, in the hall upstairs, Carla's room, which was like the inside of a shell in pale colors, with lilacs on the table, and the fragrance of the lilacs followed them as they went down the halls.

The sound of their shoes on the polished floor was like rain, but the sun came in on them wherever they went. "Here," Carla said, opening a door, "is where we have breakfast when it is warm; here," opening another door, "is the passage to the room where Mama does her letters. And that—" nodding, "—is the stairway to the tower, and *here* is where we shall have dances when my brother comes home."

"A real tower?" Margaret said.

"And *here*," Carla said, "is the old schoolroom, and my brother and I studied here before he went away, and I stayed on alone studying here until it was time for me to come to school and meet *you*."

"Can we go up into the tower?" Margaret asked.

"Down here, at the end of the hall," Carla said, "is where all my grandpapas and my grandmamas and my great-great-grandpapas and grandmamas live." She opened the door to the long gallery, where pictures of tall old people in lace and pale waistcoats leaned down to stare at Margaret and Carla. And then, to a walk at the top of the house, where they leaned over and looked at the ground below and the tower above, and Margaret looked at the gray stone of the tower and wondered who lived there, and Carla pointed out where the river ran far below, far away, and said they should walk there tomorrow.

"When my brother comes," she said, "he will take us boating on the river."

In her room, unpacking her clothes, Margaret realized that her white dress was the only one possible for dinner, and thought that she would have to send home for more things; she had intended to wear her ordinary gray downstairs most evenings before Carla's brother came, but knew she could not when she saw Carla in light blue, with pearls around her neck. When Margaret and Carla came into the drawing room before dinner Mrs. Montague greeted them very kindly, and asked had Margaret seen the painted room, or the room with the tiles?

"We had no time to go near that part of the house at all," Carla said.

"After dinner, then," Mrs. Montague said, putting her arm affectionately around Margaret's shoulders, "we will go and see the painted room and the room with the tiles, because they are particular favorites of mine."

"Come and meet my papa," Carla said.

The door was just opening for Mr. Montague, and Margaret, who felt almost at ease now with Mrs. Montague, was frightened again of Mr. Montague, who spoke loudly and said, "So this is m'girl's friend from school? Lift up your head, girl, and let's have a look at you." When Margaret looked up blindly, and smiled weakly, he patted her cheek and said, "We shall have to make you look bolder before you leave us," and then he tapped his daughter on the shoulder and said she had grown to a monstrous fine girl.

They went in to dinner, and on the walls of the dining room were tapestries of the house in the seasons of the year, and the dinner service was white china with veins of gold running through it, as though it had been mined and not molded. The fish was one Margaret did not recognize, and Mr. Montague very generously insisted upon serving her himself without smiling at her ignorance. Carla and Margaret were each given a glassful of pale spicy wine.

"When my brother comes," Carla said to Margaret, "we will not dare be so quiet at table." She looked across the white cloth to Margaret, and then to her father at the head, to her mother at the foot, with the long table between them, and said, "My brother can make us laugh all the time."

"Your mother will not miss you for these summer months?" Mrs. Montague said to Margaret.

"She has my sisters, ma'am," Margaret said, "and I have been away at school for so long that she has learned to do without me."

"We mothers never learn to do without our daughters," Mrs. Montague said, and looked fondly at Carla. "Or our sons," she added with a sigh.

"When my brother comes," Carla said, "you will see what this house can be like with life in it."

"When does he come?" Margaret asked.

"One week," Mr. Montague said, "three days, and four hours."

When Mrs. Montague rose, Margaret and Carla followed her, and Mr. Montague rose gallantly to hold the door for them all.

That evening Carla and Margaret played and sang duets, although Carla said that their voices together were too thin to be appealing without a deeper voice accompanying, and that when her brother came they should have some splendid trios. Mrs. Montague complimented their singing, and Mr. Montague fell asleep in his chair.

Before they went upstairs Mrs. Montague reminded herself of her promise to show Margaret the painted room and the room with the tiles, and so she and Margaret and Carla, holding their long dresses up away from the floor in front so that their skirts whispered behind them, went down a hall and through a passage and down another hall, and through a room filled with books and then through a painted door into a tiny octagonal room where each of the sides were paneled and painted, with pink and blue and green and gold small pictures of shepherds and nymphs, lambs and fauns, playing on the broad green lawns by the river, with the house standing lovely behind them. There was nothing else in the little room, because seemingly the paintings were furniture enough for one room, and Margaret felt surely that she could stay happily and watch the small painted people playing, without ever seeing anything more of the house. But Mrs. Montague led her on, into the room of the tiles, which was not exactly a room at all, but had one side all glass window looking out onto the same lawn of the pictures in the octagonal room. The tiles were set into the floor of this room, in tiny bright spots of color which showed, when you stood back and looked at them, that they were again a picture of the house, only now the same materials that made the house made the tiles, so that the tiny windows were tiles of glass, and the stones of the tower were chips of gray stone, and the bricks of the chimneys were chips of brick.

Beyond the tiles of the house Margaret, lifting her long skirt as she walked, so that she should not brush a chip of the tower out of place, stopped and said, "What is *this?*" And stood back to see, and then knelt down and said, "*What* is this?"

"Isn't she enchanting?" said Mrs. Montague, smiling at Margaret, "I've always loved her."

"I was wondering what Margaret would say when she saw it," said Carla, smiling also.

It was a curiously made picture of a girl's face, with blue chip eyes and a red chip mouth, staring blindly from the floor, with long light braids made of yellow stone chips going down evenly on either side of her round cheeks.

"She is pretty," said Margaret, stepping back to see her better. "What does it say underneath?"

She stepped back again, holding her head up and back to

read the letters, pieced together with stone chips and set unevenly in the floor. "Here was Margaret," it said, "who died for love."

There was, of course, not time to do everything. Before Margaret had seen half the house, Carla's brother came home. Carla came running up the great staircase one afternoon calling, "Margaret, Margaret, he's come," and Margaret, running down to meet her, hugged her and said, "I'm so glad."

He had certainly come, and Margaret, entering the drawing room shyly behind Carla, saw Mrs. Montague with tears in her eyes and Mr. Montague standing straighter and prouder than before, and Carla said, "Brother, here is Margaret."

He was tall and haughty in uniform, and Margaret wished she had met him a little later, when she had perhaps been to her room again, and perhaps tucked up her hair. Next to him stood his friend, a captain, small and dark and bitter, and smiling bleakly upon the family assembled. Margaret smiled back timidly at them both, and stood behind Carla.

Everyone then spoke at once. Mrs. Montague said, "We've missed you so," and Mr. Montague said, "Glad to have you back, m'boy," and Carla said "We shall have such times—I've promised Margaret—" and Carla's brother said "So this is Margaret?" and the dark captain said "I've been wanting to come."

It seemed that they all spoke at once, every time; there would be a long waiting silence while all of them looked around with joy at being together, and then suddenly everyone would have found something to say. It was so at dinner. Mrs. Montague said "You're not eating enough," and "You used to be more fond of pomegranates," and Carla said "We're to go boating," and "We'll have a dance, won't we?" and "Margaret and I insist upon a picnic," and "I saved the river for my brother to show to Margaret." Mr. Montague puffed and laughed and passed the wine, and Margaret hardly dared lift her eyes. The black captain said "Never realized what an attractive old place it could be, after all," and Carla's brother said

"There's much about the house I'd like to show Margaret."

After dinner they played charades, and even Mrs. Montague did Achilles with Mr. Montague, holding his heel and both of them laughing and glancing at Carla and Margaret and the captain. Carla's brother leaned on the back of Margaret's chair and once she looked up at him and said, "No one ever calls you by name. Do you actually have a name?"

"Paul," he said.

The next morning they walked on the lawn, Carla with the captain and Margaret with Paul. They stood by the lake, and Margaret looked at the pure reflection of the house and said, "It almost seems as though we could open a door and go in."

"There," said Paul, and he pointed with his stick at the front entrance, "there is where we shall enter, and it will swing open for us with an underwater crash."

"Margaret," said Carla, laughing, "you say odd things, sometimes. If you tried to go into *that* house, you'd be in the lake."

"Indeed, and not like it much, at all," the captain added.

"Or would you have the side door?" asked Paul, pointing with his stick.

"I think I prefer the front door," said Margaret.

"But you'd be drowned," Carla said. She took Margaret's arm as they started back toward the house, and said, "We'd make a scene for a tapestry right now, on the lawn before the house."

"Another tapestry?" said the captain, and grimaced.

They played croquet, and Paul hit Margaret's ball toward a wicket, and the captain accused her of cheating prettily. And they played word games in the evening, and Margaret and Paul won, and everyone said Margaret was so clever. And they walked endlessly on the lawns before the house, and looked into the still lake, and watched the reflection of the house in the water, and Margaret chose a room in the reflected house for her own, and Paul said she should have it.

"That's the room where Mama writes her letters," said Carla looking strangely at Margaret.

"Not in our house in the lake," said Paul.

"And I suppose if you like it she would lend it to you while you stay," Carla said.

"Not at all," said Margaret amiably. "I think I should prefer the tower anyway."

"Have you seen the rose garden?" Carla asked.

"Let me take you there," said Paul.

Margaret started across the lawn with him, and Carla called to her, "Where are you off to now, Margaret?"

"Why, to the rose garden," Margaret called back, and Carla said, staring, "You are really very odd, sometimes, Margaret. And it's growing colder, far too cold to linger among the roses," and so Margaret and Paul turned back.

Mrs. Montague's needlepoint was coming on well. She had filled in most of the outlines of the house, and was setting in the windows. After the first small shock of surprise, Margaret no longer wondered that Mrs. Montague was able to set out the house so well without a pattern or a plan; she did it from memory and Margaret, realizing this for the first time, thought "How amazing," and then "But of course how else *would* she do it?"

To see a picture of the house, Mrs. Montague needed only to lift her eyes in any direction, but, more than that, she had of course never used any other model for her embroidery; she had of course learned the faces of the house better than the faces of her children. The dreamy life of the Montagues in the house was most clearly shown Margaret as she watched Mrs. Montague surely and capably building doors and windows, carvings and cornices, in her embroidered house, smiling tenderly across the room to where Carla and the captain bent over a book together, while her fingers almost of themselves turned the edge of a carving Margaret had forgotten or never known about until, leaning over the back of Mrs. Montague's chair, she saw it form itself under Mrs. Montague's hands.

The small thread of days and sunlight, then, that bound Margaret to the house, was woven here as she watched. And

Carla, lifting her head to look over, might say, "Margaret, do come and look, here. Mother is always at her work, but my brother is rarely home."

They went for a picnic, Carla and the captain and Paul and Margaret, and Mrs. Montague waved to them from the doorway as they left, and Mr. Montague came to his study window and lifted his hand to them. They chose to go to the wooded hill beyond the house, although Carla was timid about going too far away—"I always like to be where I can see the roofs, at least," she said—and sat among the trees, on moss greener than Margaret had ever seen before, and spread out a white cloth and drank red wine.

It was a very proper forest, with neat trees and the green moss, and an occasional purple or yellow flower growing discreetly away from the path. There was no sense of brooding silence, and there sometimes is with trees about, and Margaret realized, looking up to see the sky clearly between the branches, that she had seen this forest in the tapestries in the breakfast room, with the house shining in the sunlight beyond.

"Doesn't the river come through here somewhere?" she asked, hearing, she thought, the sound of it through the trees. "I feel so comfortable here among these trees, so at home."

"It is possible," said Paul, "to take a boat from the lawn in front of the house and move without sound down the river, through the trees, past the fields and then, for some reason, around past the house again. The river, you see, goes almost around the house in a great circle. We are very proud of that."

"The river *is* nearby," said Carla. "It goes almost completely around the house."

"Margaret," said the captain. "You must not look rapt on a picnic unless you are contemplating nature."

"I was, as a matter of fact," said Margaret. "I was contemplating a caterpillar approaching Carla's foot."

"Will you come and look at the river?" said Paul, rising and holding his hand out to Margaret. "I think we can see much of its great circle from near here."

"Margaret," said Carla as Margaret stood up, "you are *always* wandering off."

"I'm coming right back," Margaret said, with a laugh. "It's only to look at the river."

"Don't be away long," Carla said. "We must be getting back before dark."

The river as it went through the trees was shadowed and cool, broadening out into pools where only the barest movement disturbed the ferns along its edge, and where small stones made it possible to step out and see the water all around, from a precarious island, and where without sound a leaf might be carried from the limits of sight to the limits of sight, moving swiftly but imperceptibly and turning a little as it went.

"Who lives in the tower, Paul?" asked Margaret, holding a fern and running it softly over the back of her hand. "I know someone lives there, because I saw someone moving at the window once."

"Not *lives* there," said Paul, amused. "Did you think we kept a political prisoner locked away?"

"I thought it might be the birds, at first," Margaret said, glad to be describing this to someone.

"No," said Paul, still amused. "There's an aunt, or a great-aunt, or perhaps even a great-great-great-aunt. She doesn't live there, at all, but goes there because she says she cannot *endure* the sight of tapestry." He laughed. "She has filled the tower with books, and a huge old cat, and she may practice alchemy there, for all anyone knows. The reason you've never seen her would be that she has one of her spells of hiding away. Sometimes she is downstairs daily."

"Will I ever meet her?" Margaret asked wonderingly.

"Perhaps," Paul said. "She might take it into her head to come down formally one night to dinner. Or she might wander carelessly up to you where you sat on the lawn, and introduce herself. Or you might never see her, at that."

"Suppose I went up to the tower?"

Paul glanced at her strangely. "I suppose you could, if you wanted to," he said. "*I've* been there."

"Margaret," Carla called through the woods. "Margaret, we shall be late if you do not give up brooding by the river."

All this time, almost daily, Margaret was seeing new places in the house: the fan room, where the most delicate filigree fans had been set into the walls with their fine ivory sticks painted in exquisite miniature; the small room where incredibly perfect wooden and glass and metal fruits and flowers and trees stood on glittering glass shelves, lined up against the windows. And daily she passed and repassed the door behind which lay the stairway to the tower, and almost daily she stepped carefully around the tiles on the floor which read "Here was Margaret, who died for love."

It was no longer possible, however, to put off going to the tower. It was no longer possible to pass the doorway several times a day and do no more than touch her hand secretly to the panels, or perhaps set her head against them and listen, to hear if there were footsteps up or down, or a voice calling her. It was not possible to pass the doorway once more, and so in the early morning Margaret set her hand firmly to the door and pulled it open, and it came easily, as though relieved that at last, after so many hints and insinuations, and so much waiting and such helpless despair, Margaret had finally come to open it.

The stairs beyond, gray stone and rough, were, Margaret thought, steep for an old lady's feet, but Margaret went up effortlessly, though timidly. The stairway turned around and around, going up to the tower, and Margaret followed, setting her feet carefully upon one step after another, and holding her hands against the warm stone wall on either side, looking forward and up, expecting to be seen or spoken to before she reached the top; perhaps, she thought once, the walls of the tower were transparent and she was clearly, ridiculously visible from the outside, and Mrs. Montague and Carla, on the lawn—if indeed they ever looked upward to the tower—might watch her and turn to one another with smiles, saying, "There is Margaret, going up to the tower at last," and, smiling, nod to one another.

The stairway ended, as she had not expected it would, in a heavy wooden door, which made Margaret, standing on the step below to find room to raise her hand and knock, seem smaller, and even standing at the top of the tower she felt that she was not really tall.

"Come in," said the great-aunt's voice, when Margaret had knocked twice; the first knock had been received with an expectant silence, as though inside someone had said inaudibly, "Is that someone knocking at *this* door?" and then waited to be convinced by a second knock; and Margaret's knuckles hurt from the effort of knocking to be heard through a heavy wooden door. She opened the door awkwardly from below—how much easier this all would be, she thought, if I knew the way—went in, and said politely, before she looked around, "I'm Carla's friend. They said I might come up to the tower to see it, but of course if you would rather I went away I shall." She had planned to say this more gracefully, without such an implication that invitations to the tower were issued by the downstairs Montagues, but the long climb and her being out of breath forced her to say everything at once, and she had really no time for the sounding periods she had composed.

In any case the great-aunt said politely—she was sitting at the other side of the round room, against the window, and she was not very clearly visible—"I am amazed that they told you about me at all. However, since you are here I cannot pretend that I really object to having you; you may come in and sit down."

Margaret came obediently into the room and sat down on the stone bench which ran all the way around the tower room, under the windows which of course were on all sides and open to the winds, so that the movement of the air through the tower room was insistent and constant, making talk difficult and even distinguishing objects a matter of some effort.

As though it were necessary to establish her position in the house emphatically and immediately, the old lady said, with a gesture and a grin, "My tapestries," and waved at the windows. She seemed to be not older than a great-aunt, although perhaps too old for a mere aunt, but her voice was clearly able to carry through the sound of the wind in the tower room and she seemed compact and strong beside the window, not at all as though she might be dizzy from looking out, or tired from the stairs.

"May I look out the window?" Margaret asked, almost of the cat, which sat next to her and regarded her without friendship, but without, as yet, dislike.

"Certainly," said the great-aunt. "Look out the windows, by all means."

Margaret turned on the bench and leaned her arms on the wide stone ledge of the window, but she was disappointed. Although the tops of the trees did not reach halfway up the tower, she could see only branches and leaves below and no sign of the wide lawns or the roofs of the house or the curve of the river.

"I hoped I could see the way the river went, from here."

"The river doesn't *go* from here," said the old lady, and laughed.

"I mean," Margaret said, "they told me that the river went around in a curve, almost surrounding the house."

"Who told you?" said the old lady.

"Paul."

"I see," said the old lady. "*He's* back, is he?"

"He's been here for several days, but he's going away again soon."

"And what's *your* name?" asked the old lady, leaning forward.

"Margaret."

"I see," said the old lady again. "That's my name, too," she said.

Margaret thought that "How nice" would be an inappropriate reply to this, and something like "Is it?" or "Just imagine" or "What a coincidence" would certainly make her feel more foolish than she believed she really was, so she smiled uncertainly at the old lady and dismissed the notion of saying "What a lovely name."

"He should have come and gone sooner," the old lady went on, as though to herself. "Then we'd have it all behind us."

"Have all *what* behind us?" Margaret asked, although she felt that she was not really being included in the old lady's conversation with herself, a conversation that seemed—and probably was—part of a larger conversation which the old lady had with herself constantly and on larger subjects than the matter of Margaret's name, and which even Margaret, intruder as she was, and young, could not be allowed to interrupt for very long. "Have all *what* behind us?" Margaret asked insistently.

"I say," said the old lady, turning to look at Margaret, "he should have come and gone already, and we'd all be well out of it by now."

"I see," said Margaret. "Well, I don't think he's going to be here much longer. He's talking of going." In spite of herself, her voice trembled a little. In order to prove to the old lady that the trembling in her voice was imaginary, Margaret said almost defiantly, "It will be very lonely here after he has gone."

"We'll be well out of it, Margaret, you and I," the old lady said. "Stand away from the window, child, you'll be wet."

Margaret realized with this that the storm, which had—she knew now—been hanging over the house for long sunny days had broken, suddenly, and that the wind had grown louder and was bringing with it through the windows of the tower long stinging rain. There were drops on the cat's black fur, and Margaret felt the side of her face wet. "Do your windows close?" she asked. "If I could help you—?"

"I don't mind the rain," the old lady said. "It wouldn't be the first time it's rained around the tower."

"*I* don't mind it," Margaret said hastily, drawing away from the window. She realized that she was staring back at the cat, and added nervously, "Although, of course, getting wet is—" She hesitated and the cat stared back at her without expression.

"I mean," she said apologetically, "some people don't *like* getting wet."

The cat deliberately turned its back on her and put its face closer to the window.

"What were you saying about Paul?" Margaret asked the old lady, feeling somehow that there might be a thin thread of reason tangling the old lady and the cat and the tower and the rain, and even, with abrupt clarity, defining Margaret herself and the strange hesitation which had caught at her here in the tower. "He's going away soon, you know."

"It would have been better if it were over with by now," the old lady said. "These things don't take really long, you know, and the sooner the better, I say."

"I suppose *that's* true," Margaret said intelligently.

"After all," said the old lady dreamily, with raindrops in her hair, "we don't always see ahead, into things that are going to happen."

Margaret was wondering how soon she might politely go back downstairs and dry herself off, and she meant to stay politely only so long as the old lady seemed to be talking, however remotely, about Paul. Also, the rain and the wind were coming through the window onto Margaret in great driving gusts, as though Margaret and the old lady and the books and the cat would be washed away, and the top of the tower cleaned of them.

"I *would* help you if I could," the old lady said earnestly to Margaret, raising her voice almost to a scream to be heard over the wind and the rain. She stood up to approach Margaret, and Margaret, thinking she was about to fall, reached out a hand to catch her. The cat stood up and spat, the rain came through the window in a great sweep, and Margaret, holding the old lady's hands, heard through the sounds of the wind the equal sounds of all the voices in the world, and they called to her saying, "Goodbye, goodbye," and "All is lost" and another voice saying, "I will always remember you," and still another called, "It is so dark." And, far away from the others, she could hear a voice calling, "Come back, come back." Then the old lady pulled her hands away from Margaret and the voices were gone. The cat shrank back and the old lady looked coldly at Margaret and said, "As I was saying, I would help you if I *could*."

"I'm so sorry," Margaret said weakly. "I thought you were going to fall."

"Goodbye," said the old lady.

At the ball Margaret wore a gown of thin blue lace that belonged to Carla, and yellow roses in her hair, and she carried one of the fans from the fan room, a daintily painted ivory thing which seemed indestructible, since she dropped it twice, and which had a tiny picture of the house painted on its ivory sticks, so that when the fan was closed the house was gone. Mrs. Montague had given it to her to carry, and had given Carla another, so that when Margaret and Carla passed one another dancing, or met by the punch bowl or in the halls, they said happily to one another, "Have you still got your fan? I gave mine to someone to hold for a minute; I showed mine to everyone. Are you still carrying your fan? I've got *mine*."

Margaret danced with strangers and with Paul, and when she danced with Paul they danced away from the others, up and down the long gallery hung with pictures, in and out between the pillars which led to the great hall opening into the room of the tiles. Near them danced ladies in scarlet silk, and green satin, and white velvet, and Mrs. Montague, in black with diamonds at her throat and on her hands, stood at the top of the room and smiled at the dancers, or went on Mr. Montague's arm to greet guests who came laughingly in between the pillars looking eagerly and already moving in time to the music as they walked. One lady wore white feathers in her hair, curling down against her shoulder; another had a pink scarf over her arms, and it floated behind her as she danced. Paul was in his haughty uniform, and Carla wore red roses in her hair and danced with the captain.

"Are you really going tomorrow?" Margaret asked Paul once during the evening; she knew that he was, but somehow asking the question—which she had done several times before—established a communication between them, of his right to go and her right to wonder, which was sadly sweet to her.

"I *said* you might meet the great-aunt," said Paul, as though in answer; Margaret followed his glance, and saw the old lady of the tower. She was dressed in yellow satin, and looked very regal and proud as she moved through the crowd of dancers, drawing her skirt aside if any of them came too close to her. She was coming toward Margaret and Paul where they sat on small chairs against the wall, and when she came close enough she smiled, looking at Paul, and said to him, holding out her hands, "I am very glad to see you, my dear."

Then she smiled at Margaret and Margaret smiled back, thankful that the old lady held out no hands to her.

"Margaret told me you were here," the old lady said to Paul, "and I came down to see you once more."

"I'm happy that you did," Paul said. "I wanted to see you so much that I almost came to the tower."

They both laughed and Margaret, looking from one to the other of them, wondered at the strong resemblance between them. Margaret sat very straight and stiff on her narrow chair, with her blue lace skirt falling charmingly around her and her hands folded neatly in her lap, and listened to their talk. Paul had found the old lady a chair and they sat with their heads near together, looking at one another as they talked, and smiling.

"You look very fit," the old lady said. "Very fit indeed." She sighed.

"You look wonderfully well," Paul said.

"Oh, well," said the old lady. "I've aged. I've aged, I know it."

"So have I," said Paul.

"Not noticeably," said the old lady, shaking her head and regarding him soberly for a minute. "*You* never will, I suppose."

At that moment the captain came up and bowed in front of Margaret, and Margaret, hoping that Paul might notice, got up to dance with him.

"I saw you sitting there alone," said the captain, "and I seized the precise opportunity I have been awaiting all evening."

"Excellent military tactics," said Margaret, wondering if these remarks had not been made a thousand times before, at a thousand different balls.

"I could be a splendid tactician," said the captain gallantly, as though carrying on his share of the echoing conversation, the words spoken under so many glittering chandeliers, "if my objective were always so agreeable to me."

"I saw you dancing with Carla," said Margaret.

"Carla," he said, and made a small gesture that somehow showed Carla as infinitely less than Margaret. Margaret knew that she had seen him make the same gesture to Carla, probably with reference to Margaret. She laughed.

"I forget what I'm supposed to say now," she told him.

"You're supposed to say," he told her seriously, " 'And do you really leave us so soon?' "

"And do you really leave us so soon?" said Margaret obediently.

"The sooner to return," he said, and tightened his arm around her waist. Margaret said, it being her turn, "We shall miss you very much."

"I shall miss *you*," he said, with a manly air of resignation.

They danced two waltzes, after which the captain escorted her handsomely back to the chair from which he had taken her, next to which Paul and the old lady continued in conversation, laughing and gesturing. The captain bowed to Margaret deeply, clicking his heels.

"May I leave you alone for a minute or so?" he asked. "I believe Carla is looking for me."

"I'm perfectly all right here," Margaret said. As the captain hurried away she turned to hear what Paul and the old lady were saying.

"I remember, I remember," said the old lady laughing, and she tapped Paul on the wrist with her fan. "I never imagined there would be a time when I should find it funny."

"But it *was* funny," said Paul.

"We were so young," the old lady said. "I can hardly remember."

She stood up abruptly, bowed to Margaret, and started back across the room among the dancers. Paul followed her as far as the doorway and then left her to come back to Margaret. When he sat down next to her he said, "So you met the old lady?"

"I went to the tower," Margaret said.

"She told me," he said absently, looking down at his gloves. "Well," he said finally, looking up with an air of cheerfulness. "Are they *never* going to play a waltz?"

Shortly before the sun came up over the river the next morning they sat at breakfast, Mr. and Mrs. Montague at the ends of the table, Carla and the captain, Margaret and Paul. The red roses in Carla's hair had faded and been thrown away, as had Margaret's yellow roses, but both Carla and Margaret still wore their ball gowns, which they had been wearing for so long that the soft richness of them seemed natural, as though they were to wear nothing else for an eternity in the house, and the gay confusion of helping one another dress, and admiring one another, and straightening the last folds to hang more gracefully, seemed all to have happened longer ago than memory, to be perhaps a dream that might never have happened at all, as perhaps the figures in the tapestries on the walls of the dining room might remember, secretly, an imagined process of dressing themselves and coming with laughter and light voices to sit on the lawn where they were woven. Margaret, looking at Carla, thought that she had never seen Carla so familiarly as in this soft white gown, with her hair dressed high on her head—had it really been curled and pinned that way? Or had it always, forever been so?—and the fan in her hand—had she not always had that fan, held just so?—and when Carla turned her head slightly on her long neck she captured the air of one of the portraits in the long gallery. Paul and the captain were still somehow trim in their uniforms; they were leaving at sunrise.

"Must you really leave this morning?" Margaret whispered to Paul.

"You are all kind to stay up and say goodbye," said the captain, and he leaned forward to look down the table at Margaret, as though it were particularly kind of her.

"Every time my son leaves me," said Mrs. Montague, "it is as though it were the first time."

Abruptly, the captain turned to Mrs. Montague and said, "I noticed this morning that there was a bare patch on the grass before the door. Can it be restored?"

"I had not known," Mrs. Montague said, and she looked nervously at Mr. Montague, who put his hand quietly on the table and said, "We hope to keep the house in good repair so long as we are able."

"But the broken statue by the lake?" said the captain. "And the tear in the tapestry behind your head?"

"It is wrong of you to notice these things," Mrs. Montague said, gently.

"What can I do?" he said to her. "It is impossible not to notice these things. The fish are dying, for instance. There are no grapes in the arbor this year. The carpet is worn to thread near your emboidery frame," he bowed to Mrs. Montague, "and in the house itself—" bowing to Mr. Montague, "—there is a noticeable crack over the window of the conservatory, a crack in the solid stone. Can you repair that?"

Mr. Montague said weakly, "It is very wrong of you to notice these things. Have you neglected the sun, and the bright perfection of the drawing room? Have you been recently to the gallery of portraits? Have you walked on the green portions of the lawn, or only watched for the bare places?"

"The drawing room is shabby," said the captain softly. "The green brocade sofa is torn a little near the arm. The carpet has lost its luster. The gilt is chipped on four of the small chairs in the gold room, the silver paint scratched in the silver room. A tile is missing from the face of Margaret, who died for love, and in the great gallery the paint has faded slightly on the portrait of—" bowing to Mr. Montague, "—your great-great-great-grandfather, sir."

Mr. Montague and Mrs. Montague looked at one another, and then Mrs. Montague said, "Surely it is not necessary to reproach *us* for these things?"

The captain reddened and shook his head.

"My embroidery is very nearly finished," Mrs. Montague said. "I have only to put the figures into the foreground."

"*I* shall mend the brocade sofa," said Carla.

The captain glanced once around the table, and sighed. "I must pack," he said. "We cannot delay our duties even though we have offended lovely women." Mrs. Montague, turning coldly away from him, rose and left the table, with Carla and Margaret following.

Margaret went quickly to the tile room, where the white face of Margaret who died for love stared eternally into the sky beyond the broad window. There was indeed a tile missing from the wide white cheek, and the broken spot looked like a tear, Margaret thought; she kneeled down and touched the tile face quickly to be sure that it was not a tear.

Then she went slowly back through the lovely rooms, across the broad rose and white tiled hall, and into the drawing room, and stopped to close the tall doors behind her.

"There really is a tile missing," she said.

Paul turned and frowned; he was standing alone in the drawing room, tall and bright in his uniform, ready to leave. "You are mistaken," he said. "It is not possible that anything should be missing."

"I saw it."

"It is not *true*, you know," he said. He was walking quickly up and down the room, slapping his gloves on his wrist, glancing nervously, now and then, at the door, at the tall windows opening out onto the marble stairway. "The house is the same as ever," he said. "It does not change."

"But the worn carpet . . ." It was under his feet as he walked.

"Nonsense," he said violently. "Don't you think I'd know my own house? I care for it constantly, even when *they* forget; without this house I could not exist; do you think it would begin to crack while I am here?"

"How can you keep it from aging? Carpets *will* wear, you know, and unless they are replaced . . ."

"Replaced?" he stared as though she had said something evil. "What could replace anything in this house?" He touched Mrs. Montague's embroidery frame, softly. "All we can do is add to it."

There was a sound outside; it was the family coming down the great stairway to say goodbye. He turned quickly and listened, and it seemed to be the sound he had been expecting. "I will always remember you," he said to Margaret, hastily, and turned again toward the tall windows. "Goodbye."

"It is so dark," Margaret said, going beside him. "You will come back?"

"I will come back," he said sharply. "Goodbye." He stepped across the sill of the window onto the marble stairway outside; he was black for a moment against the white marble, and Margaret stood still at the window watching him go down the steps and away through the gardens. "Lost, lost," she heard faintly, and, from far away, "all is lost."

She turned back to the room, and, avoiding the worn spot in the carpet and moving widely around Mrs. Montague's embroidery frame, she went to the great doors and opened them. Outside, in the hall with the rose and white tiled floor, Mr. and Mrs. Montague and Carla were standing with the captain.

"Son," Mrs. Montague was saying. "When will you be back?"

"Don't *fuss* at me," the captain said. "I'll be back when I can."

Carla stood silently, a little away. "Please be careful," she said, and, "Here's Margaret, come to say goodbye to you, brother."

"Don't linger, m'boy," said Mr. Montague. "Hard on the women."

"There are so many things Margaret and I planned for you while you were here," Carla said to her brother. "The time has been so short."

Margaret, standing beside Mrs. Montague, turned to Carla's brother (*and Paul; who was Paul?*) and said "Goodbye." He bowed to her and moved to go to the door with his father.

"It is hard to see him go," Mrs. Montague said. "And we do not know when he will come back." She put her hand gently on Margaret's shoulder. "We must show you more of the house," she said. "I saw you one day try the door of the ruined tower; have you seen the hall of flowers? Or the fountain room?"

"When my brother comes again," Carla said, "we shall have a musical evening, and perhaps he will take us boating on the river."

"And my visit?" said Margaret smiling. "Surely there will be an end to my visit?"

Mrs. Montague, with one last look at the door from which Mr. Montague and the captain had gone, dropped her hand from Margaret's shoulder and said, "I must go to my embroidery. I have neglected it while my son was with us."

"You will not leave us before my brother comes again?" Carla asked Margaret.

"I have only to put the figures into the foreground," Mrs. Montague said, hesitating on her way to the drawing room. "I shall have you exactly if you sit on the lawn near the river."

"We shall be models of stillness," said Carla, laughing. "Margaret, will you come and sit beside me on the lawn?"

Agatha Christie and her husband, the noted archaeologist Sir Max E. L. Mallowan

1926

THE LAST SEANCE

by Agatha Christie

The dean of them all, Dame Agatha! At eighty years of age she has eighty published books to her credit. Agatha Christie was created a Dame Commander of the British Empire by Queen Elizabeth II. Avidly read by kings, queens, and presidents as well as the common reader, her books are renowned throughout the world. Dame Agatha has given us shelves of glorious mysteries, but she is less well known for her horror tales which are published much less frequently in this country. Sit quietly at "The Last Seance."

In the psychic vocabulary, a seance is a sitting together to obtain psychic manifestations or communications with the spirit world.

Now, well on the way to the twenty-first century, there is a new interest in the occult. Perhaps within our own time it will take on more scientific aspects than it has in the past. The first scientific group to be interested in psychic phenomena was founded in 1862 by a distinguished British scientist. It was called the Ghost Club. It languished and then was revived in 1881. In 1938 it opened its membership to women, a belated recognition of the fact that women have been unusually gifted in the area most popularly known as "intuition." In the literature of spiritualism, women more often than men appear as mediums—persons who under certain states of consciousness can relay messages from the dead to the living.

Unusually sensitive to psychic phenomena, mediums are reputed to have had remarkable experiences—none more terrifying than the one we can witness in "The Last Seance."

Raoul Daubreuil crossed the Seine humming a little tune to himself. He was a good-looking young Frenchman of about thirty-two, with a fresh-coloured face and a little black moustache. By profession he was an engineer. In due course he reached the Cardonet and turned in at the door of No. 17. The concierge looked out from her lair and gave him a grudging "Good morning," to which he replied cheerfully. Then he mounted the stairs to the apartment on the third floor. As he stood there waiting for his ring at the bell to be answered he hummed once more his little tune. Raoul Daubreuil was feeling particularly cheerful this morning. The door was opened by an elderly Frenchwoman whose wrinkled face broke into smiles when she saw who the visitor was.

"Good morning, Monsieur."

"Good morning, Elise," said Raoul.

He passed into the vestibule, pulling off his gloves as he did so.

"Madame expects me, does she not?" he asked over his shoulder.

"Ah, yes, indeed, Monsieur."

Elise shut the front door and turned towards him.

"If Monsieur will pass into the little *salon* Madame will be with him in a few minutes. At the moment she reposes herself."

Raoul looked up sharply.

"Is she not well?"

"*Well!*"

Elise gave a snort. She passed in front of Raoul and opened the door of the little *salon* for him. He went in and she followed him.

"*Well!*" she continued. "How should she be well, poor lamb?

Séances, séances, and always *séances!* It is not right—not natural, not what the good God intended for us. For me, I say straight out, it is trafficking with the devil."

Raoul patted her on the shoulder reassuringly.

"There, there, Elise," he said soothingly, "do not excite yourself, and do not be too ready to see the devil in everything you do not understand."

Elise shook her head doubtingly.

"Ah, well," she grumbled under her breath, "Monsieur may say what he pleases, I don't like it. Look at Madame, every day she gets whiter and thinner, and the headaches!"

She held up her hands.

"Ah, no, it is not good, all this spirit business. Spirits indeed! All the good spirits are in Paradise, and the others are in Purgatory."

"Your view of the life after death is refreshingly simple, Elise," said Raoul as he dropped into a chair.

The old woman drew herself up.

"I am a good Catholic, Monsieur."

She crossed herself, went towards the door, then paused, her hand on the handle.

"Afterwards when you are married, Monsieur," she said pleadingly, "it will not continue—all this?"

Raoul smiled at her affectionately.

"You are a good faithful creature, Elise," he said, "and devoted to your mistress. Have no fear, once she is my wife, all this 'spirit business' as you call it, will cease. For Madame Daubreuil there will be no more *séances.*"

Elise's face broke into smiles.

"Is it true what you say?" she asked eagerly.

The other nodded gravely.

"Yes," he said, speaking almost more to himself than to her. "Yes, all this must end. Simone has a wonderful gift and she has used it freely, but now she has done her part. As you have justly observed, Elise, day by day she gets whiter and thinner. The life of a medium is a particularly trying and arduous one, involving a terrible nervous strain. All the same, Elise, your mistress is the most wonderful medium in Paris—more, in France. People from all over the world come to her because they know that with her there is no trickery, no deceit."

Elise gave a snort of contempt.

"Deceit! Ah, no, indeed. Madame could not deceive a newborn babe if she tried."

"She is an angel," said the young Frenchman with fervour. "And I—I shall do everything a man can to make her happy. You believe that?"

Elise drew herself up, and spoke with a certain simple dignity.

"I have served Madame for many years, Monsieur. With all respect I may say that I love her. If I did not believe that you adored her as she deserves to be adored—*eh bien,* Monsieur! I should be willing to tear you limb from limb."

Raoul laughed.

"Bravo, Elise! You are a faithful friend, and you must approve of me now that I have told you Madame is going to give up the spirits."

He expected the old woman to receive this pleasantry with a laugh, but somewhat to his surprise she remained grave.

"Supposing, Monsieur," she said hesitatingly, "the spirits will not give *her* up?"

Raoul stared at her.

"Eh! What do you mean?"

"I said," repeated Elise, "supposing the spirits will not give *her* up?"

"I thought you didn't believe in the spirits, Elise?"

"No more I do," said Elise stubbornly. "It is foolish to believe in them. All the same—"

"Well?"

"It is difficult for me to explain, Monsieur. You see, me, I always thought that these mediums, as they call themselves, were just clever cheats who imposed on the poor souls who had lost their dear ones. But Madame is not like that. Madame is good. Madame is honest and—"

She lowered her voice and spoke in a tone of awe.

"*Things happen.* It is not trickery, things happen, and that is why I am afraid. For I am sure of this, Monsieur, it is not right. It is against nature and le bon Dieu, and *somebody will have to pay.*"

Raoul got up from his chair and came and patted her on the shoulder.

"Calm yourself, my good Elise," he said, smiling. "See, I will give you some good news. To-day is the last of these *séances;* after to-day there will be no more."

"There *is* one to-day then?" asked the old woman suspiciously.

"The last, Elise, the last."

Elise shook her head disconsolately.

"Madame is not fit—" she began.

But her words were interrupted, the door opened and a tall, fair woman came in. She was slender and graceful, with the face of a Botticelli Madonna. Raoul's face lighted up, and Elise withdrew quickly and discreetly.

"Simone!"

He took both her long, white hands in his and kissed each in turn. She murmured his name very softly.

"Raoul, my dear one."

Again he kissed her hands and then looked intently into her face.

"Simone, how pale you are! Elise told me you were resting; you are not ill, my well-beloved?"

"No, not ill—" she hesitated.

He led her over to the sofa and sat down on it beside her.

"But tell me then."

The medium smiled faintly.

"You will think me foolish," she murmured.

"*I?* Think you foolish? Never."

Simone withdrew her hand from his grasp. She sat perfectly still for a moment or two gazing down at the carpet. Then she spoke in a low, hurried voice.

"I am afraid, Raoul."

He waited for a minute or two expecting her to go on, but as she did not he said encouragingly:

"Yes, afraid of what?"

"Just afraid—that is all."

"But—"

He looked at her in perplexity, and she answered the look quickly.

"Yes, it is absurd, isn't it, and yet I feel just that. Afraid, nothing more. I don't know what of, or why, but all the time I am possessed with the idea that something terrible—terrible, is going to happen to me."

She stared out in front of her. Raoul put an arm gently round her.

"My dearest," he said, "come, you must not give way. I know what it is, the strain, Simone, the strain of a medium's life. All you need is rest—rest and quiet."

She looked at him gratefully.

"Yes, Raoul, you are right. That is what I need, rest and quiet."

She closed her eyes and leant back a little against his arm.

"And happiness," murmured Raoul in her ear.

His arm drew her closer. Simone, her eyes still closed, drew a deep breath.

"Yes," she murmured, "yes. When your arms are round me I feel safe. I forget my life—the terrible life—of a medium. You know much, Raoul, but even you do not know all it means."

He felt her body grow rigid in his embrace. Her eyes opened again, staring in front of her.

"One sits in the cabinet in the darkness, waiting, and the darkness is terrible, Raoul, for it is the darkness of emptiness, of nothingness. Deliberately one gives oneself up to be lost in it. After that one knows nothing, one feels nothing, but at last there comes the slow, painful return, the awakening out of sleep, but so tired—so terribly tired."

"I know," murmured Raoul, "I know."

"So tired," murmured Simone again.

Her whole body seemed to droop as she repeated the words.

"But you are wonderful, Simone."

He took her hands in his, trying to rouse her to share his enthusiasm.

"You are unique—the greatest medium the world has ever known."

She shook her head, smiling a little at that.

"Yes, yes," Raoul insisted.

He drew two letters from his pocket.

"See here, from Professor Roche of the *Salpêtrière,* and this one from Dr. Genir at Nancy, both imploring that you will continue to sit for them occasionally."

"Ah, no!"

Simone sprang suddenly to her feet.

"I will not, I will not. It is to be all finished—all done with. You promised me, Raoul."

Raoul stared at her in astonishment as she stood wavering, facing him almost like a creature at bay. He got up and took her hand.

"Yes, yes," he said. "Certainly it is finished, that is understood. But I am so proud of you, Simone, that is why I mentioned those letters."

She threw him a swift sideways glance of suspicion.

"It is not that you will ever want me to sit again?"

"No, no," said Raoul, "unless perhaps you yourself would care to, just occasionally for these old friends——"

But she interrupted him, speaking excitedly.

"No, no, never again. There is a danger. I tell you. I can feel it, great danger."

She clasped her hands on her forehead a minute, then walked across to the window.

"Promise me never again," she said in a quieter voice over her shoulder.

Raoul followed her and put his arms round her shoulders.

"My dear one," he said tenderly, "I promise you after to-day you shall never sit again."

He felt the sudden start she gave.

"To-day," she murmured. "Ah, yes— I had forgotten Madame Exe."

Raoul looked at his watch.

"She is due any minute now; but perhaps, Simone, if you do not feel well——"

Simone hardly seemed to be listening to him; she was following out her own train of thought.

"She is—a strange woman, Raoul, a very strange woman. Do you know I—I have almost a horror of her."

"Simone!"

There was reproach in his voice, and she was quick to feel it.

"Yes, yes, I know, you are like all Frenchmen, Raoul. To you a mother is sacred and it is unkind of me to feel like that about her when she grieves so for her lost child. But—I cannot explain it, she is so big and black, and her hands—have you ever noticed her hands, Raoul? Great big strong hands, as strong as a man's. Ah!"

She gave a little shiver and closed her eyes. Raoul withdrew his arm and spoke almost coldly.

"I really cannot understand you, Simone. Surely you, a woman, should have nothing but sympathy for another woman, a mother bereft of her only child."

Simone made a gesture of impatience.

"Ah, it is you who do not understand, my friend! One cannot help these things. The first moment I saw her I felt——"

She flung her hands out.

"*Fear!* You remember, it was a long time before I would consent to sit for her? I felt sure in some way she would bring me misfortune."

Raoul shrugged his shoulders.

"Whereas, in actual fact, she brought you the exact opposite," he said dryly. "All the sittings have been attended with marked success. The spirit of the little Amelie was able to control you at once, and the materialisations have really been striking. Professor Roche ought really to have been present at the last one."

"Materialisations," said Simone in a low voice. "Tell me, Raoul (you know that I know nothing of what takes place while I am in the trance), are the materialisations really so wonderful?"

He nodded enthusiastically.

"At the first few sittings the figure of the child was visible in a kind of nebulous haze," he explained, "but at the last *séance*——"

"Yes?"

He spoke very softly.

"Simone, the child that stood there was an actual living child of flesh and blood. I even touched her—but seeing that the touch was acutely painful to you, I would not permit Madame Exe to do the same. I was afraid that her self-control might break down, and that some harm to you might result."

Simone turned away again towards the window.

"I was terribly exhausted when I woke," she murmured. "Raoul, are you sure—are you really sure that all this is *right?* You know what dear old Elise thinks, that I am trafficking with the devil?"

She laughed rather uncertainly.

"You know what I believe," said Raoul gravely. "In the handling of the unknown there must always be danger, but the cause is a noble one, for it is the cause of Science. All over the world there have been martyrs to Science, pioneers who have paid the price so that others may follow safely in their footsteps. For ten years now you have worked for Science at the cost of a terrific nervous strain. Now your part is done, from to-day onward you are free to be happy."

She smiled at him affectionately, her calm restored. Then she glanced quickly up at the clock.

"Madame Exe is late," she murmured. "She may not come."

"I think she will," said Raoul. "Your clock is a little fast, Simone."

Simone moved about the room, rearranging an ornament here and there.

"I wonder who she is, this Madame Exe?" she observed. "Where she comes from, who her people are? It is strange that we know nothing about her."

Raoul shrugged his shoulders.

"Most people remain incognito if possible when they come to a medium," he observed. "It is an elementary precaution."

"I suppose so," agreed Simone listlessly.

A little china vase she was holding slipped from her fingers and broke to pieces on the tiles of the fireplace. She turned sharply on Raoul.

"You see," she murmured, "I am not myself. Raoul, would you think me very—very cowardly if I told Madame Exe I could not sit to-day?"

His look of pained astonishment made her redden.

"You promised, Simone——" he began gently.

She backed against the wall.

"I won't do it, Raoul. I won't do it."

And again that glance of his, tenderly reproachful, made her wince.

"It is not of the money I am thinking, Simone, though you must realise that the money this woman has offered you for a last sitting is enormous—simply enormous."

She interrupted him defiantly.

"There are things that matter more than money."

"Certainly there are," he agreed warmly. "That is just what I am saying. Consider—this woman is a mother, a mother who has lost her only child. If you are not really ill, if it is only a whim on your part—you can deny a rich woman a caprice, can you deny a mother one last sight of her child?"

The medium flung her hands out despairingly in front of her.

"Oh, you torture me," she murmured. "All the same you are

right. I will do as you wish, but I know now what I am afraid of—it is the word 'mother.' "

"Simone!"

"There are certain primitive elementary forces, Raoul. Most of them have been destroyed by civilisation, but motherhood stands where it stood at the beginning. Animals—human beings, they are all the same. A mother's love for her child is like nothing else in the world. It knows no law, no pity, it dares all things and crushes down remorselessly all that stands in its path."

She stopped, panting a little, then turned to him with a quick, disarming smile.

"I am foolish to-day, Raoul. I know it."

He took her hand in his.

"Lie down for a minute or two," he urged. "Rest till she comes."

"Very well." She smiled at him and left the room.

Raoul remained for a minute or two lost in thought, then he strode to the door, opened it, and crossed the little hall. He went into a room the other side of it, a sitting-room very much like the one he had left, but at one end was an alcove with a big armchair set in it. Heavy black velvet curtains were arranged so as to pull across the alcove. Elise was busy arranging the room. Close to the alcove she had set two chairs and a small round table. On the table was a tambourine, a horn, and some paper and pencils.

"The last time," murmured Elise with grim satisfaction. "Ah, Monsieur, I wish it were over and done with."

The sharp *ting* of an electric bell sounded.

"There she is, the great gendarme of a woman," continued the old servant. "Why can't she go and pray decently for her little one's soul in a church, and burn a candle to Our Blessed Lady? Does not the good God know what is best for us?"

"Answer the bell, Elise," said Raoul peremptorily.

She threw him a look, but obeyed. In a minute or two she returned ushering in the visitor.

"I will tell my mistress you are here, Madame."

Raoul came forward to shake hands with Madame Exe. Simone's words floated back to his memory.

"So big and so black."

She *was* a big woman, and the heavy black of French mourning seemed almost exaggerated in her case. Her voice when she spoke was very deep.

"I fear I am a little late, Monsieur."

"A few moments only," said Raoul, smiling. "Madame Simone is lying down. I am sorry to say she is far from well, very nervous and overwrought."

Her hand, which she was just withdrawing, closed on his suddenly like a vice.

"But she will sit?" she demanded sharply.

"Oh, yes, Madame."

Madame Exe gave a sigh of relief, and sank into a chair, loosening one of the heavy black veils that floated round her.

"Ah, Monsieur!" she murmured, "you cannot imagine, you cannot conceive the wonder and the joy of these *séances* to me! My little one! My Amelie! To see her, to hear her, even—perhaps—yes, perhaps to be even able to—stretch out my hand and touch her."

Raoul spoke quickly and peremptorily.

"Madame Exe—how can I explain?—on no account must you do anything except under my express directions, otherwise there is the gravest danger."

"Danger to me?"

"No, Madame," said Raoul, "to the medium. You must understand that the phenomena that occur are explained by Science in a certain way. I will put the matter very simply, using no technical terms. A spirit, to manifest itself, has to use the actual physical substance of the medium. You have seen the vapour of fluid issuing from the lips of the medium. This finally condenses and is built up into the physical semblance of the spirit's dead body. But this ectoplasm we believe to be the actual substance of the medium. We hope to prove this some day by careful weighing and testing—but the great difficulty is the danger and pain which attends the medium on any handling of the phenomena. Were anyone to seize hold of the materialisation roughly the death of the medium might result."

Madame Exe had listened to him with close attention.

"That is very interesting, Monsieur. Tell me, shall not a time come when the materialisations shall advance so far that it shall be capable of detachment from its parent, the medium?"

"That is a fantastic speculation, Madame."

She persisted.

"But, on the facts, not impossible?"

"Quite impossible to-day."

"But perhaps in the future?"

He was saved from answering, for at that moment Simone entered. She looked languid and pale, but had evidently regained entire control of herself. She came forward and shook hands with Madame Exe, though Raoul noticed the faint shiver that passed through her as she did so.

"I regret, Madame, to hear that you are indisposed," said Madame Exe.

"It is nothing," said Simone rather brusquely. "Shall we begin?"

She went to the alcove and sat down in the arm-chair. Suddenly Raoul in his turn felt a wave of fear pass over him.

"You are not strong enough," he exclaimed. "We had better cancel the *séance*. Madame Exe will understand."

"Monsieur!"

Madame Exe rose indignantly.

"Yes, yes, it is better not, I am sure of it."

"Madame Simone promised me one last sitting."

"That is so," agreed Simone quietly, "and I am prepared to carry out my promise."

"I hold you to it, Madame," said the other woman.

"I do not break my word," said Simone coldly. "Do not fear, Raoul," she added gently, "after all, it is for the last time—the last time, thank God."

At a sign from her Raoul drew the heavy black curtains across the alcove. He also pulled the curtains of the window so that the room was in semi-obscurity. He indicated one of the chairs to Madame Exe and prepared himself to take the other. Madame Exe, however, hesitated.

"You will pardon me, Monsieur, but—you understand I believe absolutely in your integrity and in that of Madame Simone. All the same, so that my testimony may be the more valuable, I took the liberty of bringing this with me."

From her handbag she drew a length of fine cord.

"Madame!" cried Raoul. "This is an insult!"

"A precaution."

"I repeat it is an insult."

"I don't understand your objection, Monsieur," said Madame Exe coldly. "If there is no trickery you have nothing to fear."

Raoul laughed scornfully.

"I can assure you that I have nothing to fear, Madame. Bind me hand and foot if you will."

His speech did not produce the effect he hoped, for Madame Exe merely murmured unemotionally:

"Thank you, Monsieur," and advanced upon him with her roll of cord.

Suddenly Simone from behind the curtain gave a cry.

"No, no, Raoul, don't let her do it."

Madame Exe laughed derisively.

"Madame is afraid," she observed sarcastically.

"Yes, I am afraid."

"Remember what you are saying, Simone," cried Raoul. "Madame Exe is apparently under the impression that we are charlatans."

"I must make sure," said Madame Exe grimly.

She went methodically about her task, binding Raoul securely to his chair.

"I must congratulate you on your knots, Madame," he observed ironically when she had finished. "Are you satisfied now?"

Madame Exe did not reply. She walked round the room

examining the panelling of the walls closely. Then she locked the door leading into the hall, and, removing the key, returned to her chair.

"Now," she said in an indescribable voice, "I am ready."

The minutes passed. From behind the curtain the sound of Simone's breathing became heavier and more stertorous. Then it died away altogether, to be succeeded by a series of moans. Then again there was silence for a little while, broken by the sudden clattering of the tambourine. The horn was caught up from the table and dashed to the ground. Ironic laughter was heard. The curtains of the alcove seemed to have been pulled back a little, the medium's figure was just visible through the opening, her head fallen forward on her breast. Suddenly Madame Exe drew in her breath sharply. A ribbon-like stream of mist was issuing from the medium's mouth. It condensed and began gradually to assume a shape, the shape of a little child.

"Amelie! My little Amelie!"

The hoarse whisper came from Madame Exe. The hazy figure condensed still further. Raoul stared almost incredulously. Never had there been a more successful materialisation. Now, surely it was a real child, a real flesh and blood child standing there.

"*Maman!*"

The soft childish voice spoke.

"My child!" cried Madame Exe. "My child!"

She half rose from her seat.

"Be careful, Madame," cried Raoul warningly.

The materialisation came hesitatingly through the curtains. It was a child. She stood there, her arms held out.

"*Maman!*"

"Ah!" cried Madame Exe.

Again she half rose from her seat.

"Madame," cried Raoul, alarmed, "the medium——"

"I must touch her," cried Madame Exe hoarsely.

She moved a step forward.

"For God's sake, Madame, control yourself," cried Raoul.

He was really alarmed now.

"Sit down at once."

"My little one, I must touch her."

"Madame, I command you, sit down!"

He was writhing desperately with his bonds, but Madame Exe had done her work well; he was helpless. A terrible sense of impending disaster swept over him.

"In the name of God, Madame, sit down!" he shouted. "Remember the medium."

Madame Exe paid no attention to him. She was like a woman transformed. Ecstasy and delight showed plainly in her face. Her outstretched hand touched the little figure that stood in the opening of the curtains. A terrible moan came from the medium.

"My God!" cried Raoul. "My God! This is terrible. The medium——"

Madame Exe turned on him with a harsh laugh.

"What do I care for your medium?" she cried. "I want my child."

"You are mad!"

"My child, I tell you. Mine! My own! My own flesh and blood! My little one come back to me from the dead, alive and breathing."

Raoul opened his lips, but no words would come. She was terrible, this woman! Remorseless, savage, absorbed by her own passion. The baby lips parted, and for the third time the same word echoed:

"*Maman!*"

"Come then, my little one," cried Madame Exe.

With a sharp gesture she caught up the child in her arms. From behind the curtains came a long-drawn scream of utter anguish.

"Simone!" cried Raoul. "Simone!"

He was aware vaguely of Madame Exe rushing past him, of the unlocking of the door, of retreating footsteps down the stairs.

From behind the curtain there still sounded the terrible high long-drawn scream—such a scream as Raoul had never heard. It died away in a horrible kind of gurgle. Then there came the thud of a body falling. . . .

Raoul was working like a maniac to free himself from his bonds. In his frenzy he accomplished the impossible, snapping the rope by sheer strength. As he struggled to his feet, Elise rushed in crying "Madame!"

"Simone!" cried Raoul.

Together they rushed forward and pulled the curtain.

Raoul staggered back.

"My God!" he murmured. "Red—all red. . . ."

Elise's voice came beside him harsh and shaking.

"So Madame is dead. It is ended. But tell me, Monsieur, what has happened. *Why is Madame all shrunken away—why is she half her usual size? What has been happening here?*"

"I do not know," said Raoul.

His voice rose to a scream.

"I do not know. I do not know. But I think—I am going mad. . . . Simone! Simone!"

A Victorian woman writer, from a print by J. W. Orr

BIOGRAPHICAL NOTES

MARY W. SHELLEY, novelist and short story writer, was born in London in 1797, the only daughter of William Godwin and Mary Wollstonecraft. In 1816 she eloped with Percy Bysshe Shelley to the Continent. While abroad, she saw much of Lord Byron, and it was at his villa on the Lake of Geneva that she conceived the idea for her famous novel *Frankenstein*. She wrote other novels and short stories, contributed biographies of foreign artists and authors to Lardner's *Cabinet Cyclopaedia*, and edited her husband's poems after his death. She died in 1851.

CLEMENCE HOUSMAN, British novelist, short story writer, and wood engraver, was born at Longmeadow, Somerset, England, in 1861. Born into a family of writers and artists (her brothers were A. E. Housman, the poet and scholar, and Laurence Housman, the dramatist, novelist, and artist), she studied art in London and had many exhibitions of her wood engravings in the Tate Gallery. Late in the autumn of 1896 she broke into print with her long short story *The Werewolf*, which was illustrated by her brother Laurence. Miss Housman died in 1955.

MARY ELEANOR WILKINS FREEMAN, American writer, was born in Randolph, Massachusetts, in 1852, of Puritan ancestry. Her early education, chiefly from reading and observation, was supplemented by a course at Mount Holyoke Seminary, South Hadley, Massachusetts. She subsequently lived in Brattleboro, Vermont, until her marriage in 1902 to Dr. Charles M. Freeman of Metuchen, New Jersey. She contributed poems and stories to magazines and published several books for children, including *Young Lucretia and Other Stories* (1892), and *Once Upon a Time and Other Child Verses* (1887). *A Humble Romance and Other Stories* (1887) and *A New England Nun and Other Stories* (1891) gave her a prominent place among American short story writers. Her tales are honest, realistic pictures of the severe and frustrating life of rural New England and helped to preserve some of its vanishing aspects. She died at Metuchen, New Jersey, in 1930.

GERTRUDE BACON, British writer, was born in 1874, the daughter of the Reverend John Bacon, the pioneer aeronaut. Her story, *The Gorgon's Head*, first published in 1899, reflects the contemporary interest in the archaeological discoveries of Troy and other ancient sites mentioned in the *Iliad* and the *Odyssey*, by the Greek poet Homer. These exciting finds caused many writers of the period to break away from the traditional ghost story and find their inspiration among the myths and legends of the past. Besides her ghost stories, Miss Bacon wrote several books about her father's exploits. She died in 1916.

E. (EDITH) NESBIT, British novelist and writer of children's books, was born in 1858. Educated at a French convent, in Germany, and at Brighton, she spent her early youth in the country at Halstead Hall, Kent. Her first appearance in print was with a poem, *The Dawn*, in *The Sunday Magazine* in 1876. She married Hubert Bland, the socialist writer, in 1880, and with him helped found the Fabian Society. They also collaborated on a novel, *The Prophet's Mantle* (1885). She continued writing articles, stories and poems, but did not find her true vocation until *The Story of the Treasure Seekers*, a story for children, brought her fame in 1899. *The Wouldbegoods* (1901) and *Five Children and It* (1902) were other favorites among her children's books. Although she is now best remembered for her books for children, she wrote a number of excellent ghost stories. Miss Nesbit died in 1924.

MARY ELIZABETH BRADDON, British novelist and short story writer, was born in 1837. She was the daughter of Henry Braddon, solicitor of Skirdon Lodge, Cornwall, and sister of Sir Edward Braddon, premier of Tasmania. Her first novel, *Three Times Dead*, written when she was nineteen, failed to be published only because the publisher went bankrupt; later it was rewritten as *The Trail of the Serpent* (1861). In 1862 her reputation as a novelist was made by the success of *Lady Audley's Secret*. This novel, translated into many languages, has been dramatized, filmed, and in its original narrative form has been reprinted innumerable times. For a considerable period Miss Braddon edited *Belgravia*, in which several of her novels appeared. She was a tireless worker and in her long series of novels, plays, and stories maintained a freshness and inventiveness which endeared her to millions of readers. In 1874 she married John Maxwell, a publisher. She died in 1915.

CHARLOTTE PERKINS GILMAN, American feminist and reformer, writer and lecturer, was born in Hartford, Connecticut, in 1860. She was married twice, in 1884 to C. W. Stetson, an American painter, and in 1900 to George H. Gilman. Prominent as a lecturer and writer on the labor movement and feminism, she edited the *Forerunner*, a liberal journal. Among her many books are *Women and Economics* (1898), *Concerning Children* (1900), *Human Work* (1904), and *This Man-made World* (1911). Her verses were collected in *This Our World* (1898). Her story *The Yellow Wall Paper* has few rivals in the class of horror stories. Her autobiography, *The Living of Charlotte Perkins Gilman*, appeared in 1935, the year of her death.

ELIZABETH BOWEN, Anglo-Irish author, daughter of an Irish barrister, was born in Dublin in 1899; *Seven Winters* (1942) tells of her childhood there. At an early age she was taken to the south of England, and was educated at Downe House in Kent. Leaving home at the age of nineteen, she lived alone in London, with winters in Italy. One of the latter, spent partly in tutoring her aunt's children at Bordighera, later produced her first novel, *The Hotel* (1927). In 1923 she married Alan Charles Cameron, and after his appointment to a teaching position at Oxford the Camerons settled in Old Headington. Her first short stories, written when she was twenty years old, were published as *Encounters* (1923); other collections are *Encounters and Ann Lee's* (1951), *The Cat Jumps* (1934), and *Demon Lovers* (1945). Among her other novels are *Friends and Relations* (1951), *To the North* (1932), *The House in Paris* (1935), *The Death of the Heart* (1938), and *The Heat of the Day* (1949). Her writing displays careful craftsmanship and a subtle sense of character. In 1948 she was created a Companion of the British Empire.

ROSE MACAULAY, British novelist and short story writer, was born in 1881 in Cambridge, where her father was a lecturer in English, but spent most of her childhood in Italy. She went to school and college at Oxford, and her first novel, *The Valley of Captives* (1911), was published while she was there. She first came into prominence with her satirical novel *Potterism* (1920); this was followed by *Dangerous Ages* (1921), which was awarded one of France's top literary honors, the *Prix Femina—Vie Heureuse,* and *Told by an Idiot* (1923), *Orphan Island* (1924), *Crewe Train* (1926), *Staying with Relations* (1930), *I Would Be Private* (1937), *The World My Wilderness* (1950), and *The Towers of Trebizond* (1957). Besides short stories and poetry, she also published studies of Milton and E. M. Forster. Clever and critical, she belonged to the Bloomsbury group of authors. In 1958, the year of her death, she was created a Dame Commander of the British Empire.

DAPHNE DU MAURIER, British novelist, born in London in 1907, is a daughter of Sir Gerald du Maurier, the famous actor, and granddaughter of George du Maurier, the artist and novelist. Two of her most interesting books are *Gerald, a Portrait* (1934), a study of her father, and *The du Mauriers* (1937), which relates the story of three generations. She was educated at home and in Paris. In 1932 she married Sir Frederick A. M. Browning of the Grenadier Guards, who became Comptroller of Princess Elizabeth's Household in 1947. *The Loving Spirit,* Lady Browning's first novel, was published in 1931. It was followed by *I'll Never Be Young Again* (1932) and *The Progress of Julius* (1933). She is a prolific and compelling storyteller. Her best-known work is *Rebecca,* which has been widely imitated since its publication in 1938. Among her other books are: *Jamaica Inn* (1936), *Frenchman's Creek* (1941), *Kiss Me Again Stranger* (1953), *My Cousin Rachel* (1952), and *The Scapegoat* (1957). She was created a Dame Commander of the British Empire in 1971.

MARY ELIZABETH COUNSELMAN, a native of Alabama, has been writing stories of the macabre for over twenty-five years. Her short story "*The Three Marked Pennies,*" now a classic, was written when she was only fifteen years old. Her stories have been published in nine countries and in over one hundred magazines and books, and many have been dramatized for television, appearing in this country, England, Canada, and Australia.

VIRGINIA LAYEFSKY was born in Seattle, Washington, and studied music at the Juilliard School of Music in New York. She is the wife of a violinist in the Pittsburgh symphony orchestra. *Moonlight–Starlight* is one of her first stories.

SHIRLEY JACKSON was born in San Francisco in 1919 and spent most of her early life in California. She studied for a year at the University of Rochester, and then transferred to Syracuse

University, where she took her B.A. degree in 1940. The same year she married a classmate, Stanley Edgar Hyman, the literary critic and author. Fame first came to her in 1948 for "The Lottery," a hair-raising intellectual horror story. Her last two novels were *The Haunting of Hill House* (1959), which was made into a motion picture, and *We Have Always Lived in the Castle* (1962). Her stories appeared regularly in *The New Yorker* magazine, and many were dramatized for television and radio. She died in 1965.

AGATHA CHRISTIE was born in 1891 in Torquay, England, of an English mother and an American father. Her first attempt at writing, toward the end of World War I, was rejected by several publishers. It was entitled *The Mysterious Affair at Styles,* and in this work she introduced the now famous Belgian detective, Hercule Poirot. The book was eventually accepted and was published in 1920. In 1926, after averaging a book a year, she wrote what is still considered her masterpiece, *The Murder of Roger Ackroyd.* In private life she is Lady Mallowan, the wife of the noted British archaeologist Sir Max E. L. Mallowan, and has often accompanied him on his expeditions, using the experiences as background for some of her books. In 1971, on her eightieth birthday, her eightieth book was published. She was created a Dame Commander of the British Empire in 1971.

4 5 75 74 73